ADVENTUREGAME COMICS

2

THE BEYOND

JASON SHIGA

INKING BY ELENA DIAZ
COLORING BY LARK PIEN
STORY BY YOU

AMULET BOOKS • NEW YORK

Library of Congress Control Number 2022948605

ISBN 978-1-4197-5781-5

Text and illustrations © 2023 Jason Shiga
Book design by Charice Silverman

Printed and bound in China
10 9 8 7 6 5 4 3 2 1

ABRAMS The Art of Books
195 Broadway, New York, NY 10007
abramsbooks.com

For Kazuo

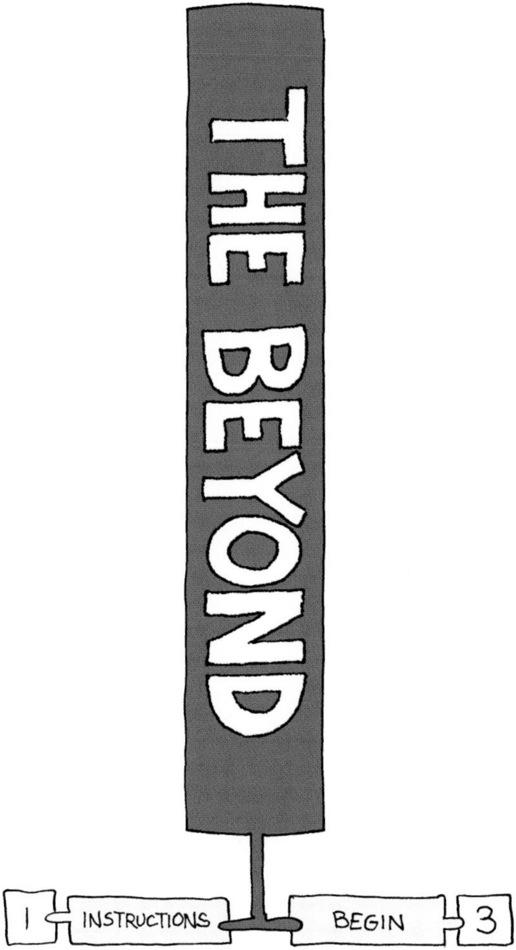
THE BEYOND
1
INSTRUCTIONS
BEGIN
3

STOP

THIS IS NOT AN ORDINARY COMIC!

Hi! I'm Jason Shiga, the author of this book. The comic you are holding in your hands is unlike any ever written.

Instead of one story, this comic splits off into hundreds of different adventures and endings.

It sounds complicated, but to read this comic all you have to do is remember these 2 rules.

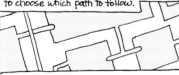

1) Each panel is connected to the next one by a tube. Tubes can travel right, left, up, down and sometimes even split! When that happens, YOU the reader get to choose which path to follow.

2) Sometimes a tube will lead to a box containing a number. When that happens, turn to the page indicated by the number.

One last thing. Sometimes a box will be blank. In that case, you can write in your own number, turn to that page and see if you're right.

That's it! Remember these rules. But also keep in mind you may have to think outside the box to unlock all the secrets of this book.

Now turn to page 3, and let's begin the adventure!

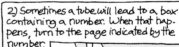

3

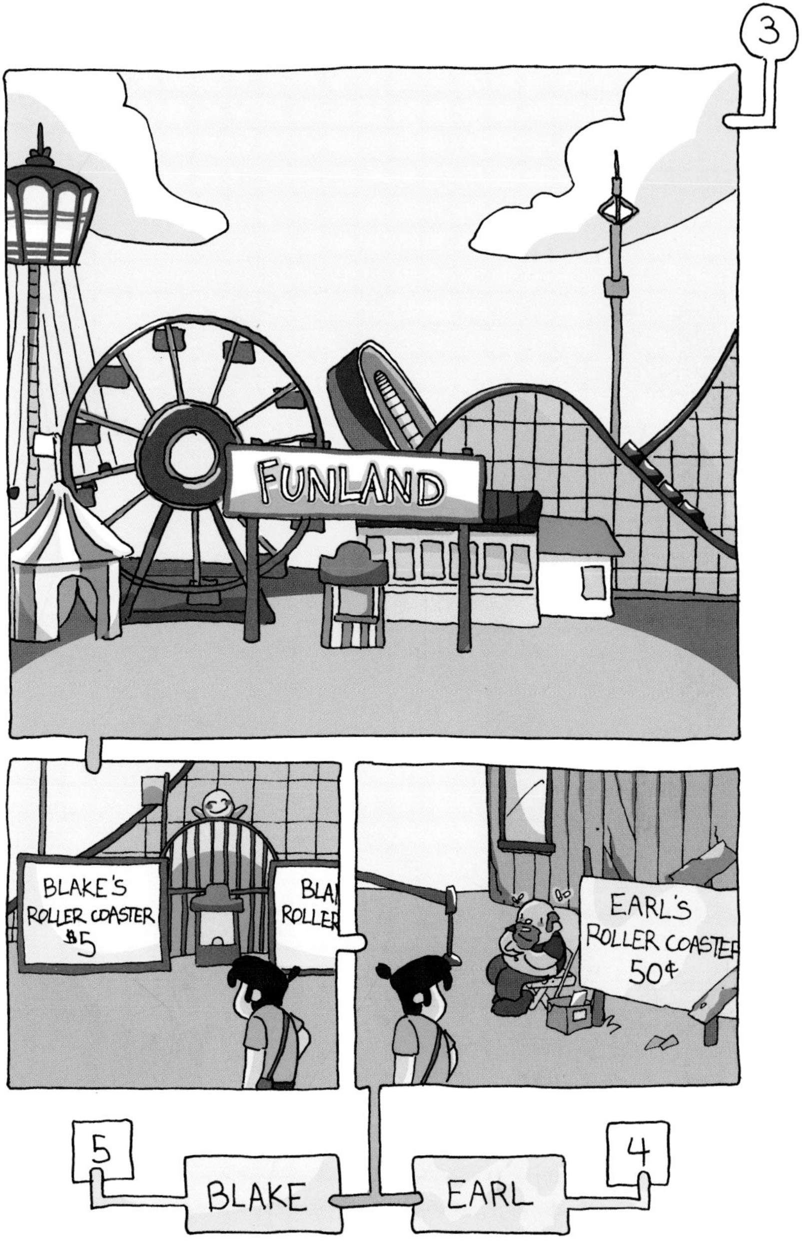
3
FUNLAND
BLAKE'S
ROLLER COASTER
$5
EARL'S
ROLLER COASTER
50¢
5
BLAKE
EARL
4

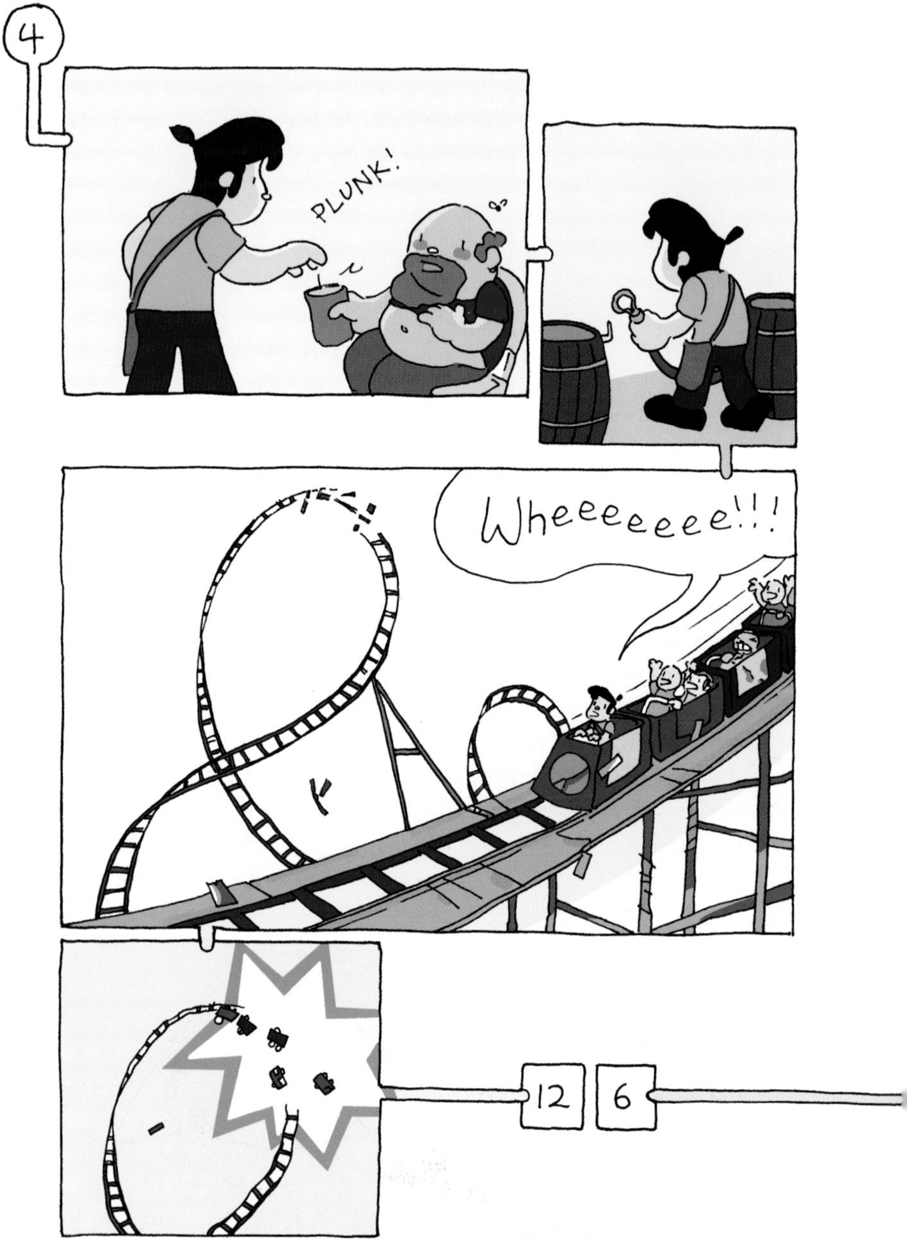
4
PLUNK!
Wheeeeeee!!!
12
6

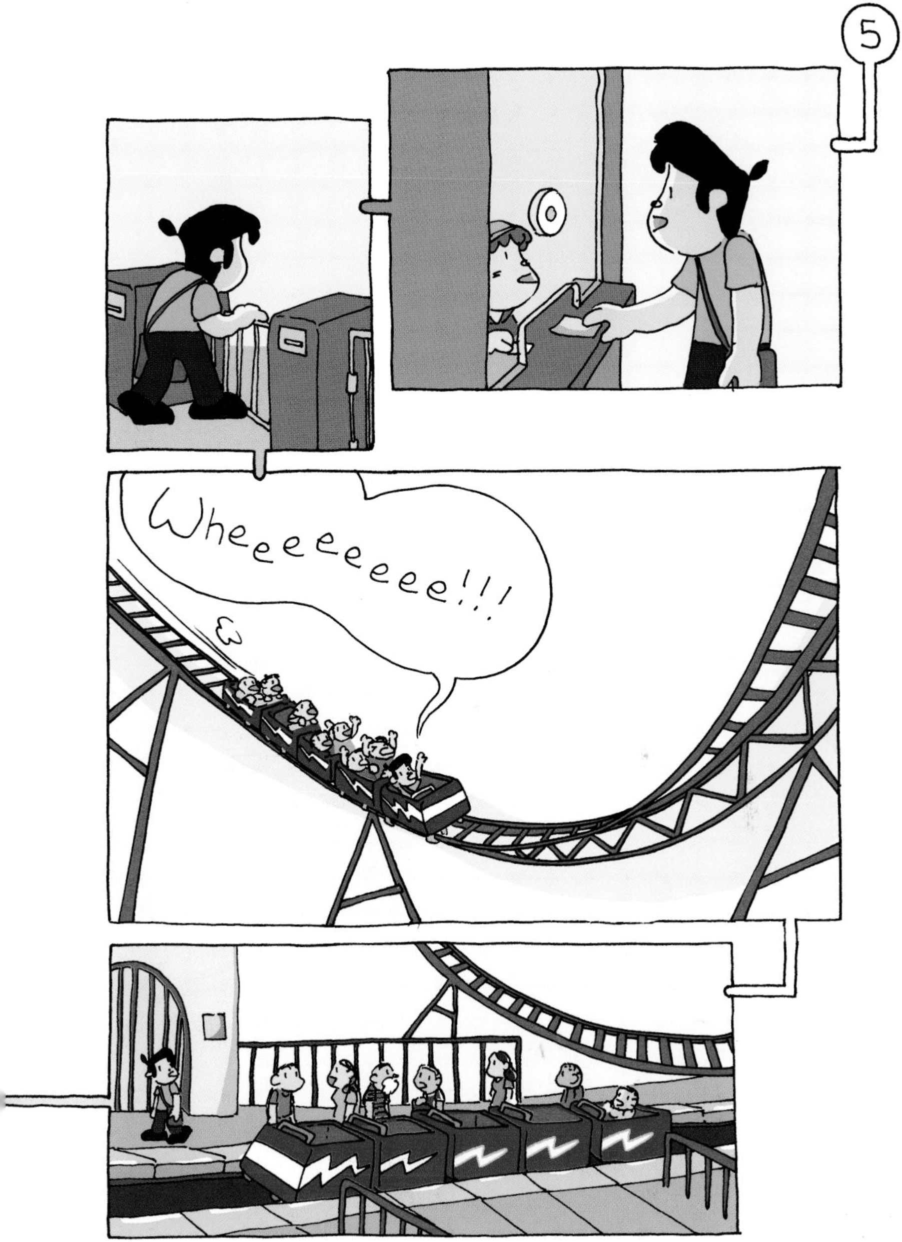
5
Wheeeeeeeee!!!

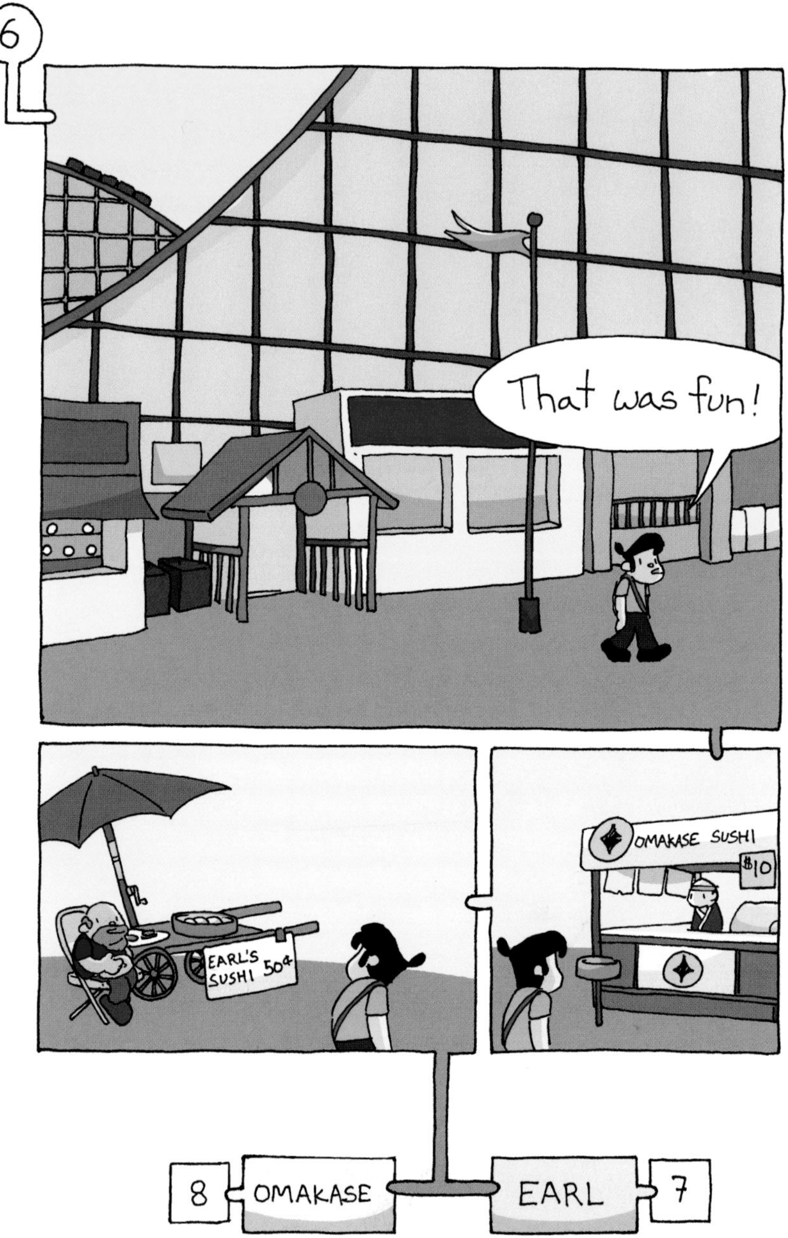
That was fun!
EARL'S SUSHI 50¢
OMAKASE SUSHI
$10
8
OMAKASE
EARL
7

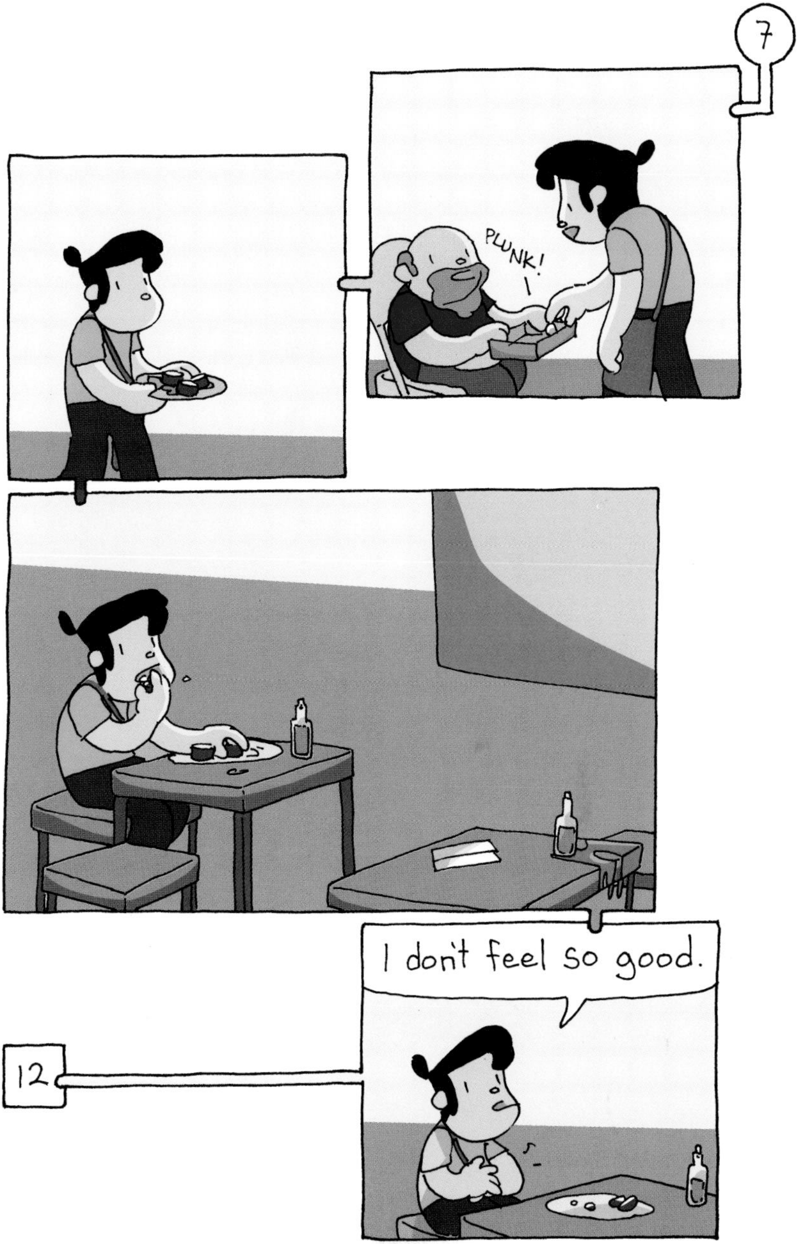
7
PLUNK!
12
I don't feel so good.

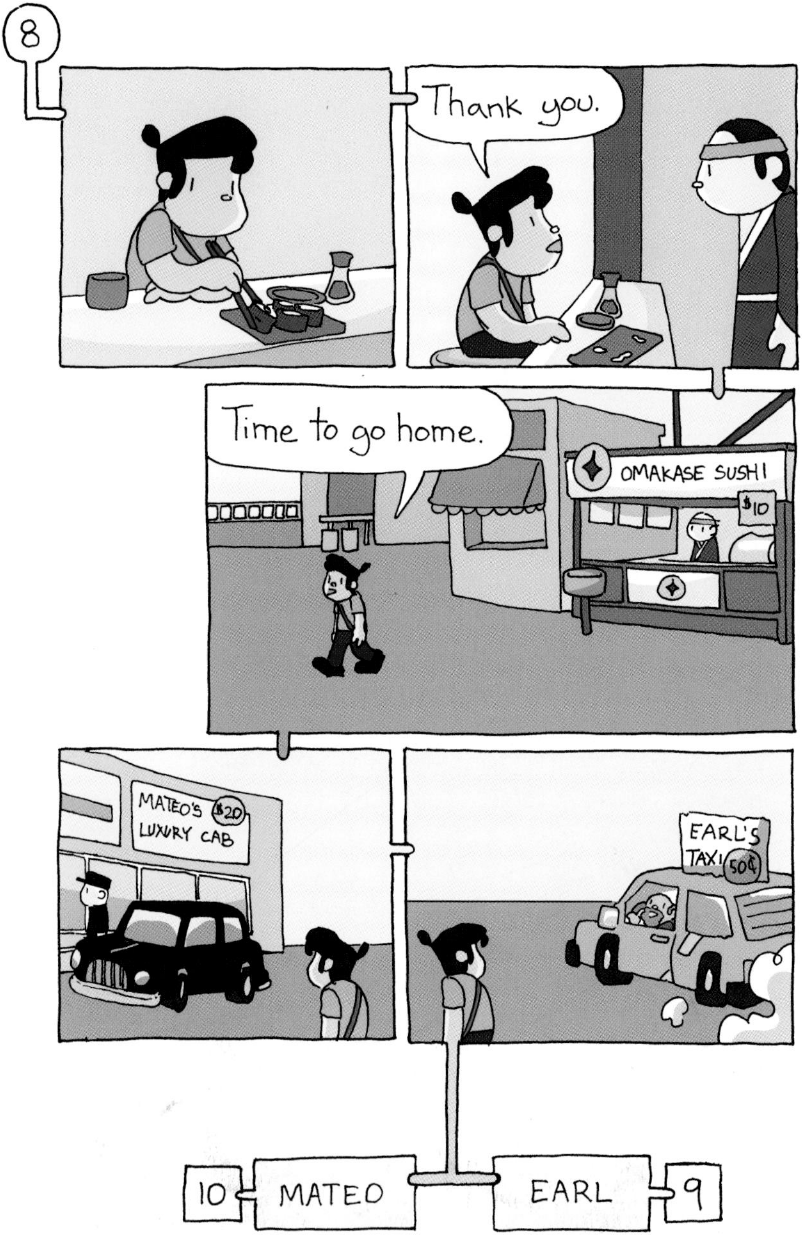
8
Thank you.
Time to go home.
OMAKASE SUSHI
$10
MATEO'S $20
LUXURY CAB
EARL'S
TAXI 50¢
10
MATEO
EARL
9

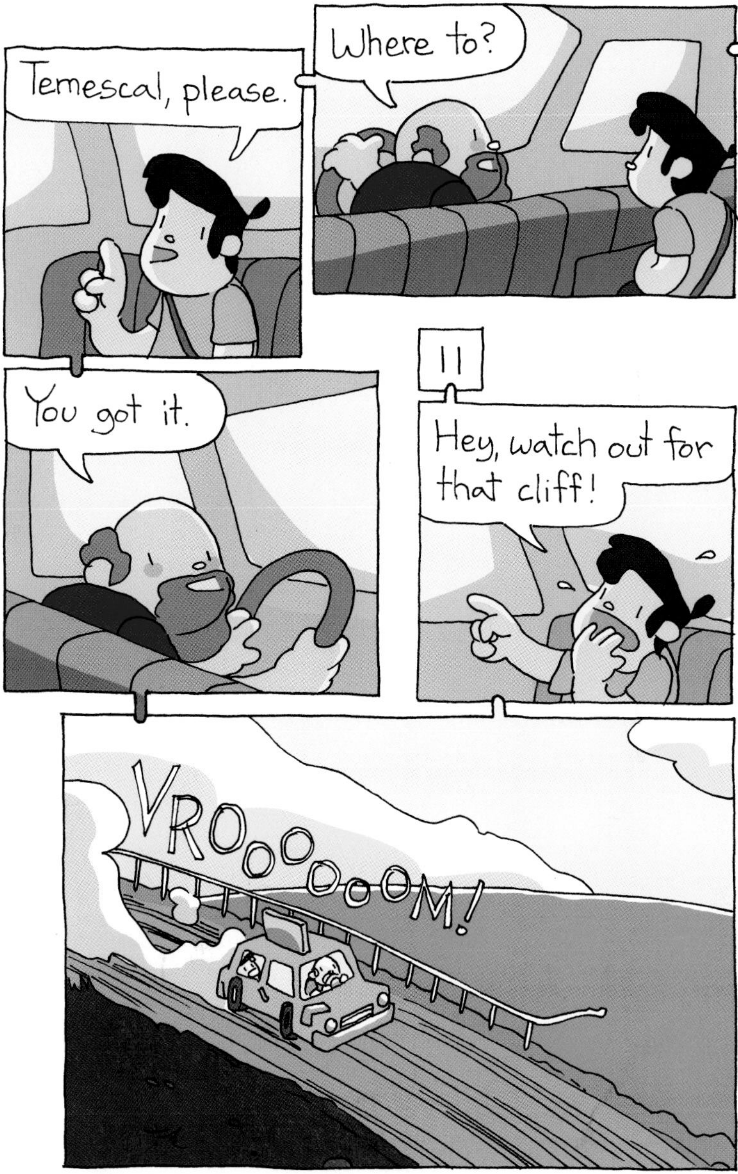
Where to?
Temescal, please.
You got it.
11
Hey, watch out for that cliff!
VROOOOOOOM!

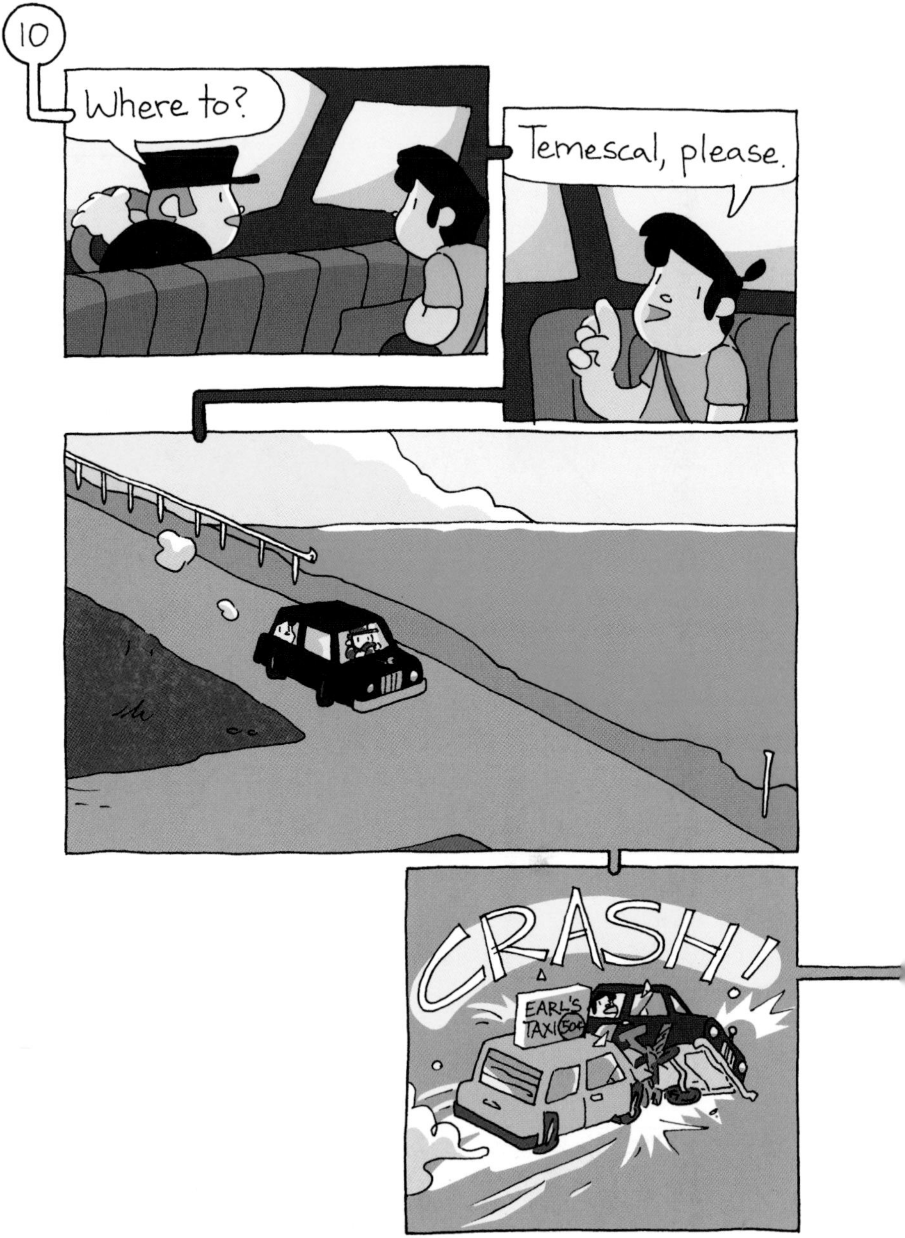
10
Where to?
Temescal, please.
CRASH!
EARL'S TAXI

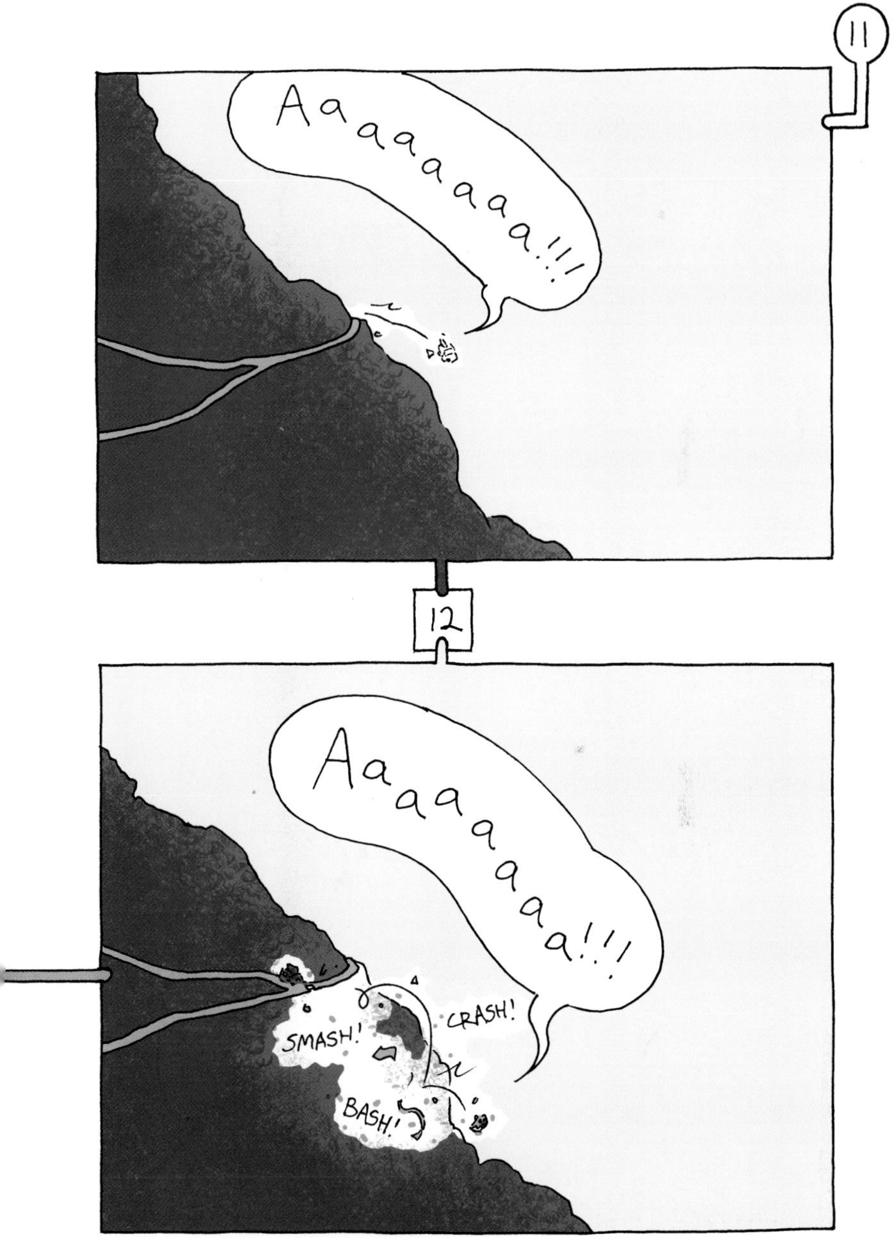
11
Aaaaaaaaaa!!!
12
Aaaaaaaaaa!!!
SMASH!
CRASH!
BASH!

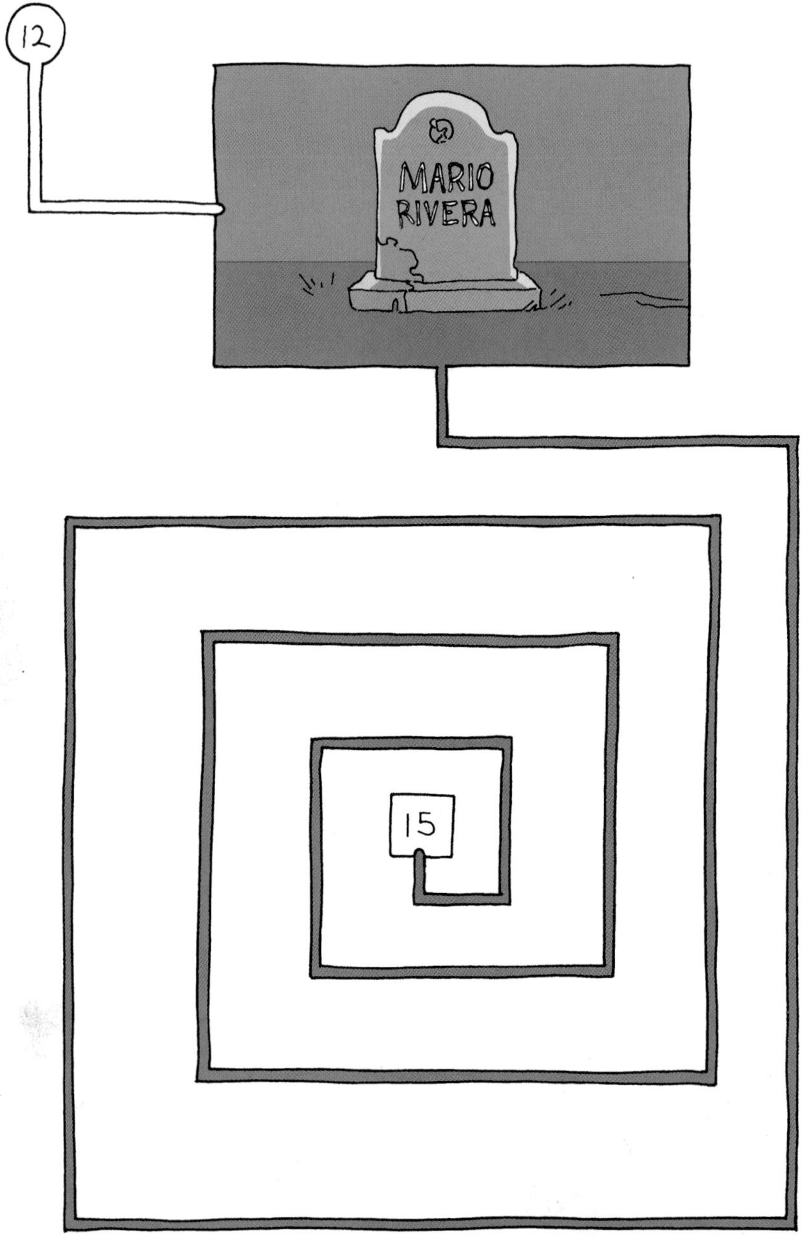
12
MARIO
RIVERA
15

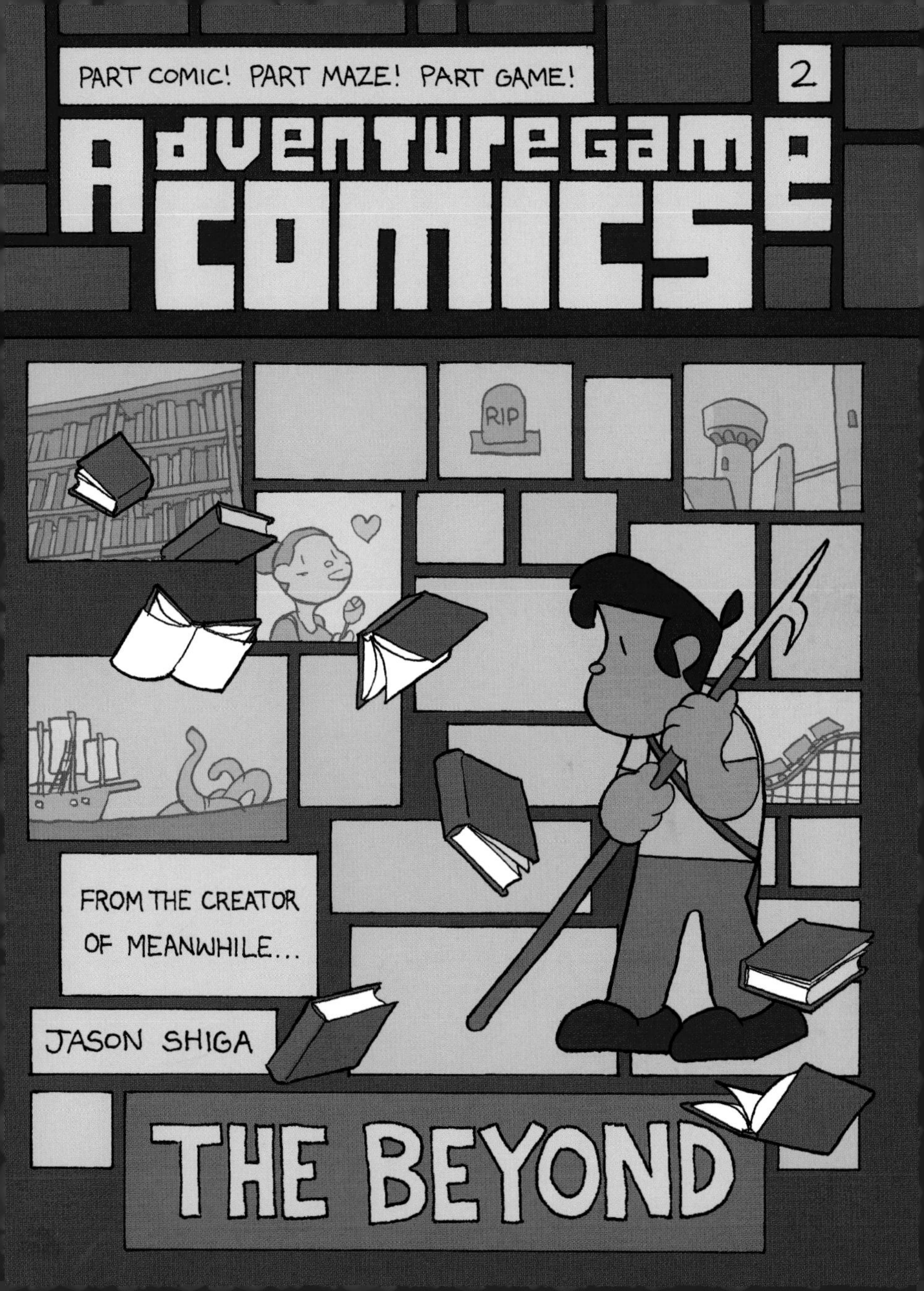

PART COMIC! PART MAZE! PART GAME!
2
ADVENTUREGAME COMICS
RIP
FROM THE CREATOR OF MEANWHILE...
JASON SHIGA
THE BEYOND

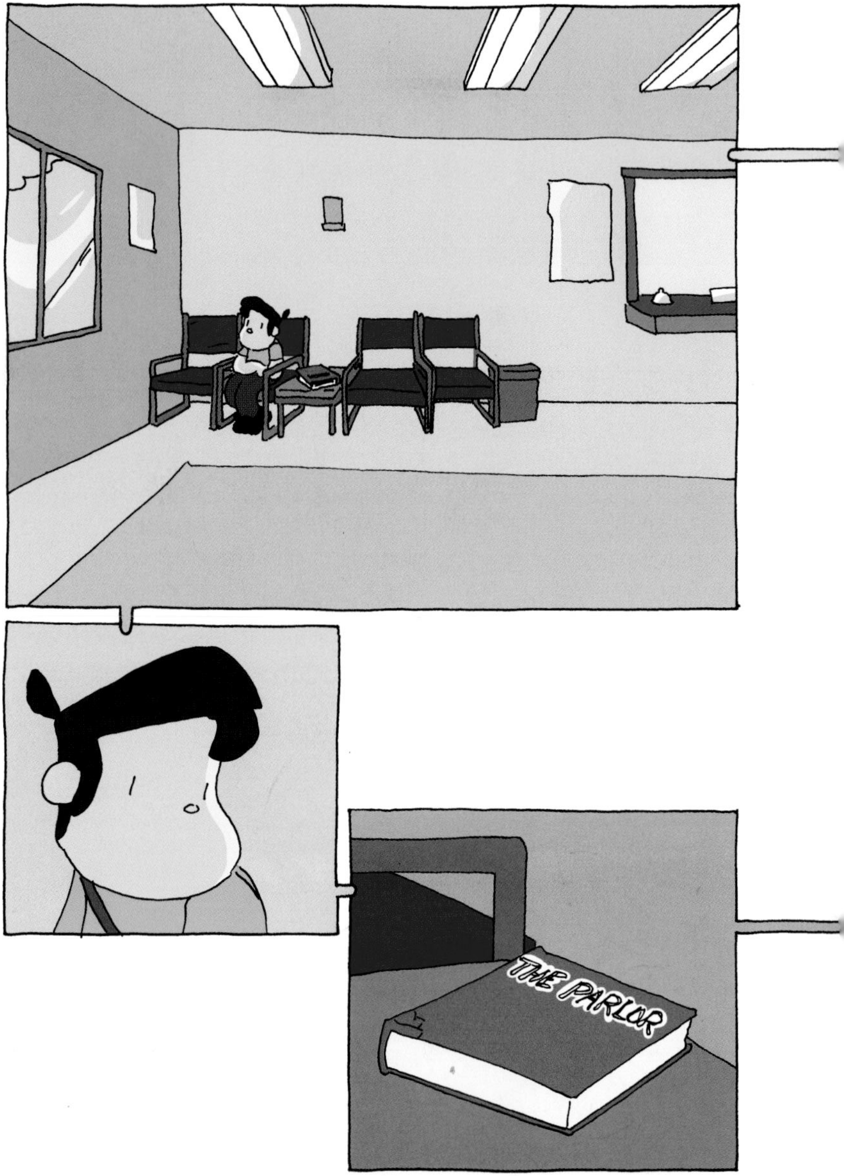
THE PARLOR

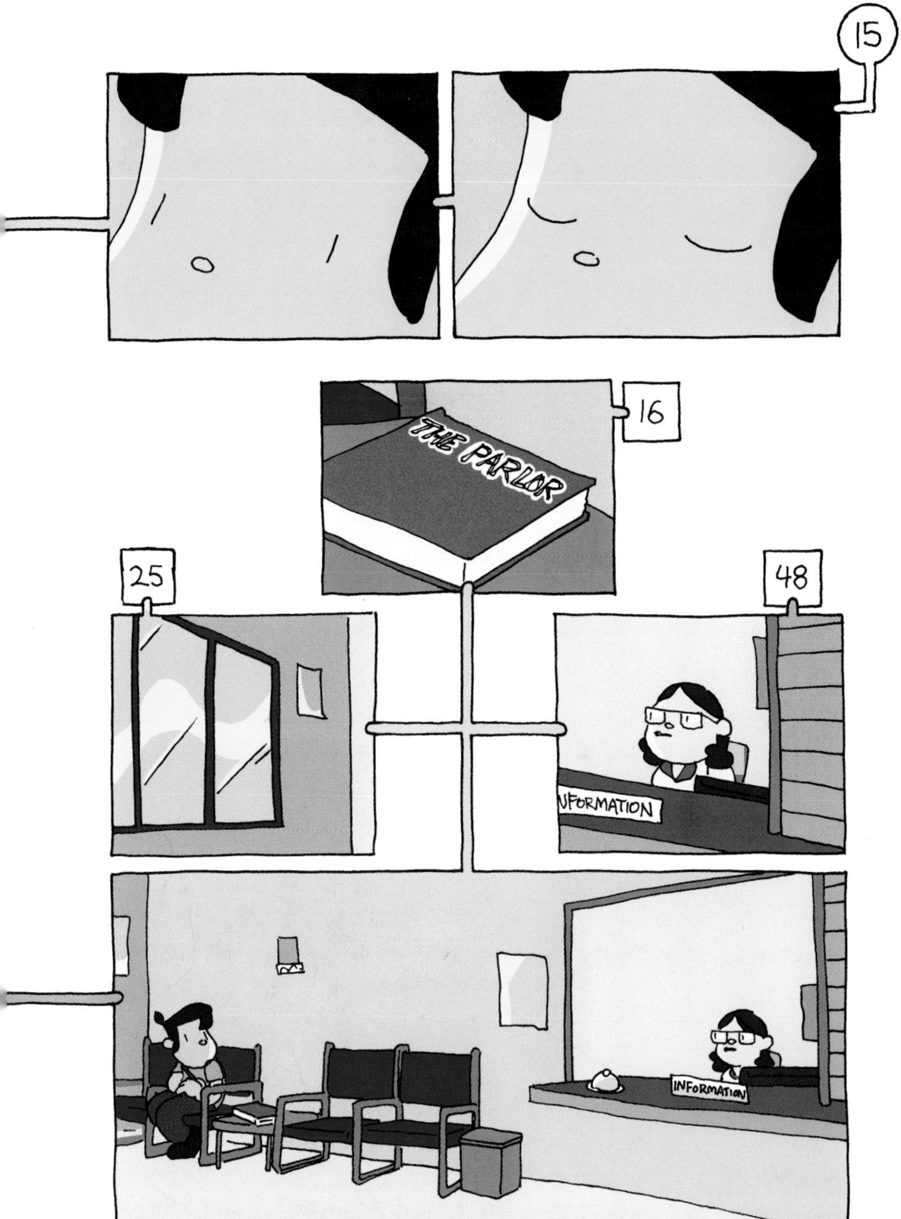
15
16
THE PARLOR
25
48
INFORMATION
INFORMATION

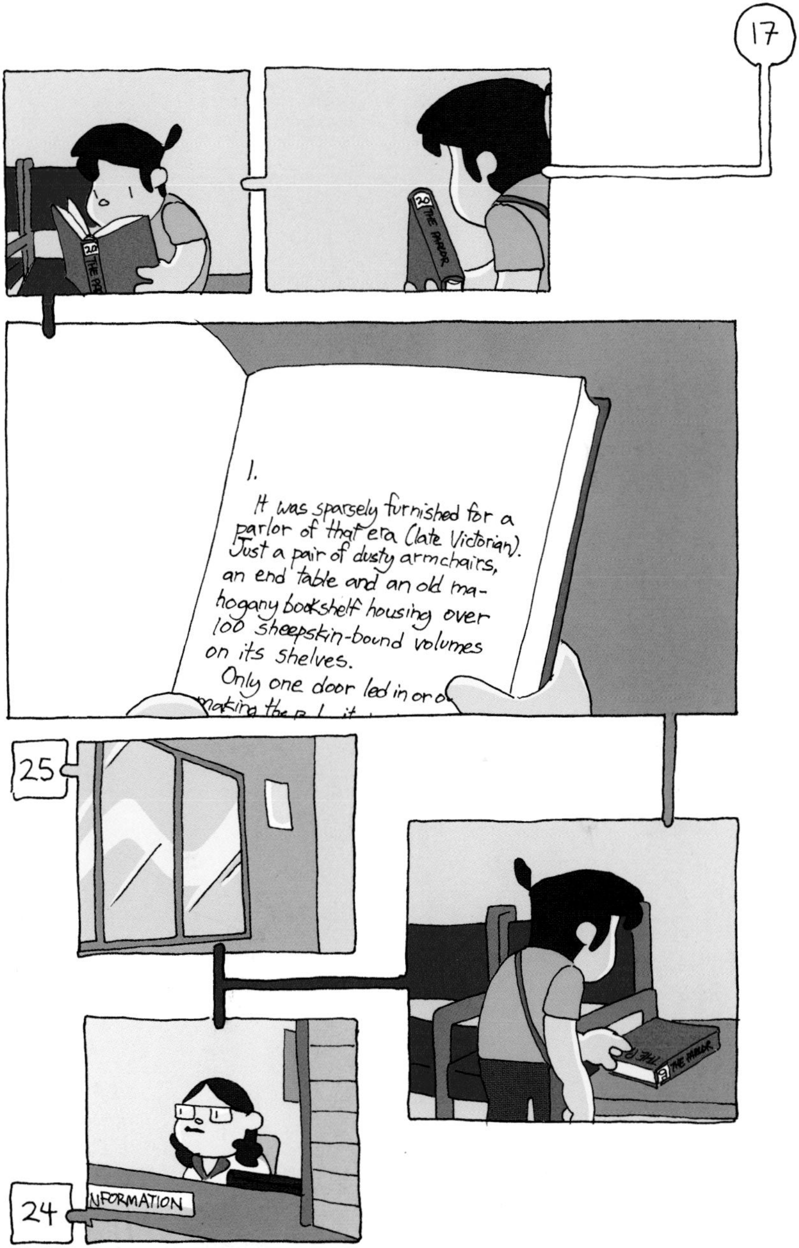
17
20 THE PARLOR
1.
It was sparsely furnished for a parlor of that era (late Victorian). Just a pair of dusty armchairs, an end table and an old mahogany bookshelf housing over 100 sheepskin-bound volumes on its shelves.
Only one door led in or o
25
THE PARLOR
NFORMATION
24

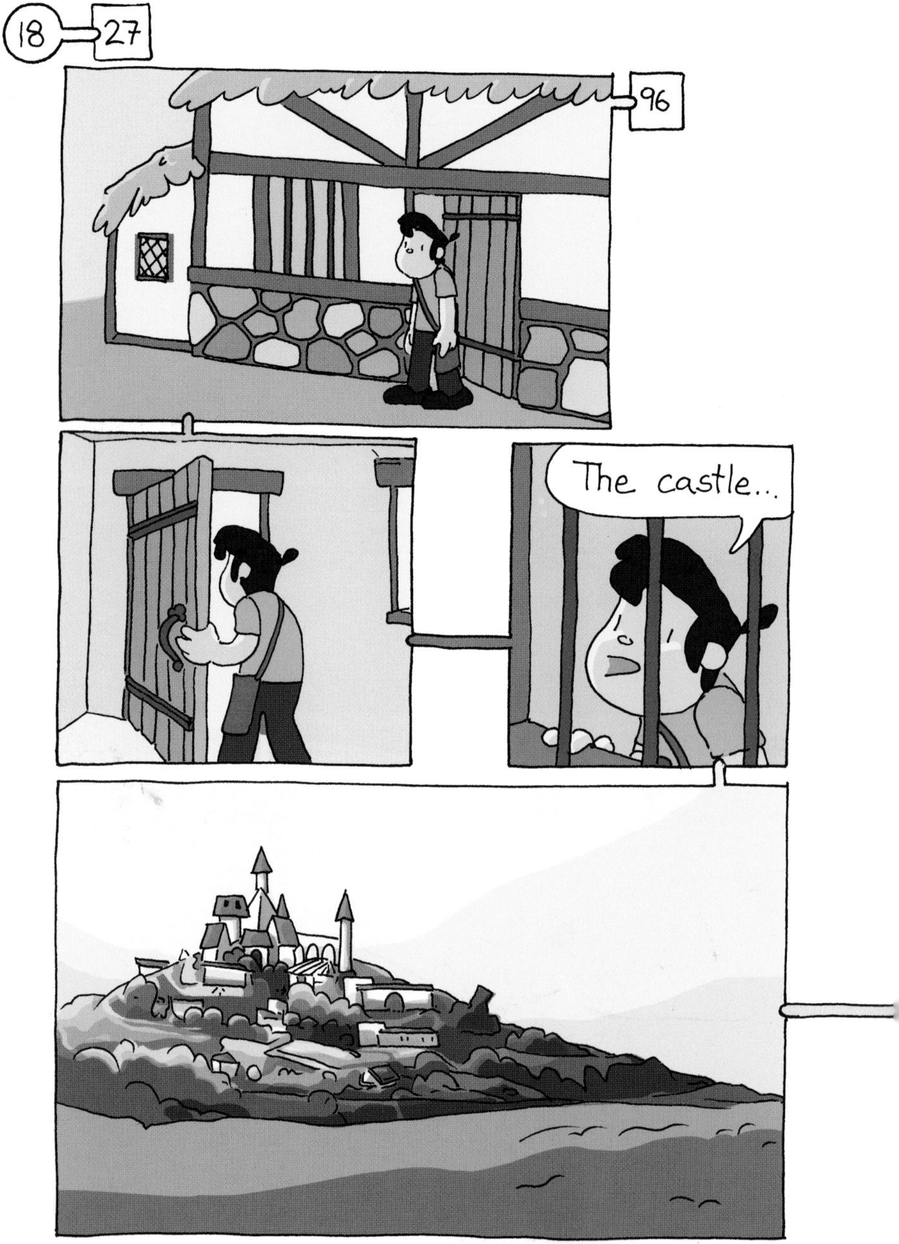
18
27
96
The castle...

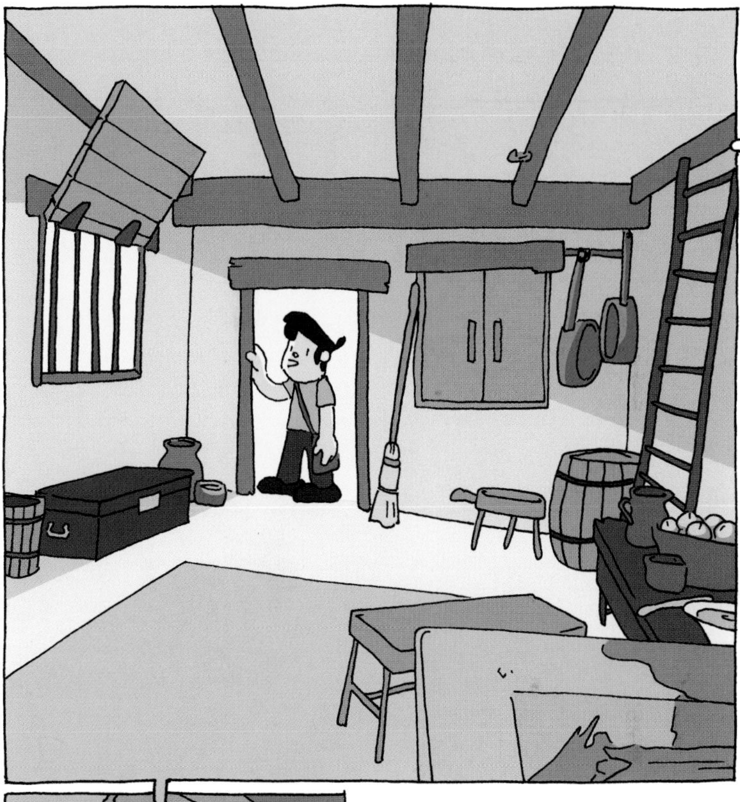

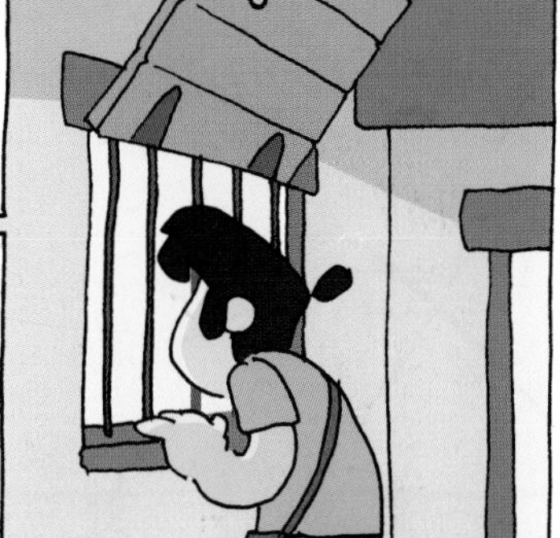

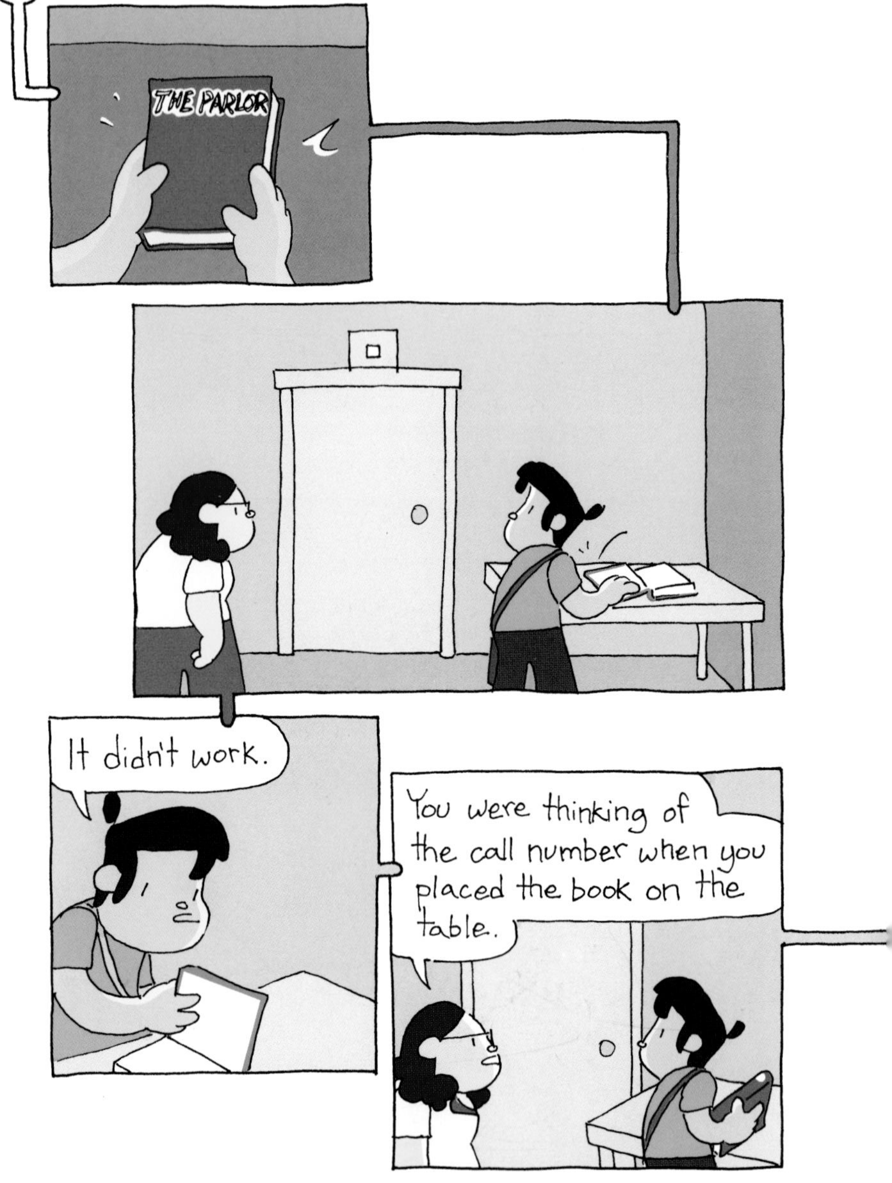
THE PARLOR
It didn't work.
You were thinking of the call number when you placed the book on the table.

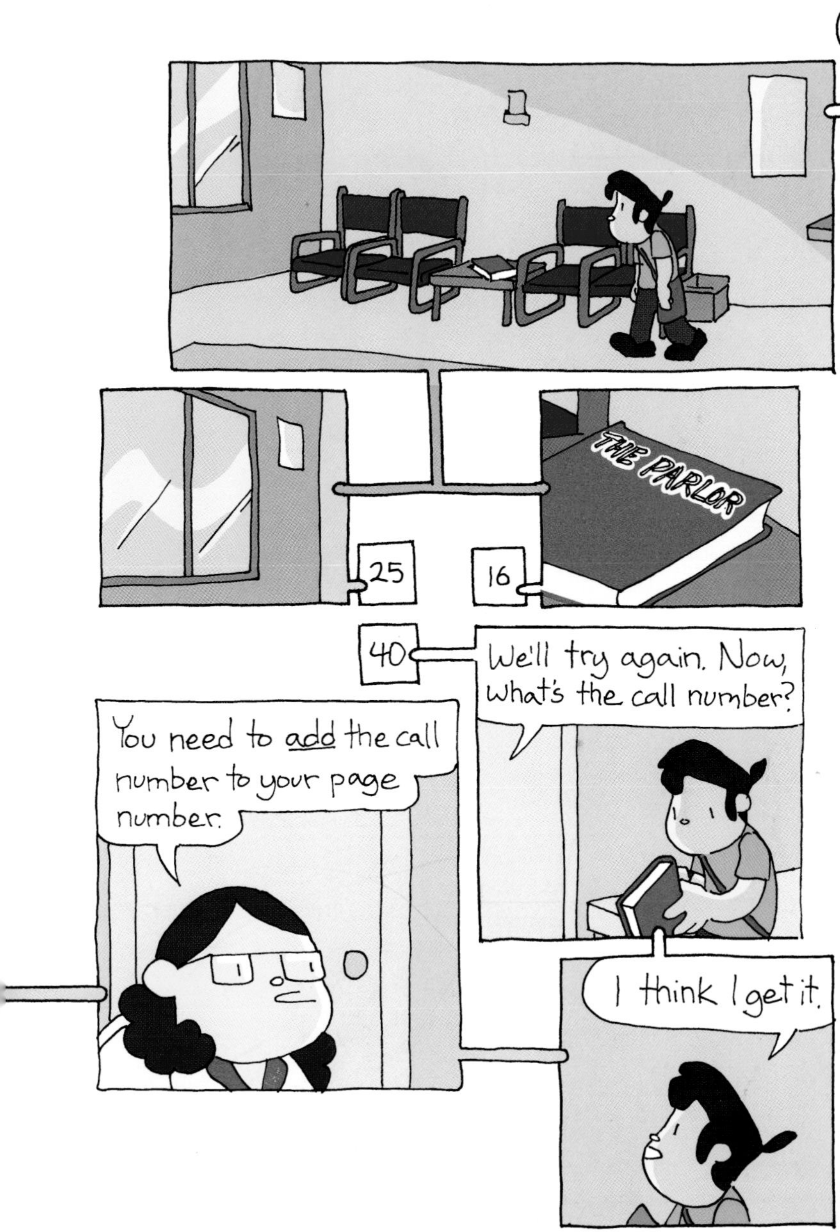
21
THE PARLOR
25
16
40
We'll try again. Now, what's the call number?
You need to add the call number to your page number.
I think I get it.

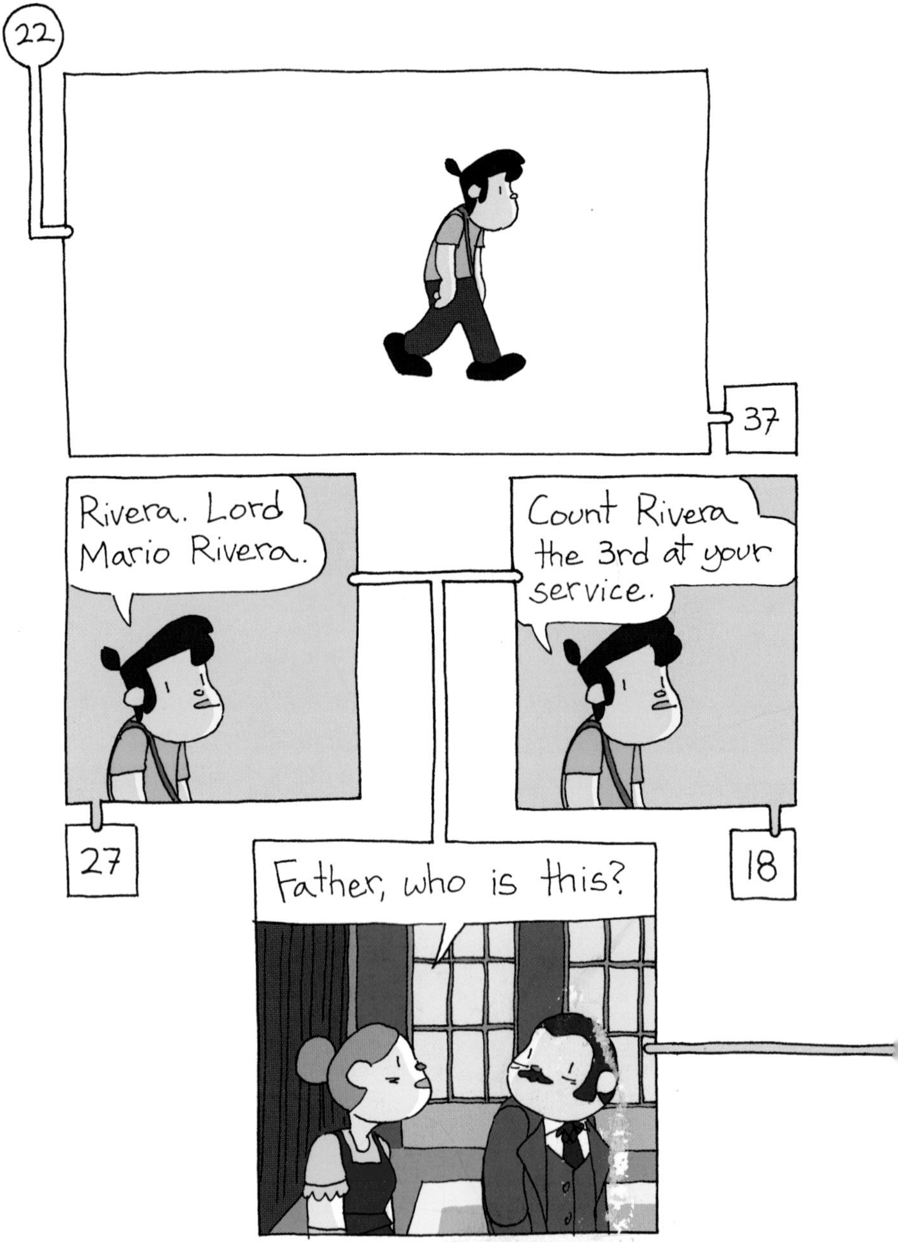
22
37
Rivera. Lord Mario Rivera.
27
Count Rivera the 3rd at your service.
18
Father, who is this?

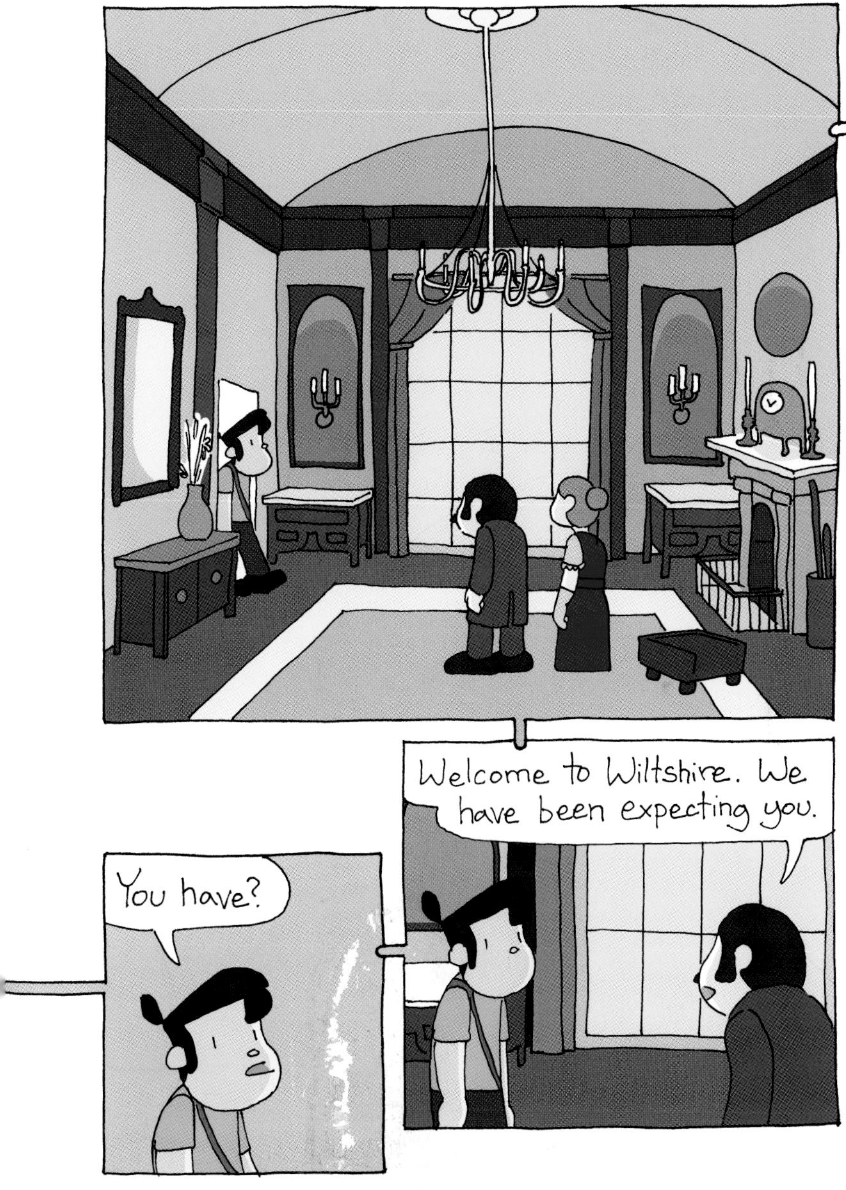
Welcome to Wiltshire. We have been expecting you.
You have?

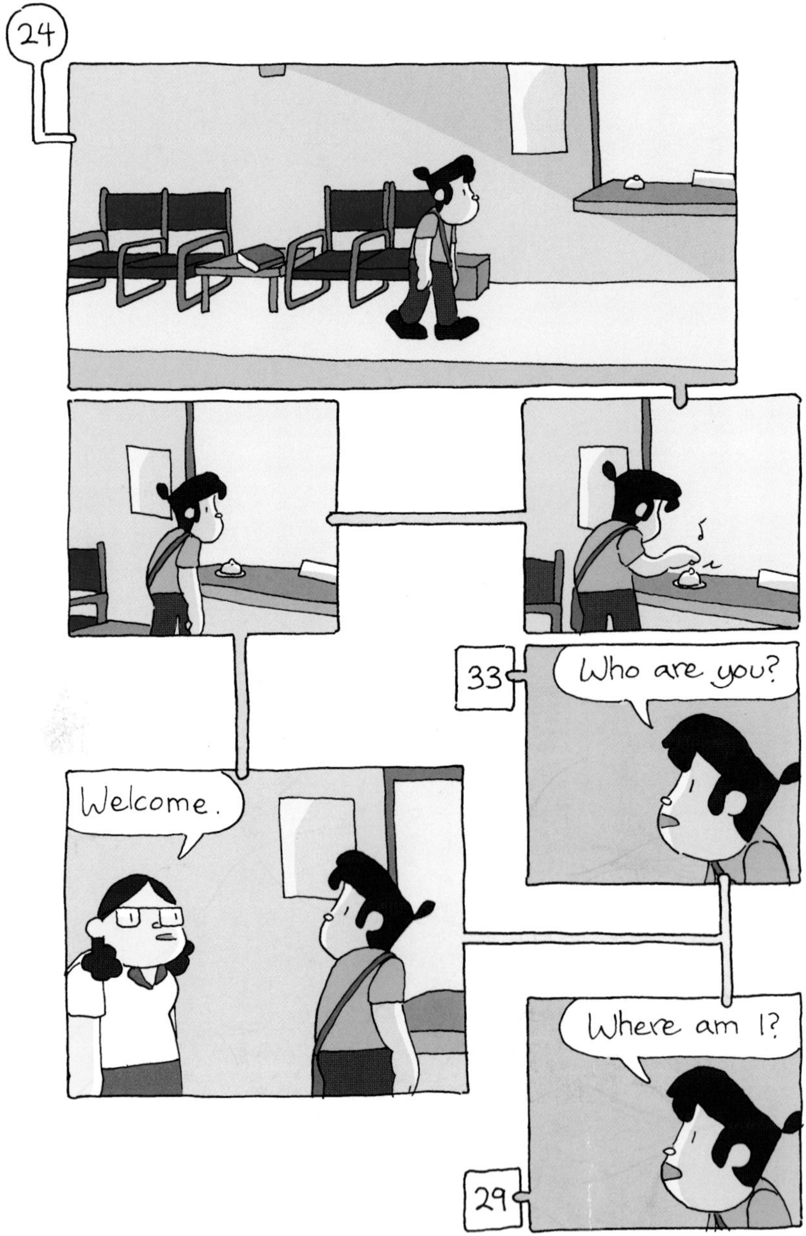
24
Welcome.
33
Who are you?
Where am I?
29

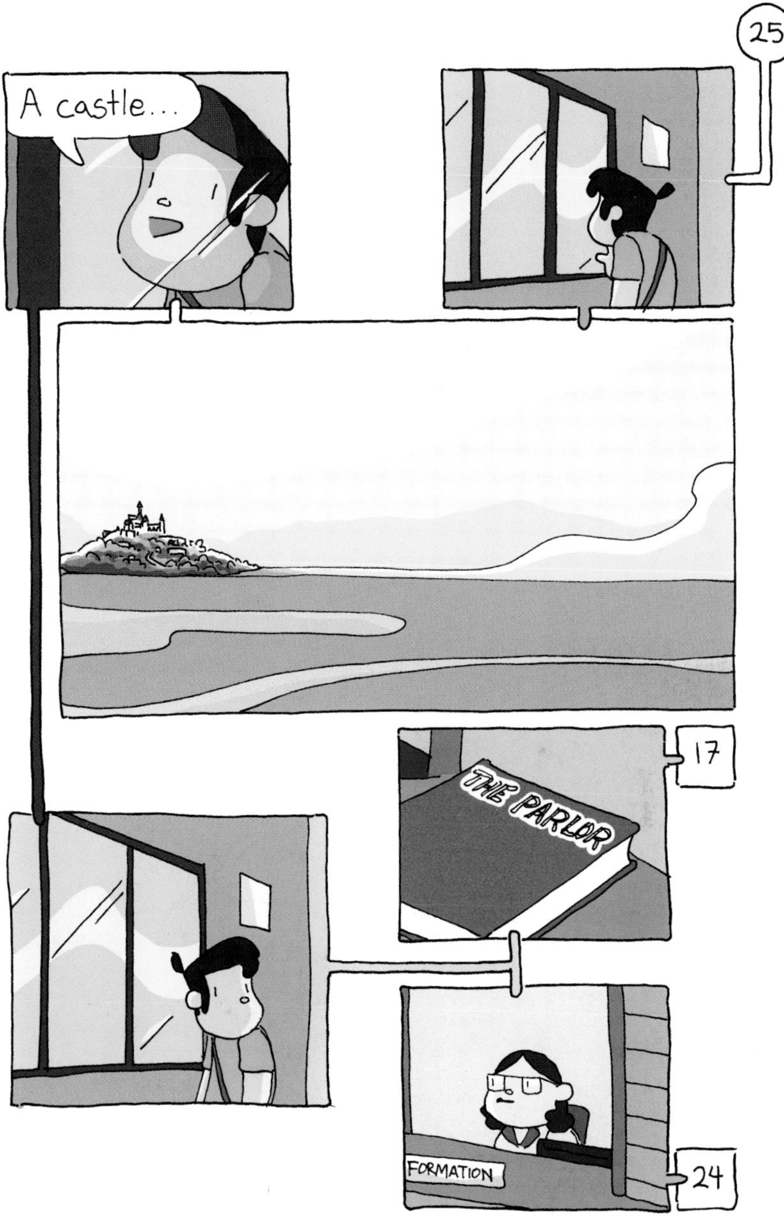

25
A castle...
17
THE PARLOR
FORMATION
24

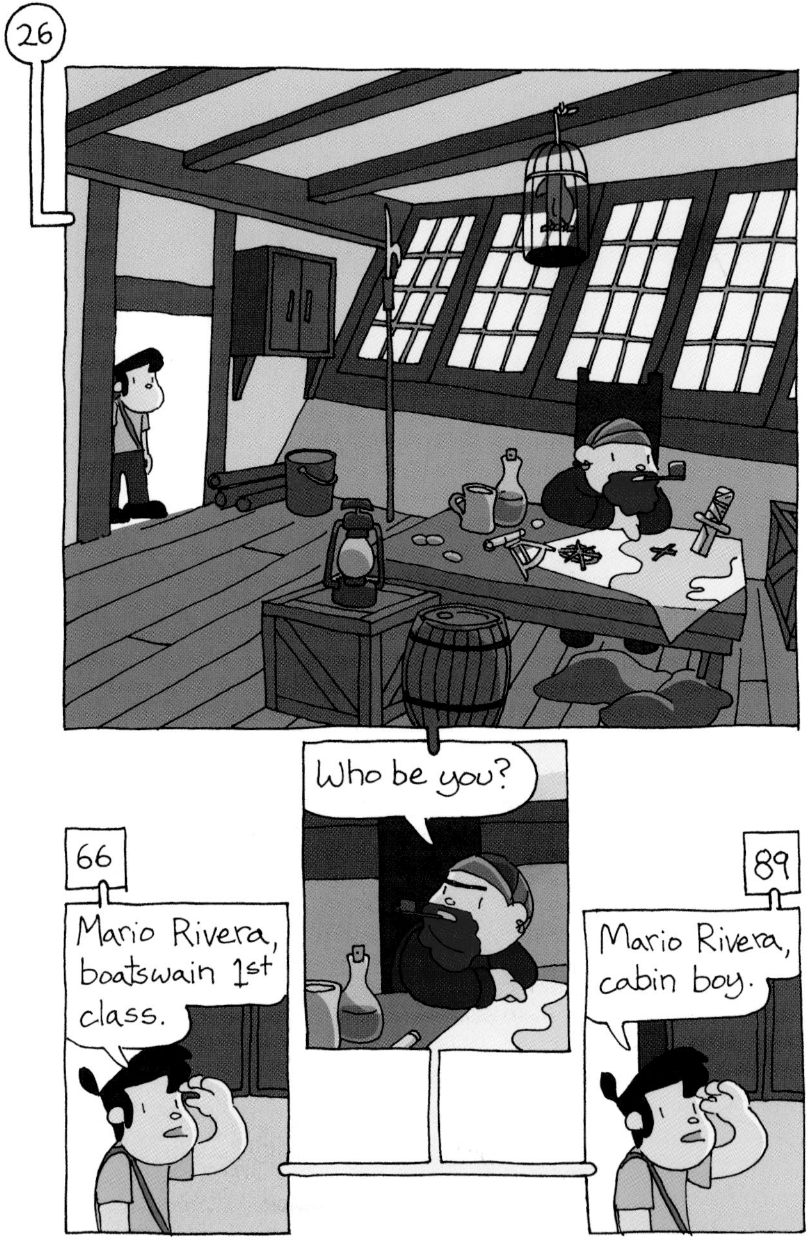
26
Who be you?
66
Mario Rivera, boatswain 1st class.
89
Mario Rivera, cabin boy.

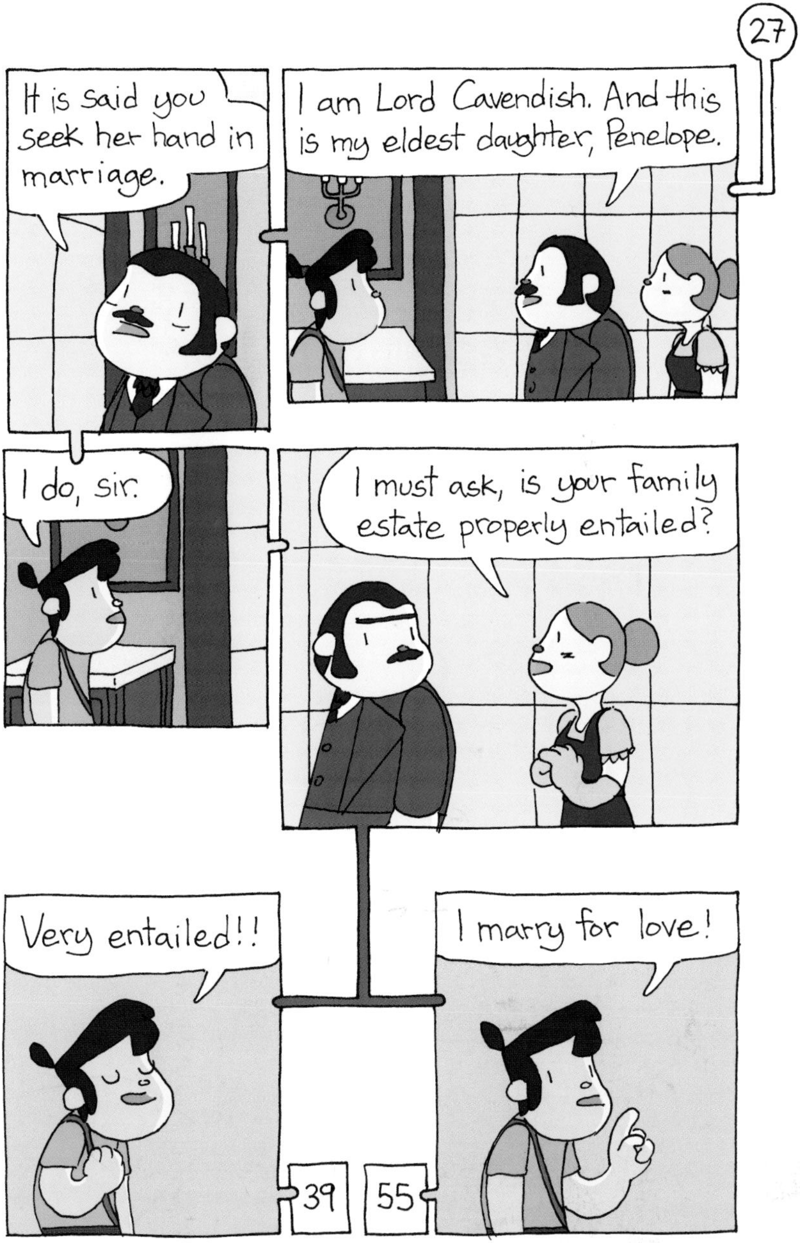
27
It is said you seek her hand in marriage.
I am Lord Cavendish. And this is my eldest daughter, Penelope.
I do, sir.
I must ask, is your family estate properly entailed?
Very entailed!!
I marry for love!
39
55

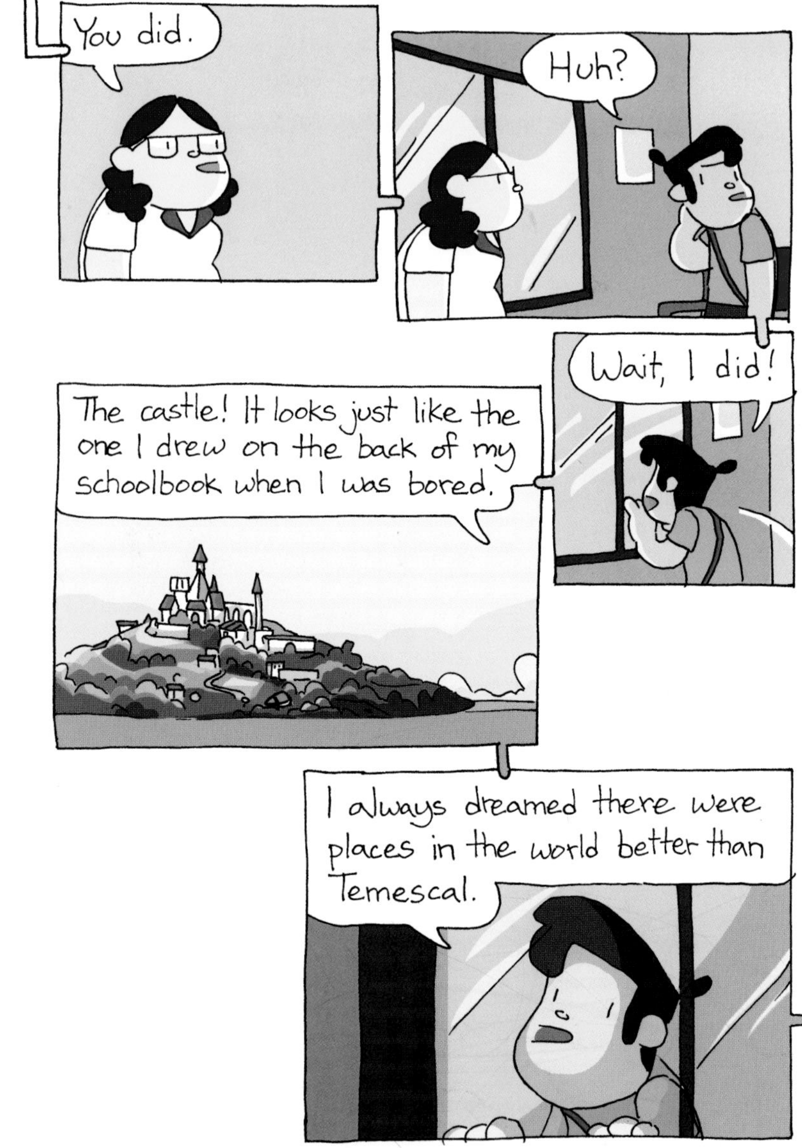
You did.
Huh?
Wait, I did!
The castle! It looks just like the one I drew on the back of my schoolbook when I was bored.
I always dreamed there were places in the world better than Temescal.

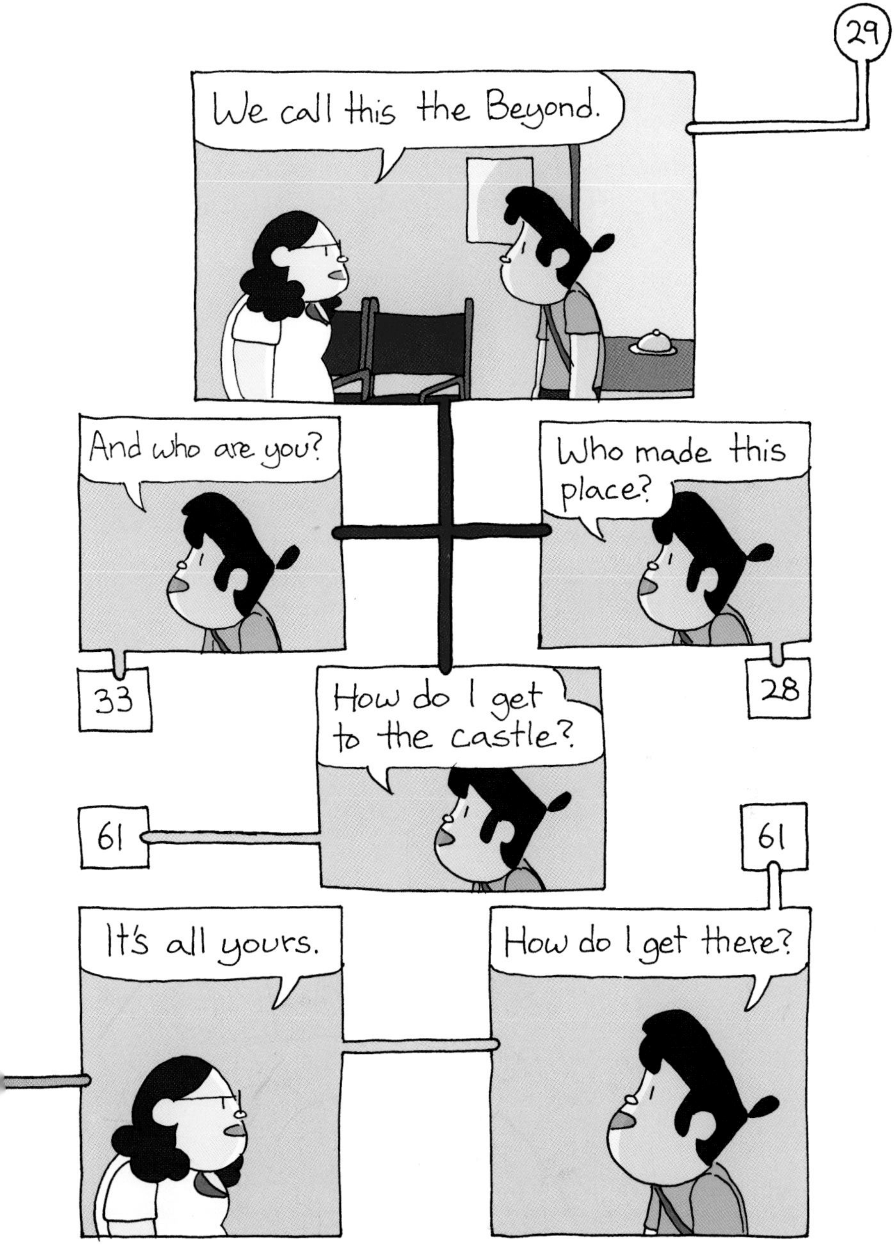
29
We call this the Beyond.
And who are you?
33
Who made this place?
28
How do I get to the castle?
61
61
It's all yours.
How do I get there?

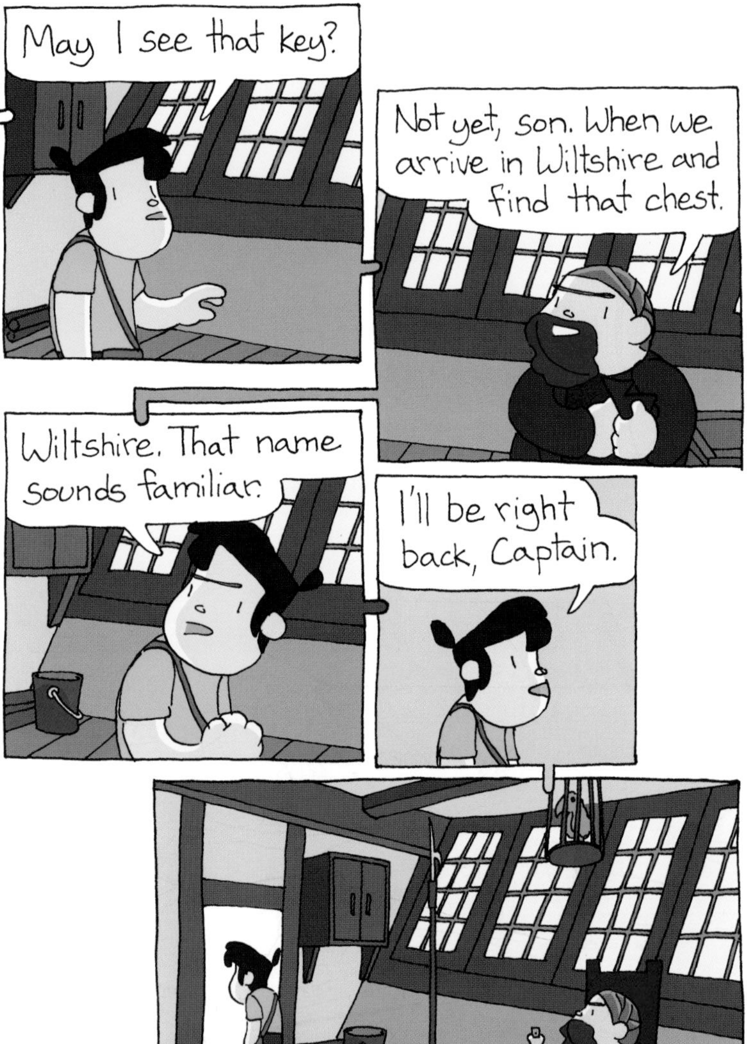
May I see that key?
Not yet, son. When we arrive in Wiltshire and find that chest.
Wiltshire. That name sounds familiar.
I'll be right back, Captain.

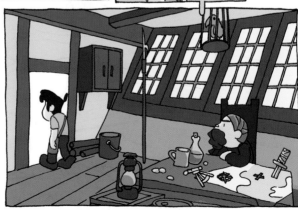

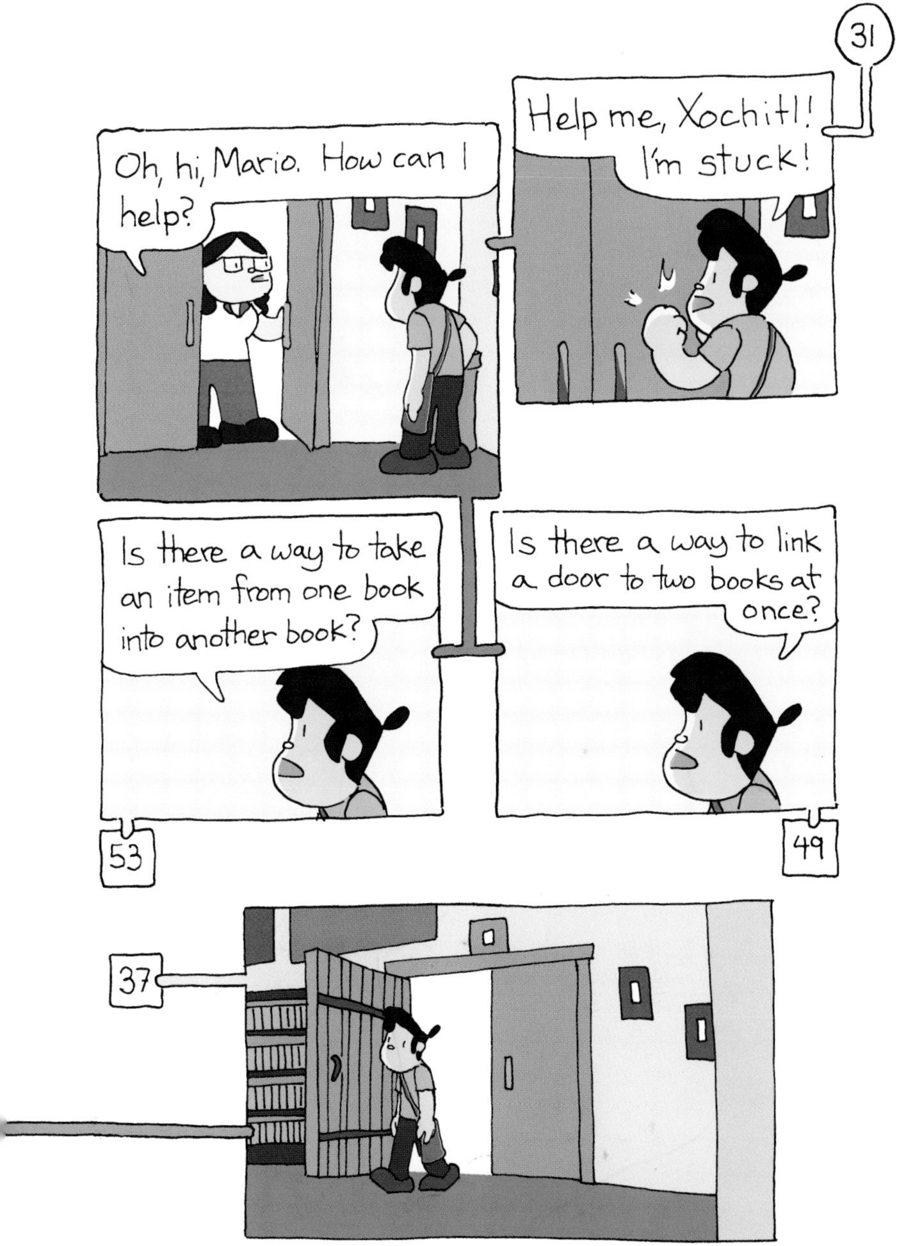
31
Oh, hi, Mario. How can I help?
Help me, Xochitl! I'm stuck!
Is there a way to take an item from one book into another book?
53
Is there a way to link a door to two books at once?
49
37

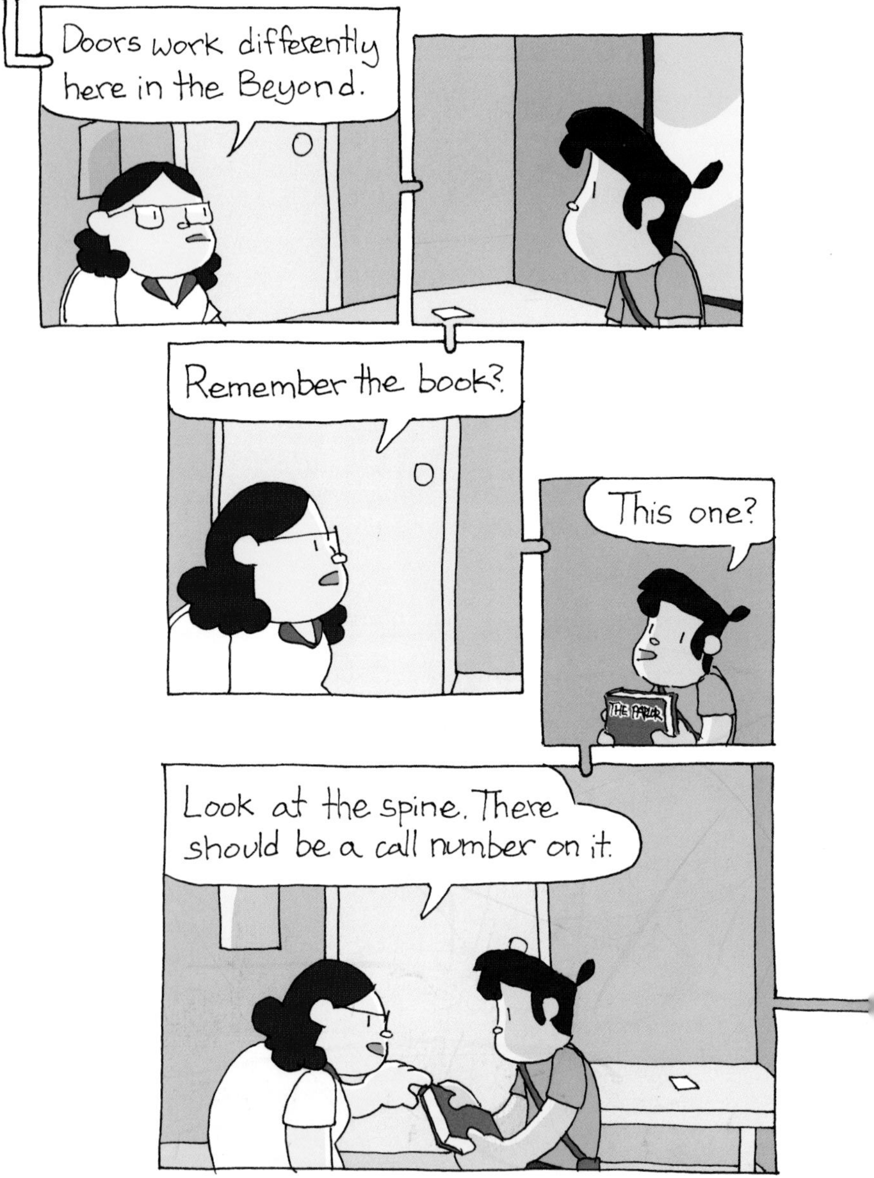
Doors work differently here in the Beyond.
Remember the book?
This one?
THE PARLOR
Look at the spine. There should be a call number on it.

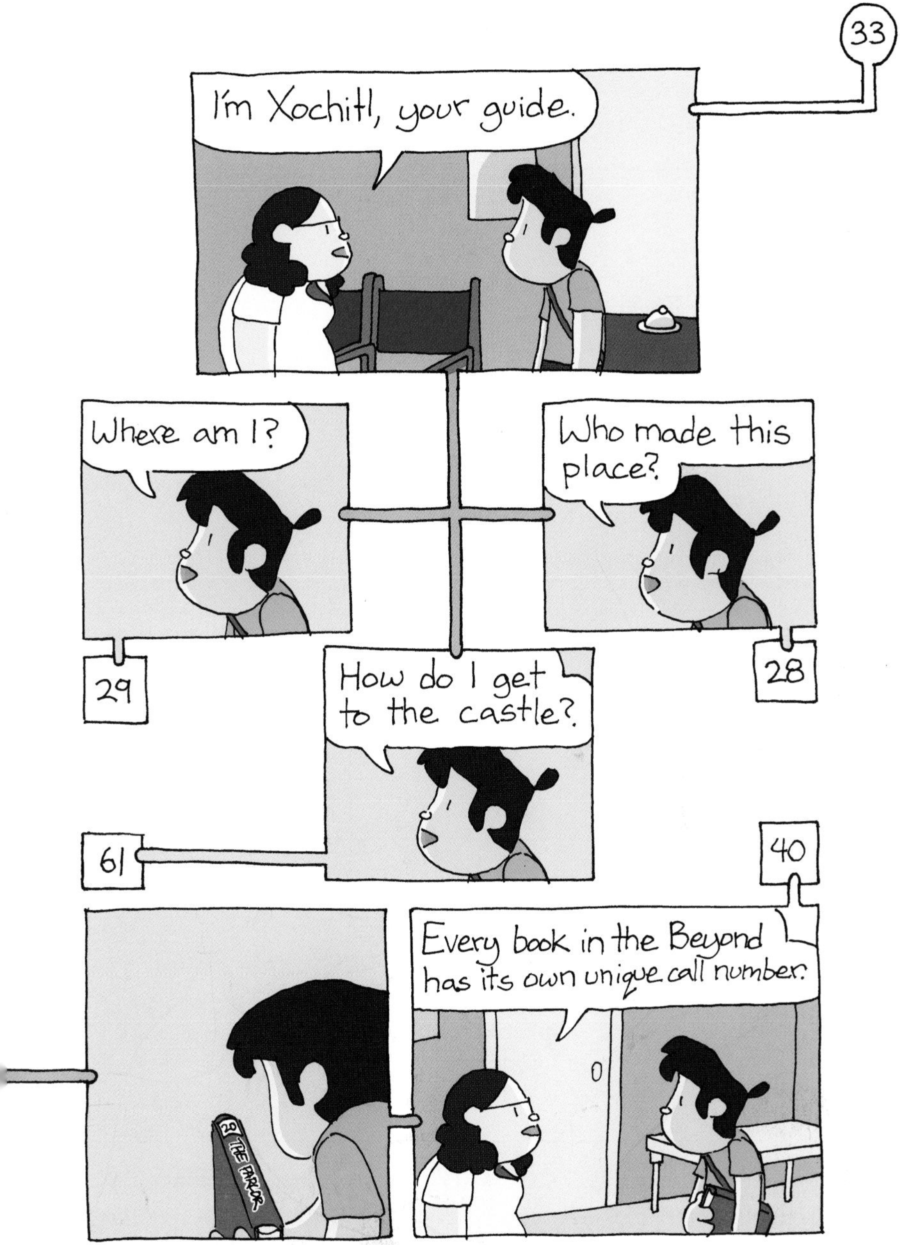
33
I'm Xochitl, your guide.
Where am I?
29
Who made this place?
28
How do I get to the castle?
61
40
Every book in the Beyond has its own unique call number.
29 THE PARLOR

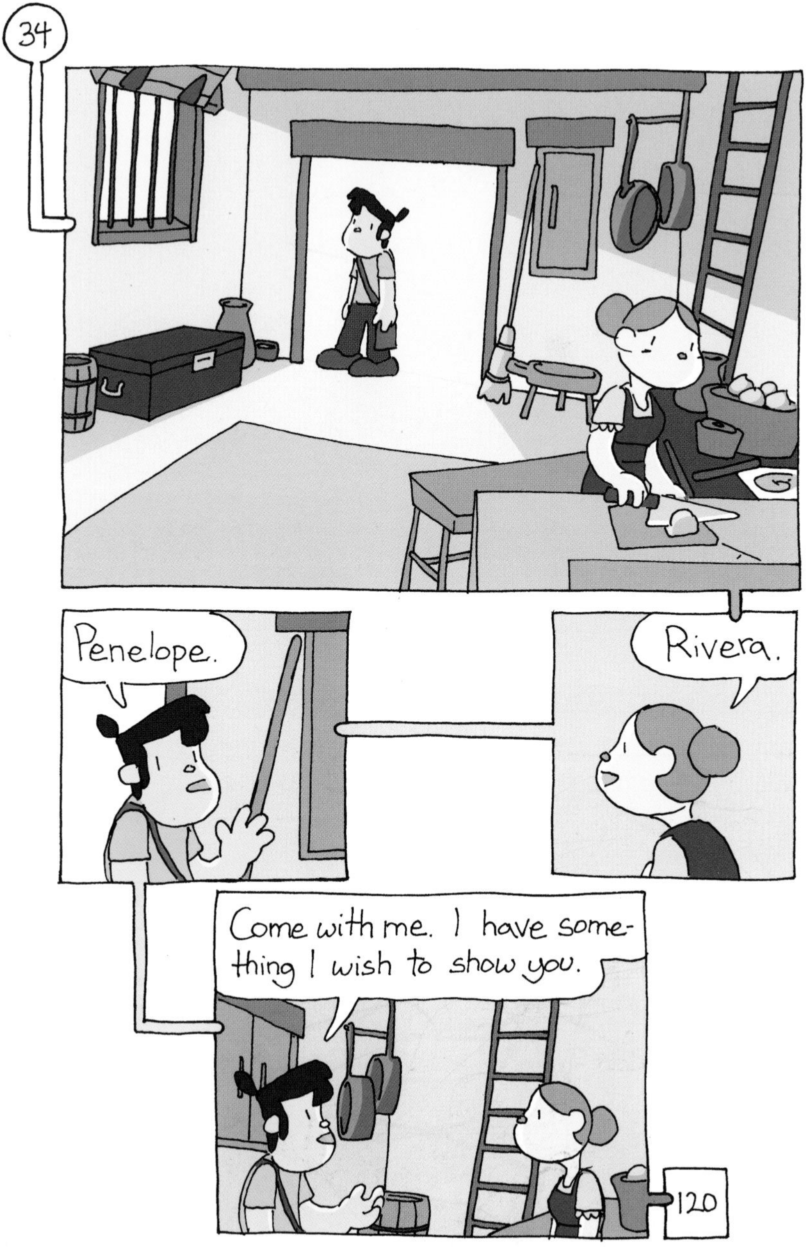
34
Penelope.
Rivera.
Come with me. I have something I wish to show you.
120

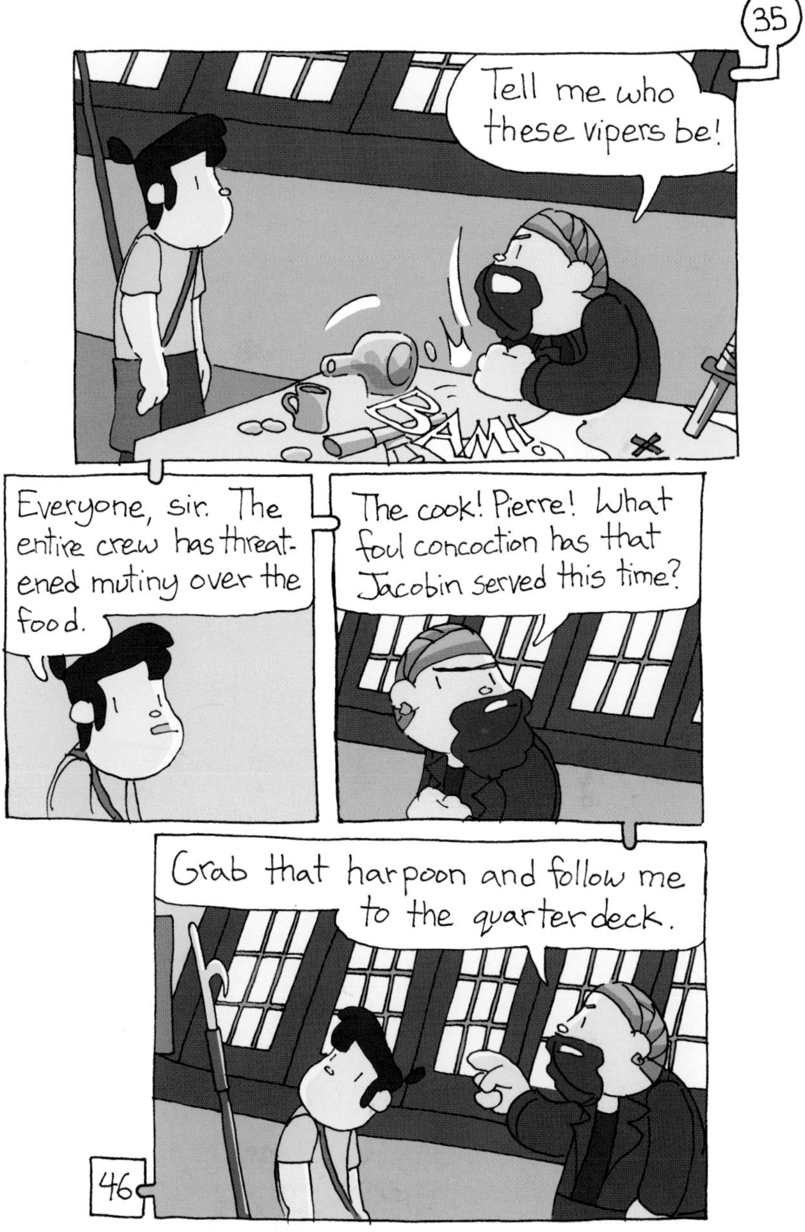
35
Tell me who these vipers be!
BAM!
Everyone, sir. The entire crew has threat-ened mutiny over the food.
The cook! Pierre! What foul concoction has that Jacobin served this time?
Grab that harpoon and follow me to the quarterdeck.
46

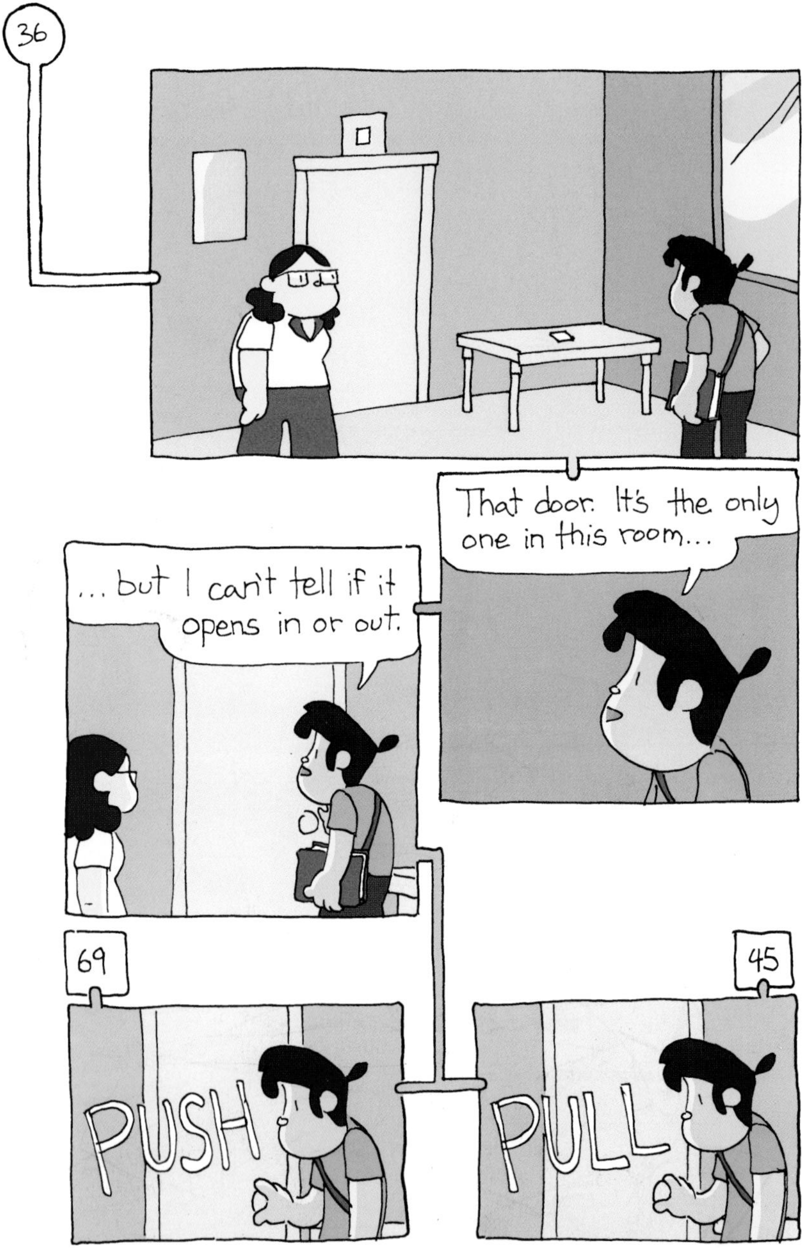
36
That door. It's the only one in this room...
...but I can't tell if it opens in or out.
69
PUSH
45
PULL

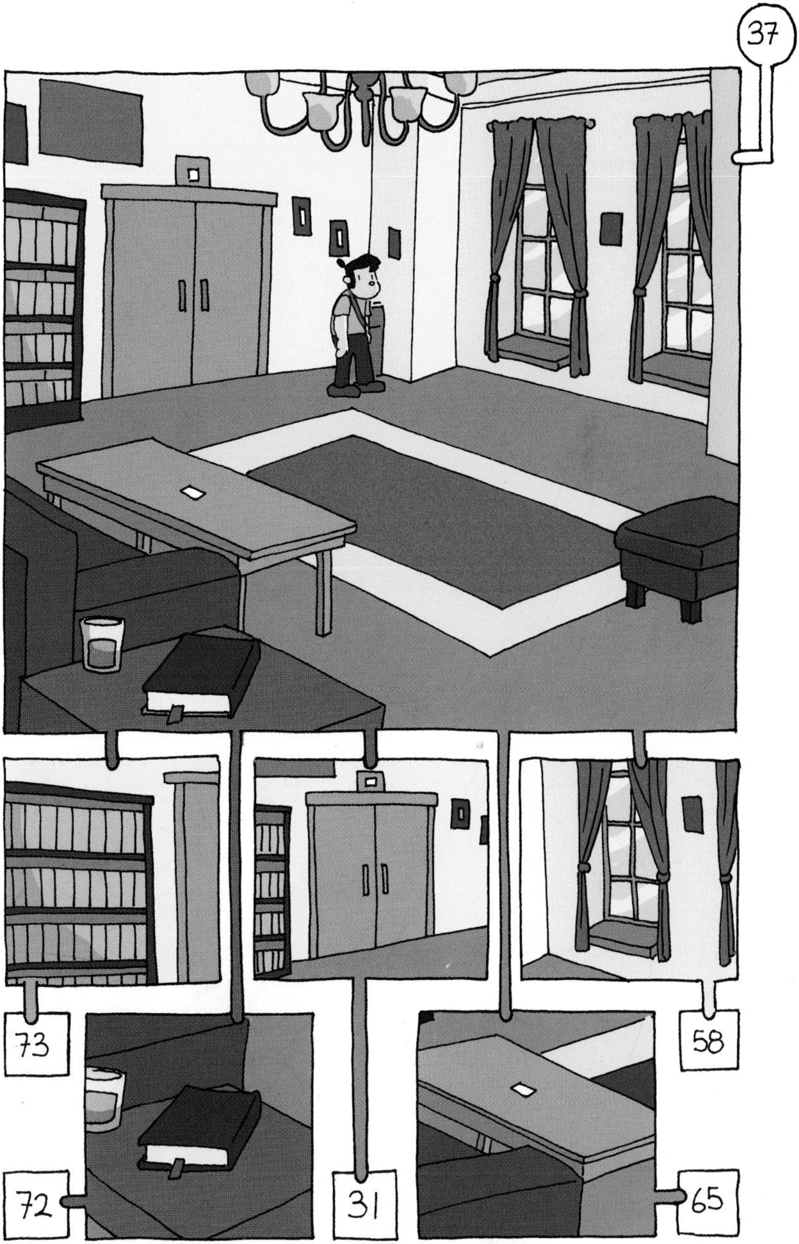
37
73
72
31
58
65

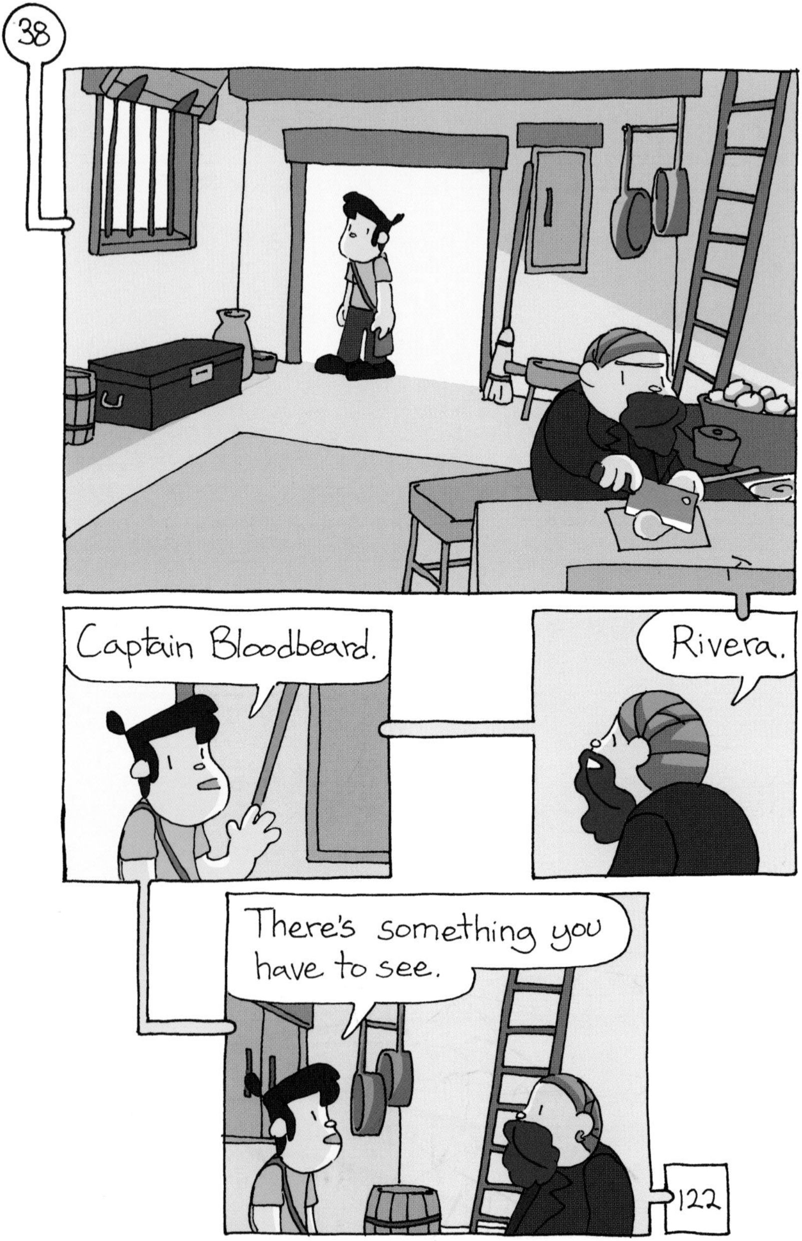
38
Captain Bloodbeard.
Rivera.
There's something you have to see.
122

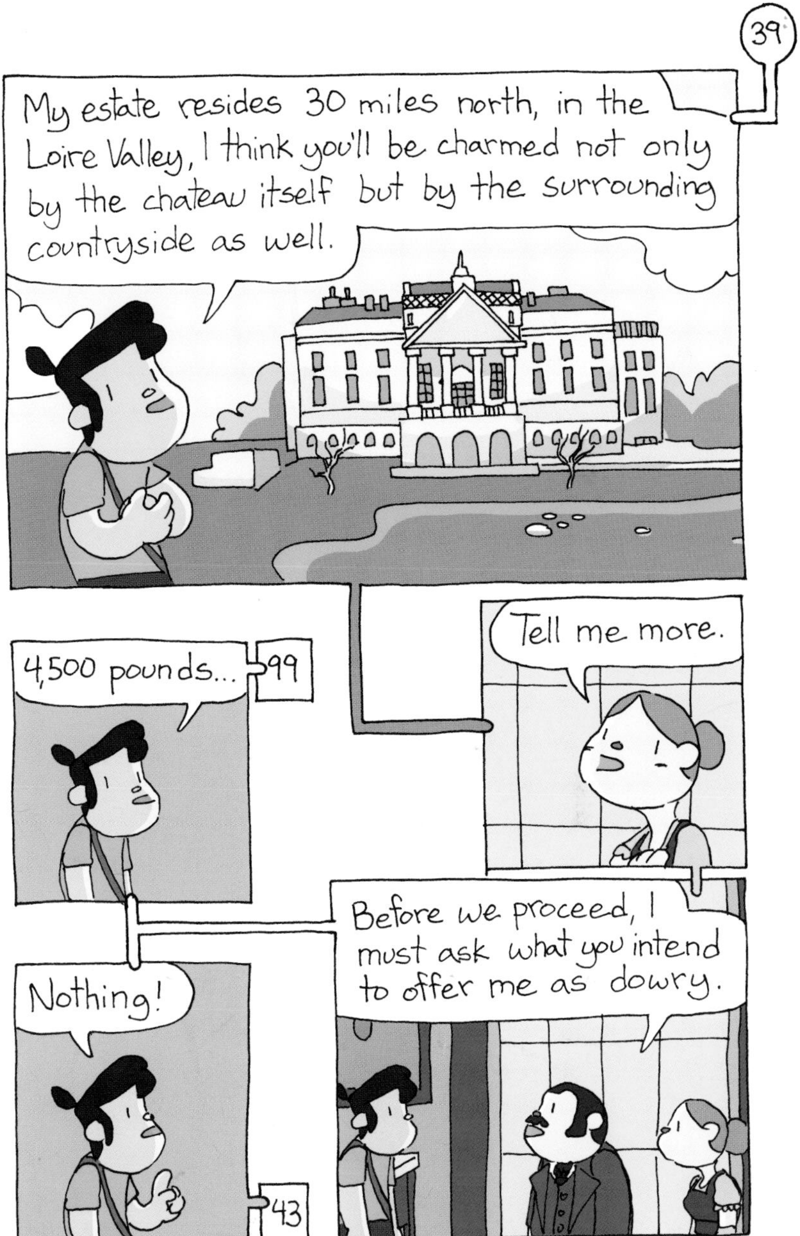

39
My estate resides 30 miles north, in the Loire Valley, I think you'll be charmed not only by the chateau itself but by the surrounding countryside as well.
Tell me more.
4,500 pounds...
99
Before we proceed, I must ask what you intend to offer me as dowry.
Nothing!
43

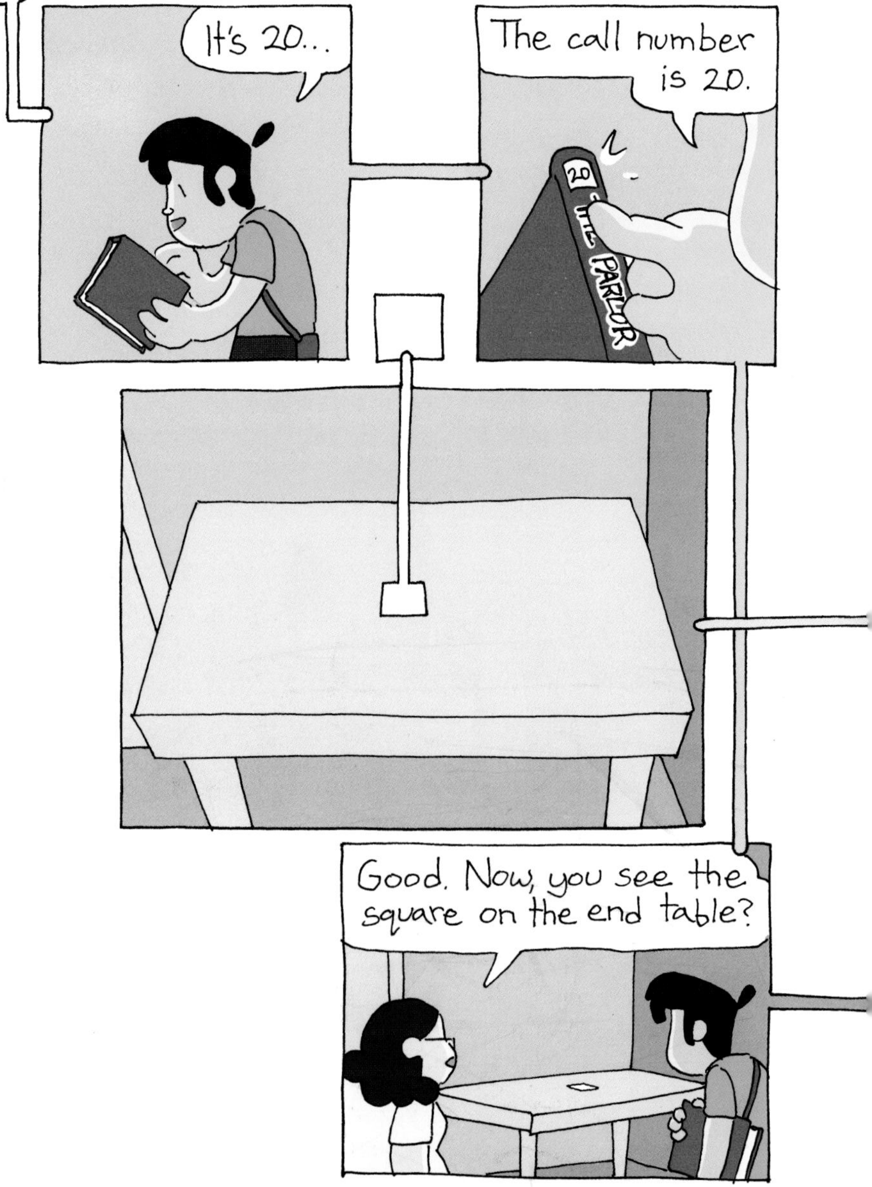
It's 20...
The call number is 20.
20
PARLOR
Good. Now, you see the square on the end table?

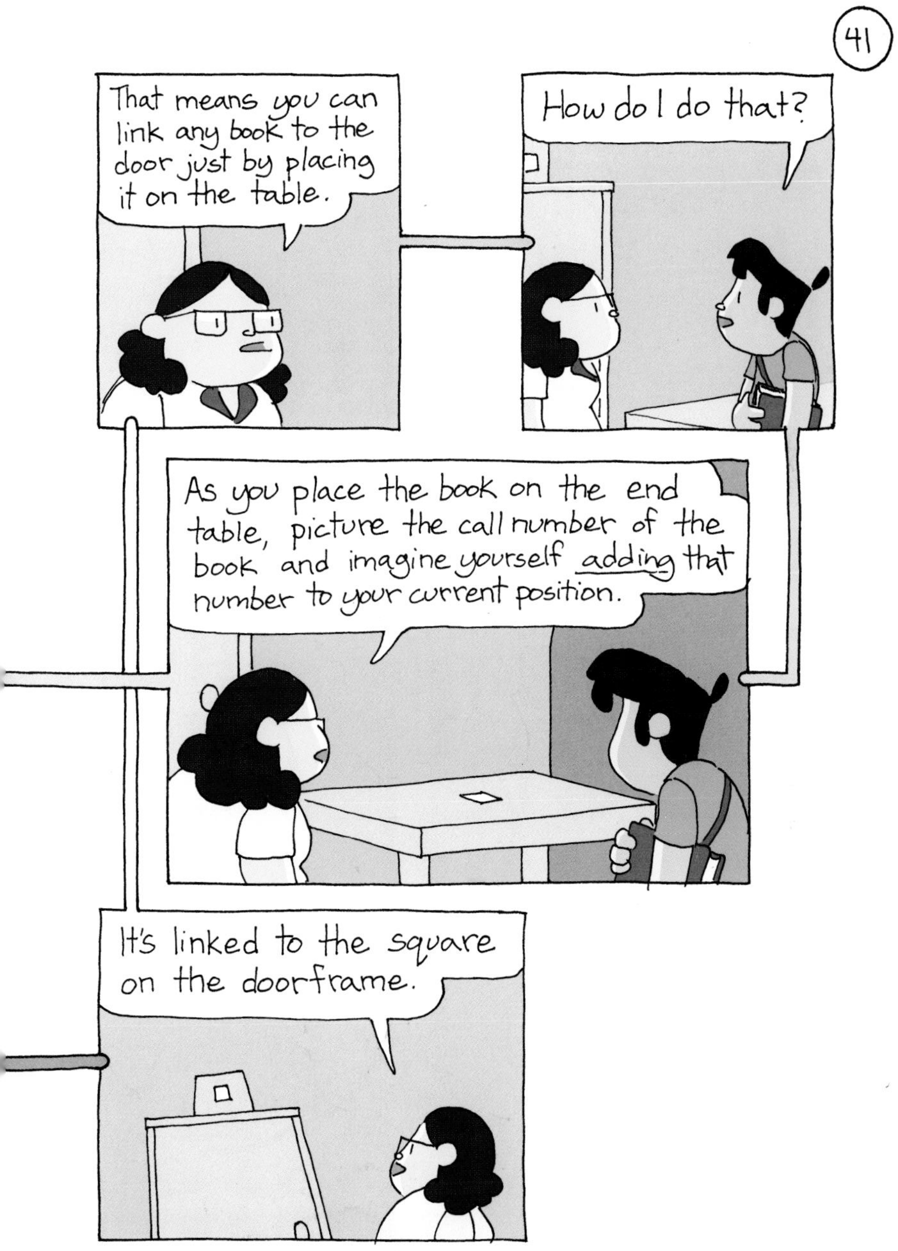
That means you can link any book to the door just by placing it on the table.
How do I do that?
As you place the book on the end table, picture the call number of the book and imagine yourself adding that number to your current position.
It's linked to the square on the doorframe.

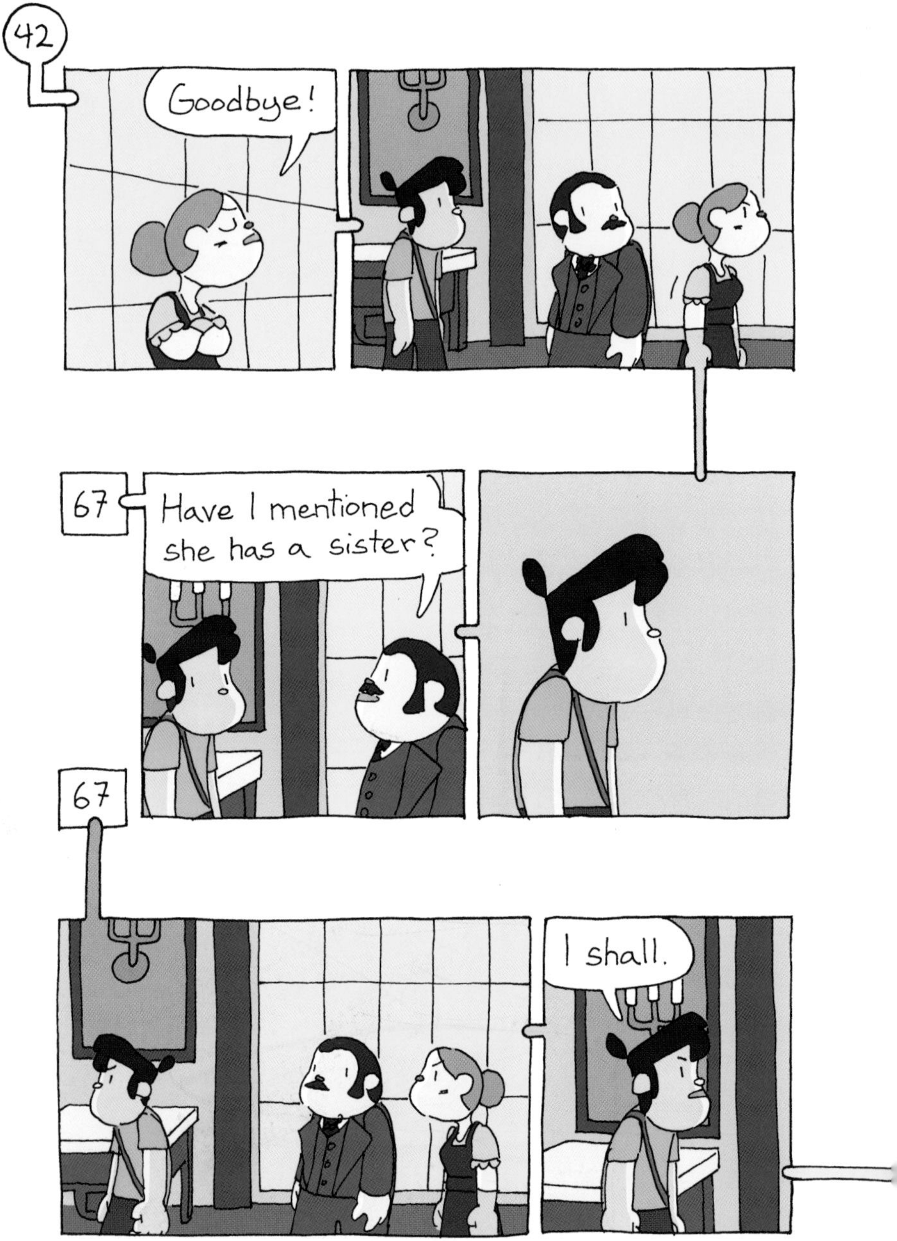
42
Goodbye!
67
Have I mentioned she has a sister?
67
I shall.

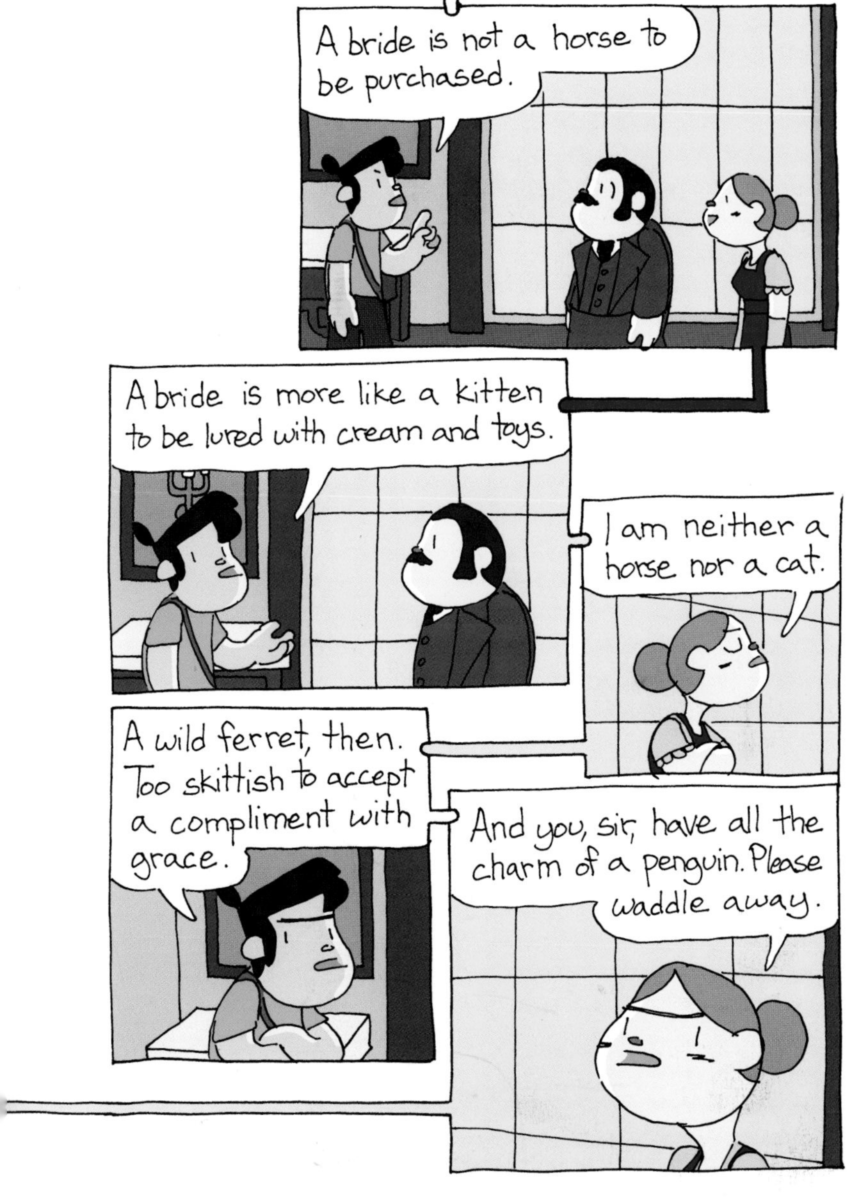
A bride is not a horse to be purchased.
A bride is more like a kitten to be lured with cream and toys.
I am neither a horse nor a cat.
A wild ferret, then. Too skittish to accept a compliment with grace.
And you, sir, have all the charm of a penguin. Please waddle away.

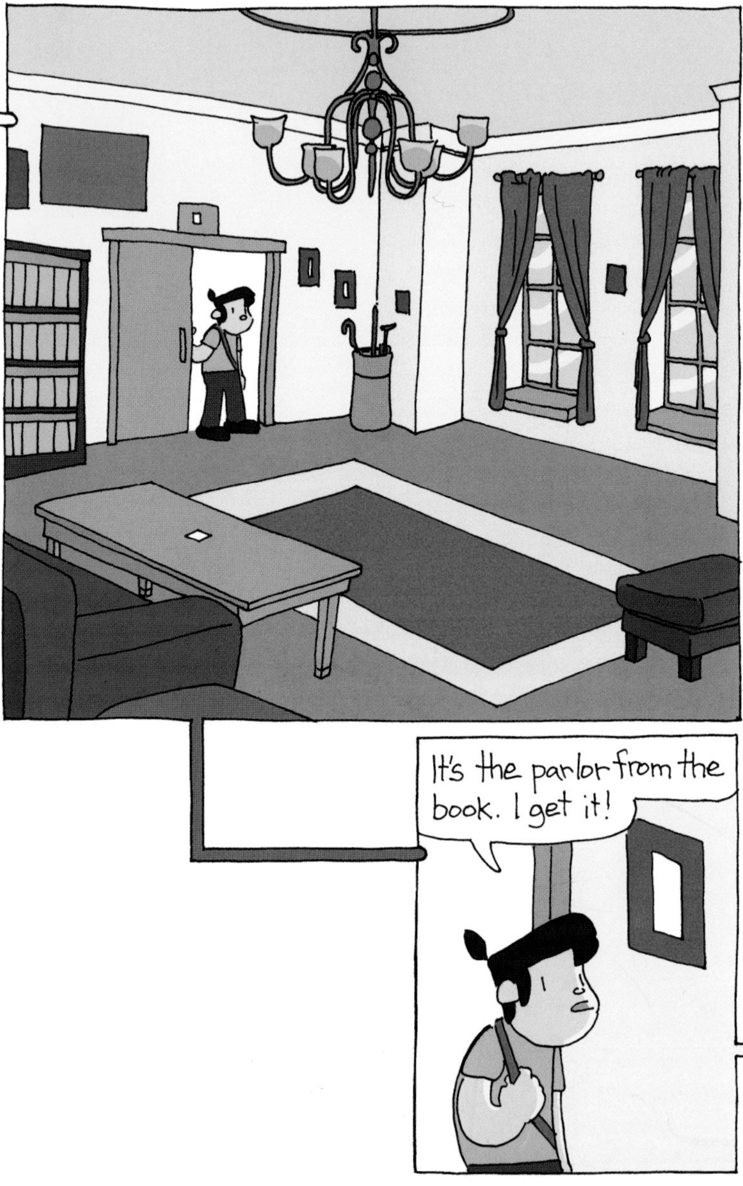
It's the parlor from the book. I get it!

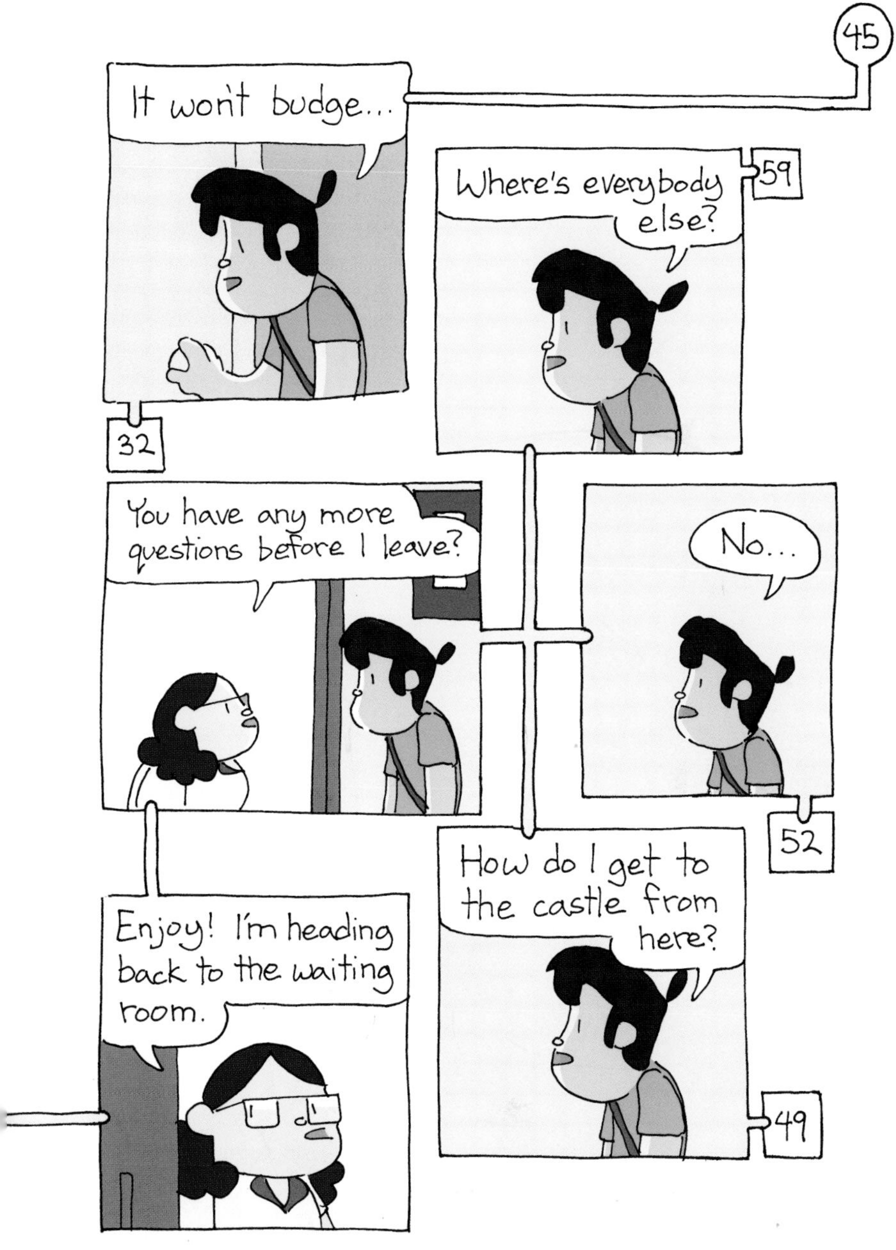
45
It won't budge...
32
Where's everybody else?
59
You have any more questions before I leave?
No...
52
How do I get to the castle from here?
49
Enjoy! I'm heading back to the waiting room.

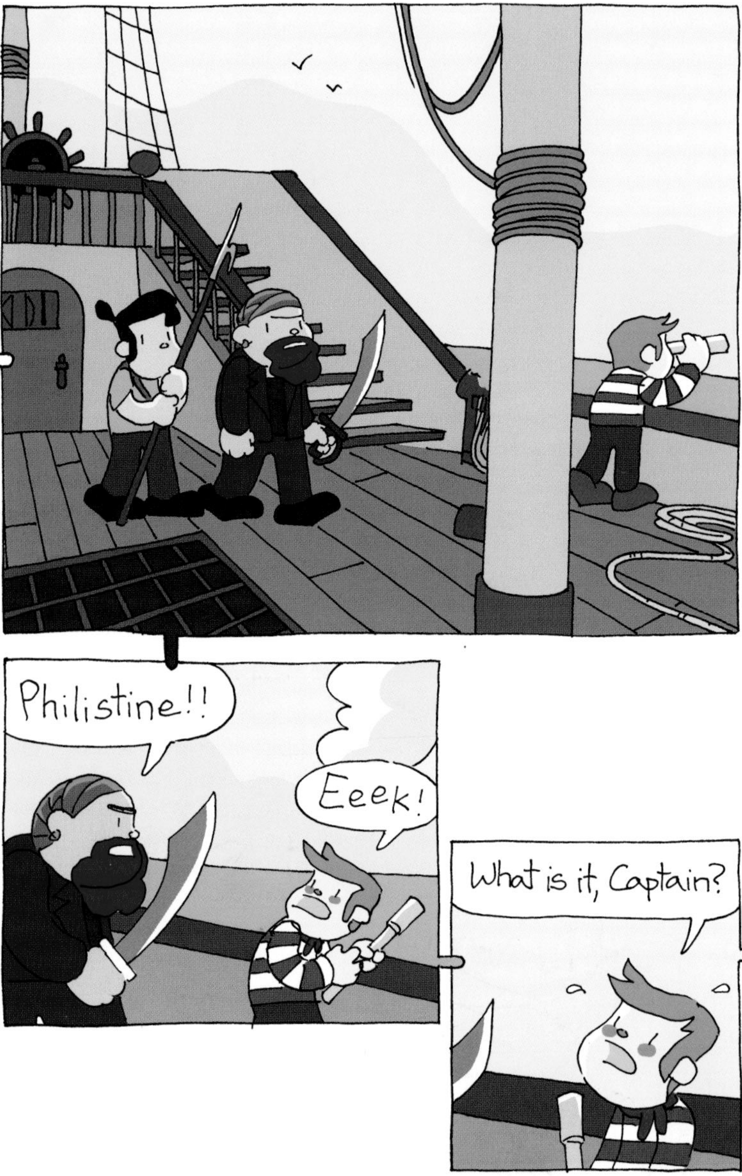
Philistine!!
Eeek!
What is it, Captain?

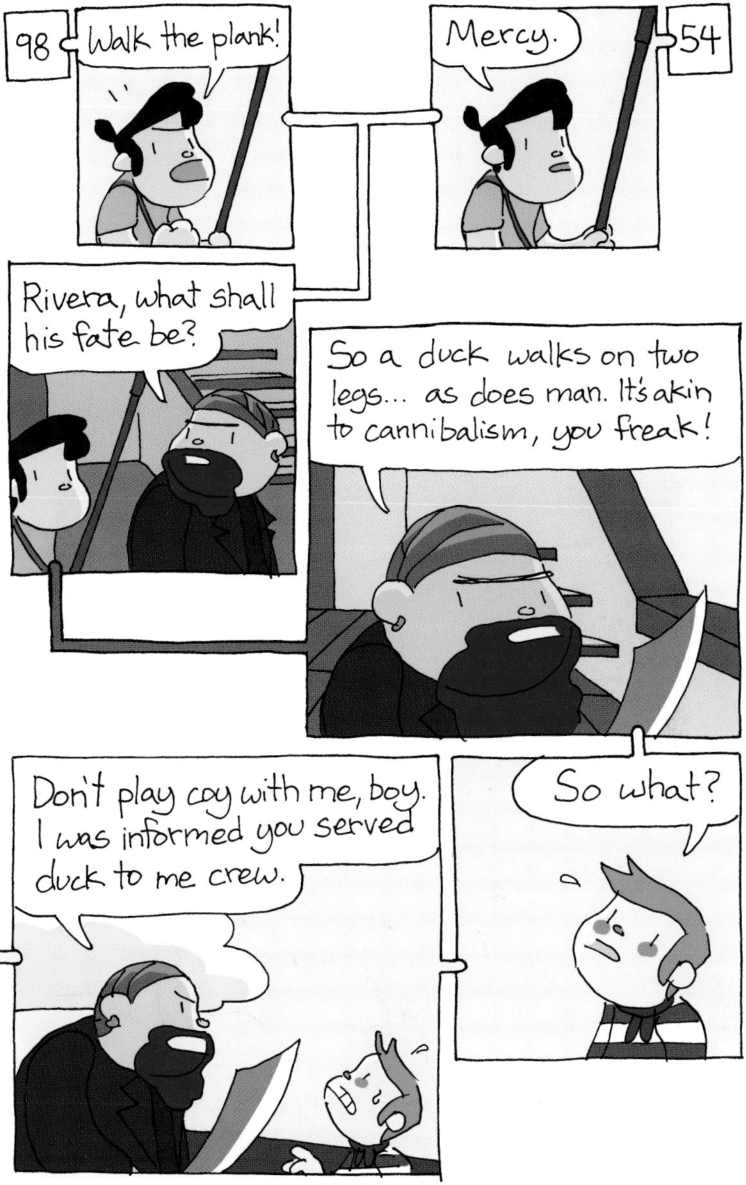
98
Walk the plank!
Mercy.
54
Rivera, what shall his fate be?
So a duck walks on two legs... as does man. It's akin to cannibalism, you freak!
So what?
Don't play coy with me, boy. I was informed you served duck to me crew.

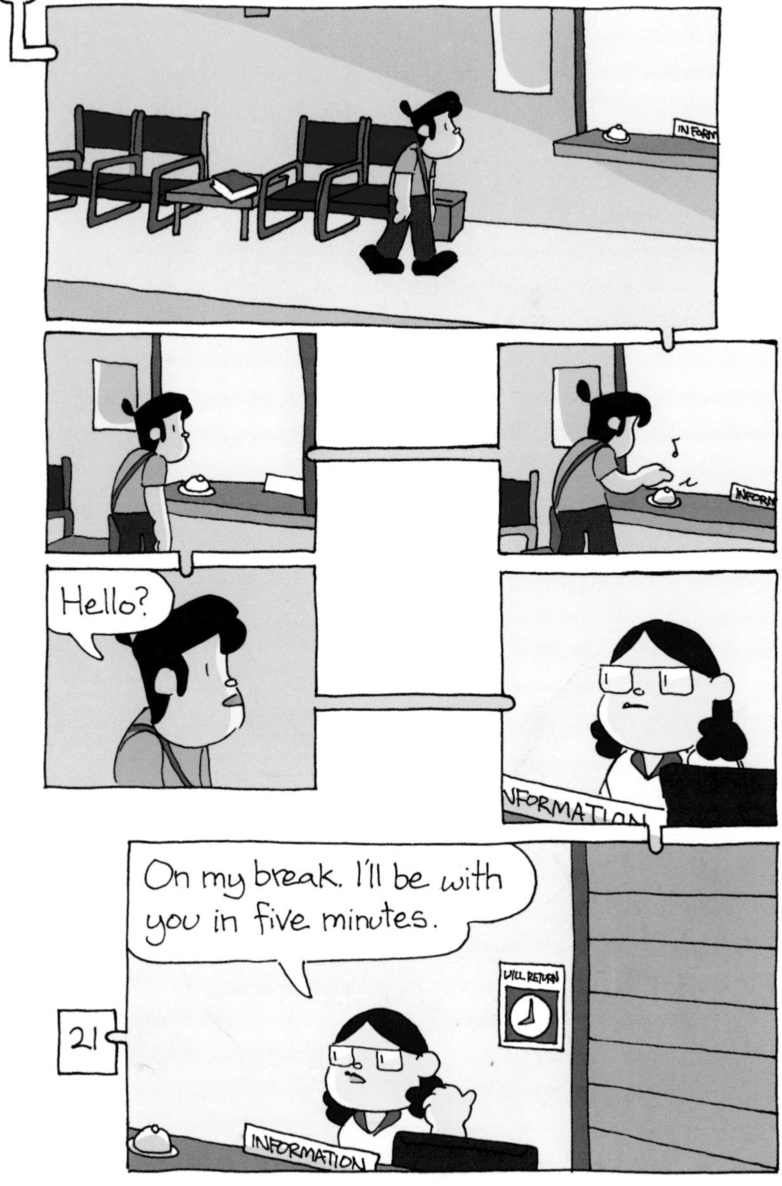
INFORM
INFORM
Hello?
NFORMATION
On my break. I'll be with you in five minutes.
WILL RETURN
21
INFORMATION

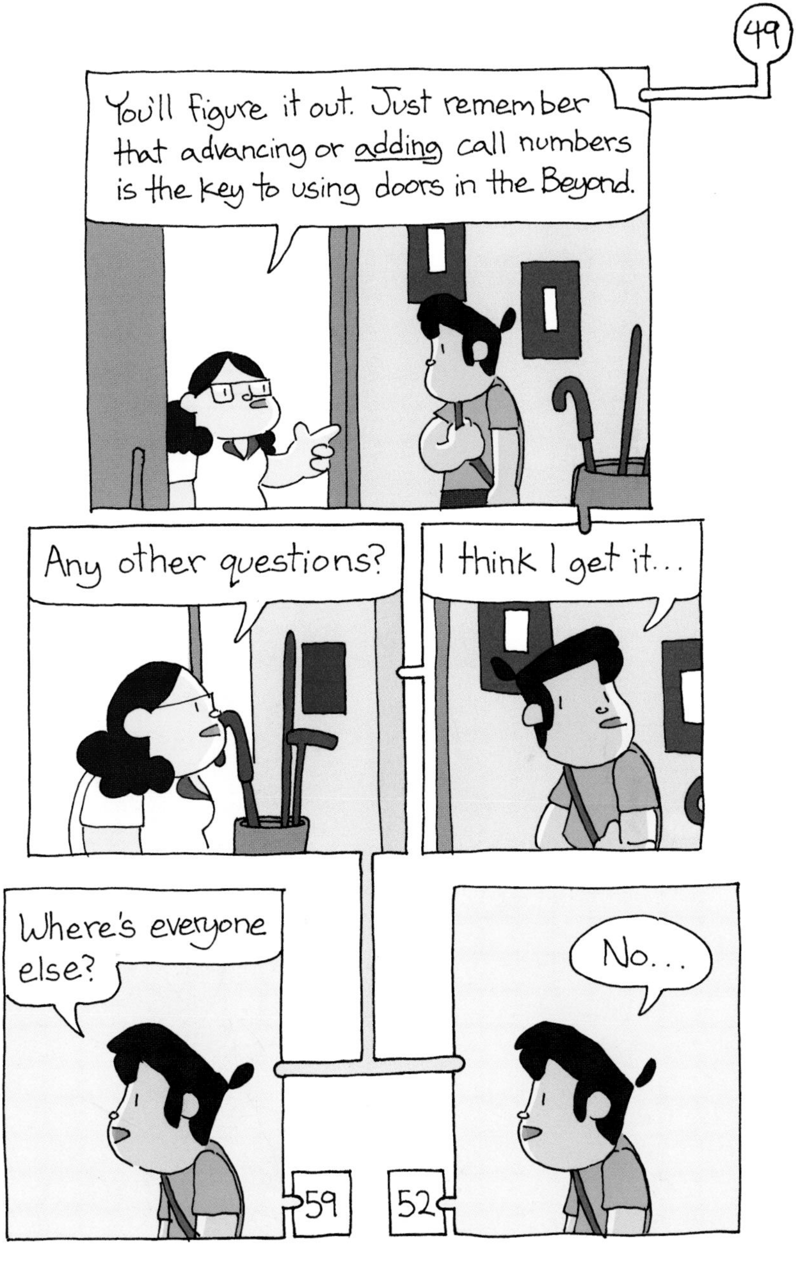
49
You'll figure it out. Just remember that advancing or adding call numbers is the key to using doors in the Beyond.
Any other questions?
I think I get it...
Where's everyone else?
No...
59
52

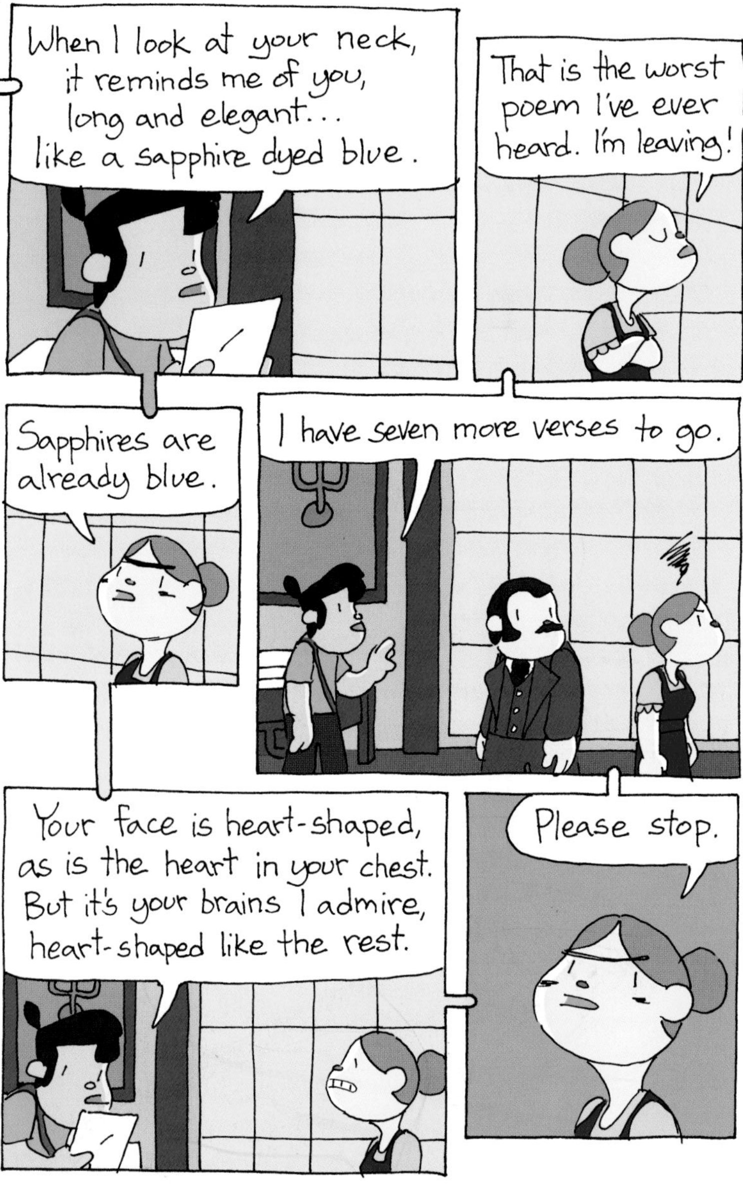
When I look at your neck,
it reminds me of you,
long and elegant...
like a sapphire dyed blue.
That is the worst poem I've ever heard. I'm leaving!
Sapphires are already blue.
I have seven more verses to go.
Your face is heart-shaped,
as is the heart in your chest.
But it's your brains I admire,
heart-shaped like the rest.
Please stop.

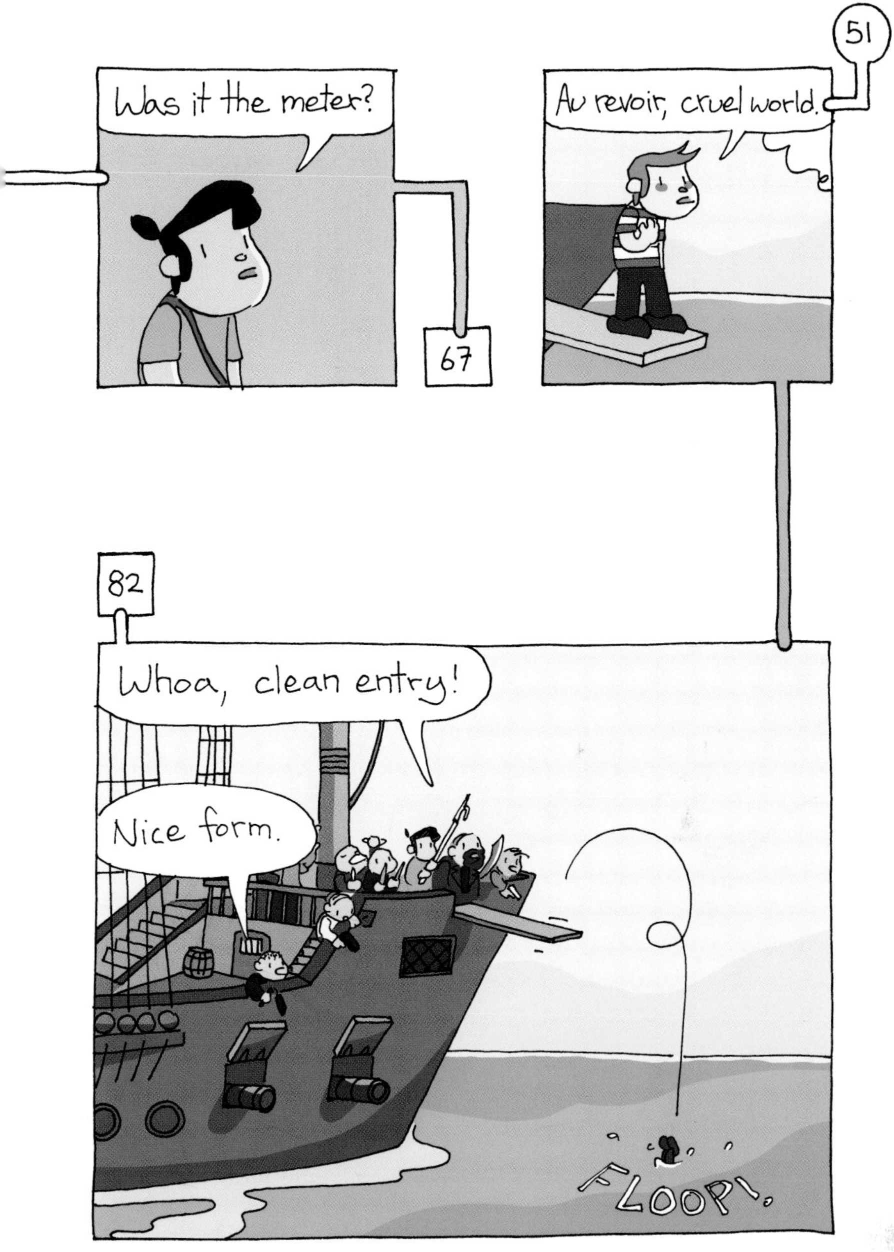
Was it the meter?
67
51
Au revoir, cruel world.
82
Whoa, clean entry!
Nice form.
FLOOP!

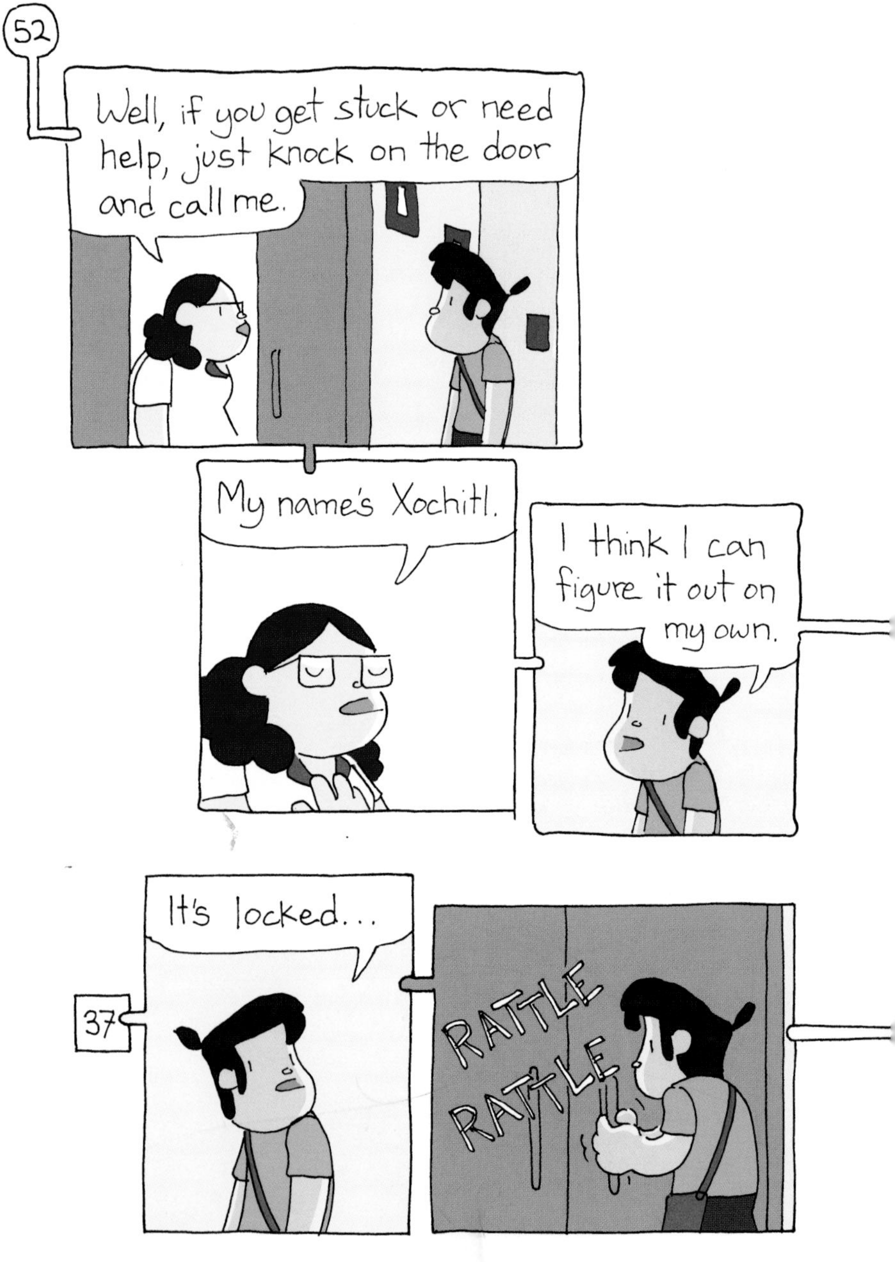
52
Well, if you get stuck or need help, just knock on the door and call me.
My name's Xochitl.
I think I can figure it out on my own.
37
It's locked...
RATTLE
RATTLE

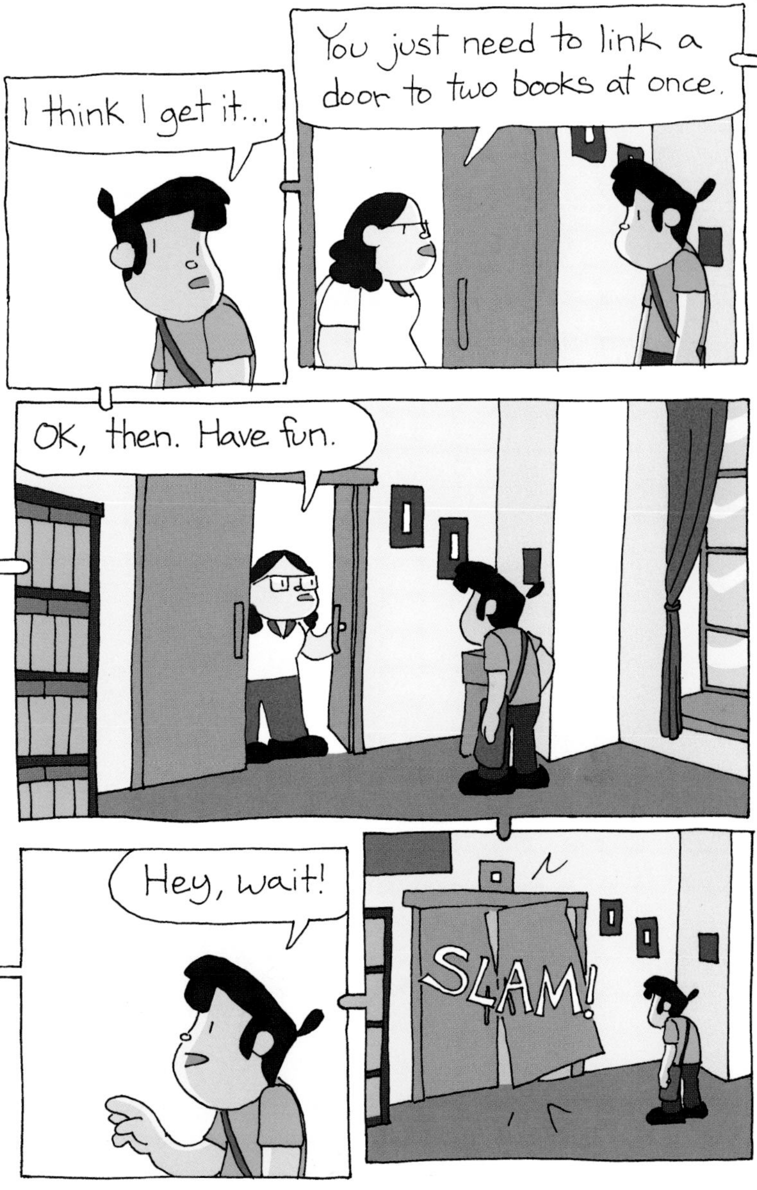
I think I get it...
You just need to link a door to two books at once.
OK, then. Have fun.
Hey, wait!
SLAM!

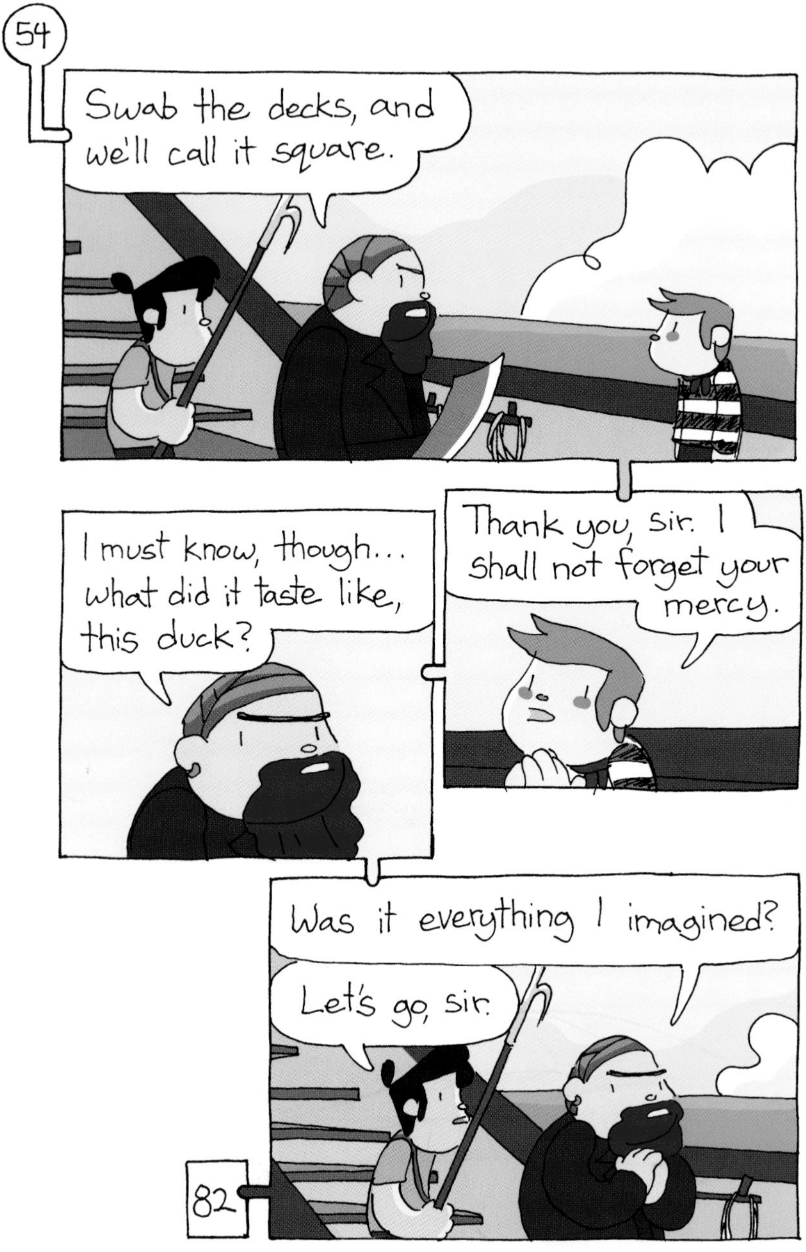
54
Swab the decks, and we'll call it square.
Thank you, sir. I shall not forget your mercy.
I must know, though... what did it taste like, this duck?
Was it everything I imagined?
Let's go, sir.
82

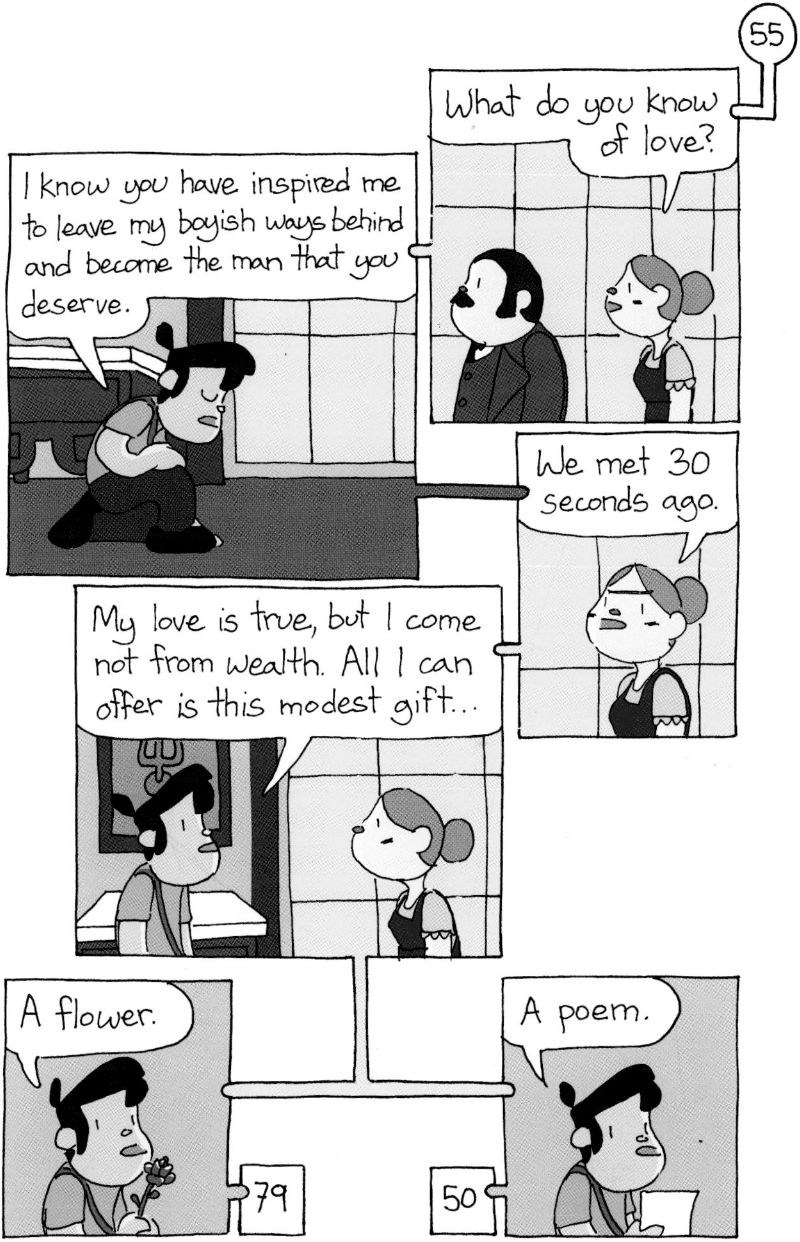
55
What do you know of love?
I know you have inspired me to leave my boyish ways behind and become the man that you deserve.
We met 30 seconds ago.
My love is true, but I come not from wealth. All I can offer is this modest gift...
A flower.
79
A poem.
50

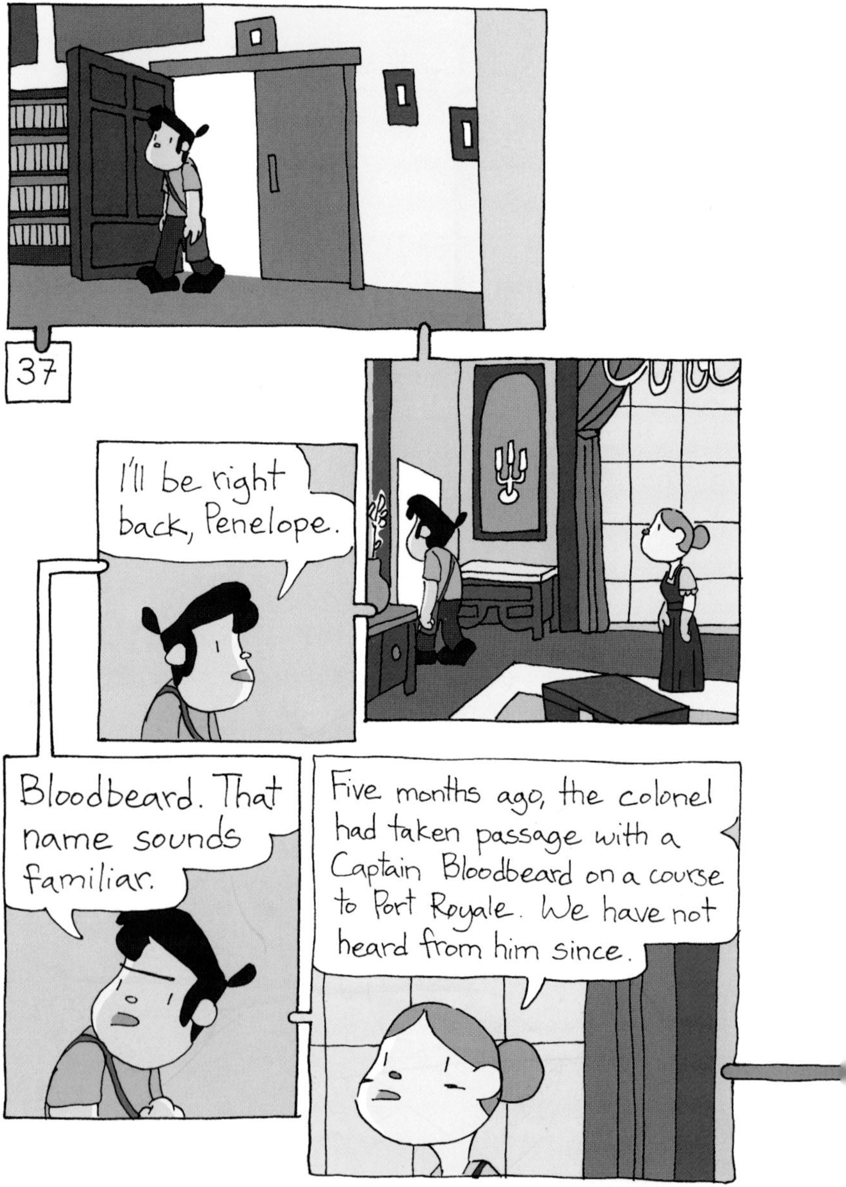
37
I'll be right back, Penelope.
Bloodbeard. That name sounds familiar.
Five months ago, the colonel had taken passage with a Captain Bloodbeard on a course to Port Royale. We have not heard from him since.

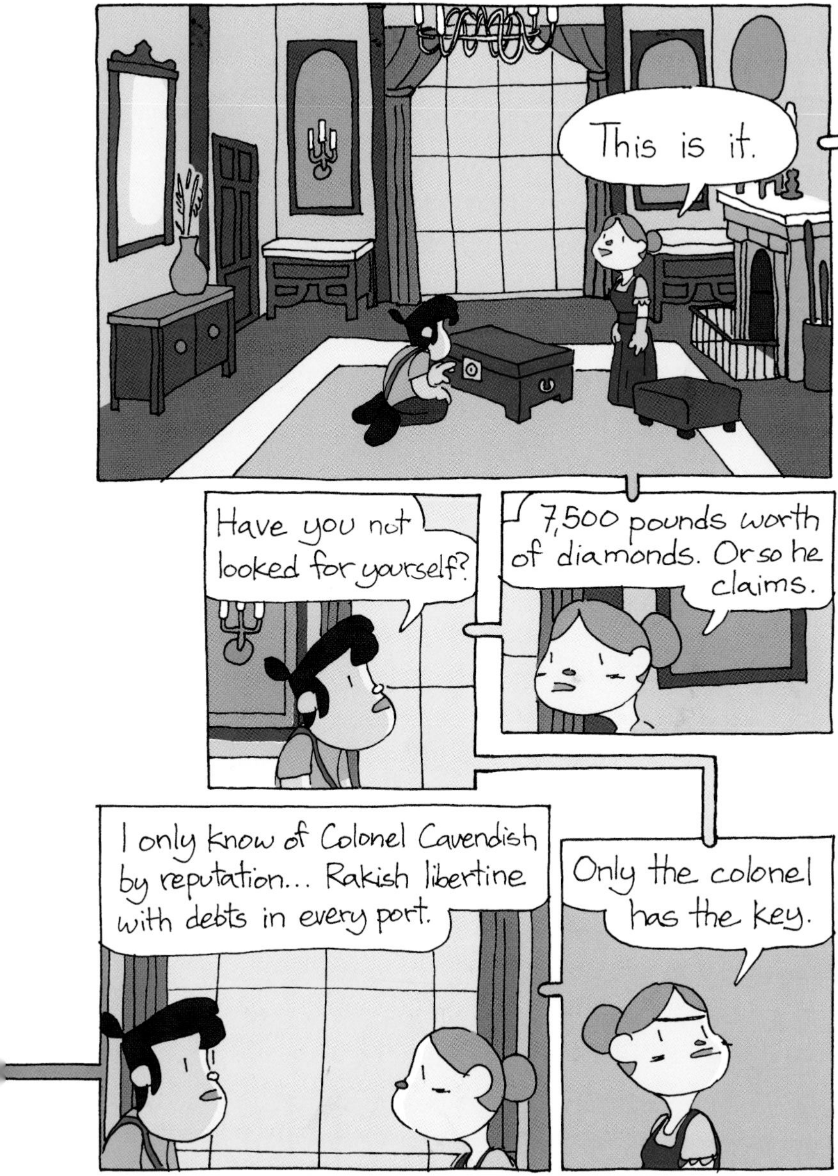
This is it.
Have you not looked for yourself?
7,500 pounds worth of diamonds. Or so he claims.
I only know of Colonel Cavendish by reputation... Rakish libertine with debts in every port.
Only the colonel has the key.

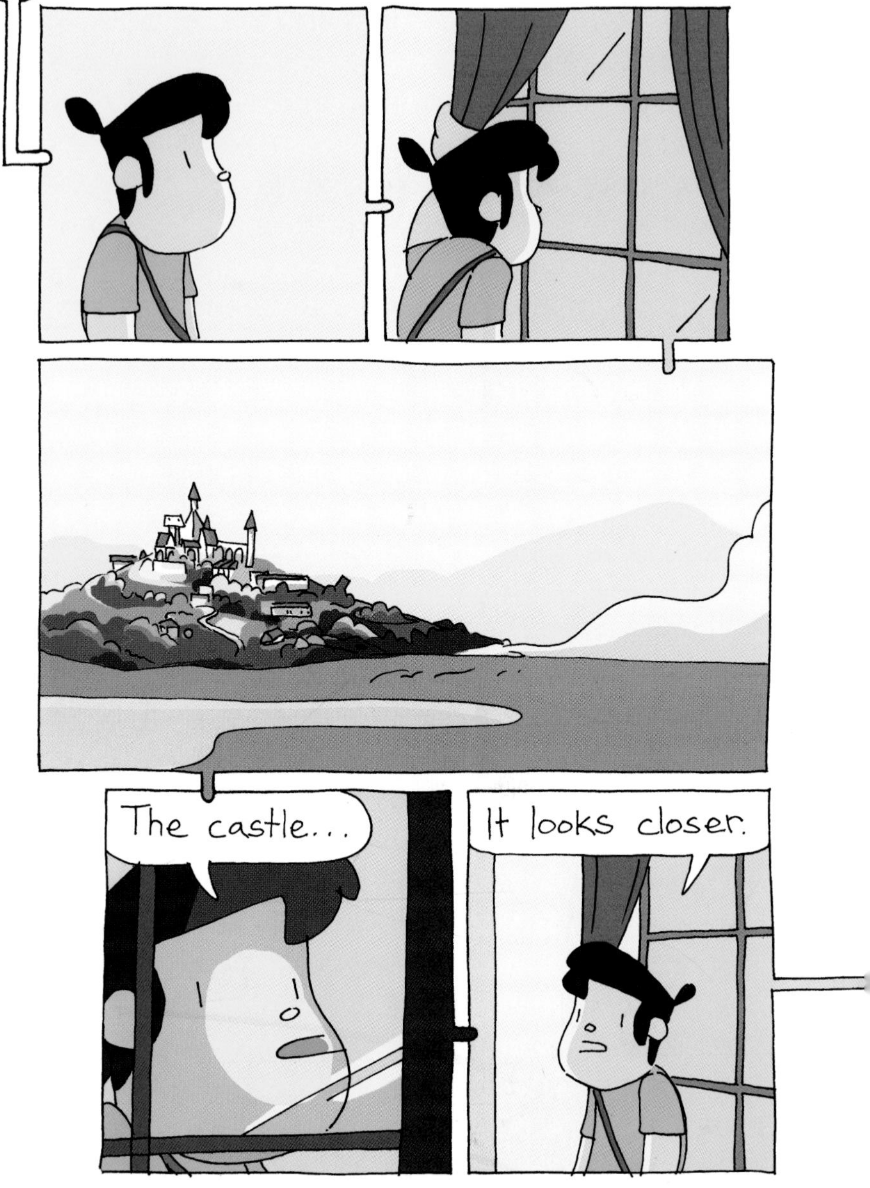
The castle...
It looks closer.

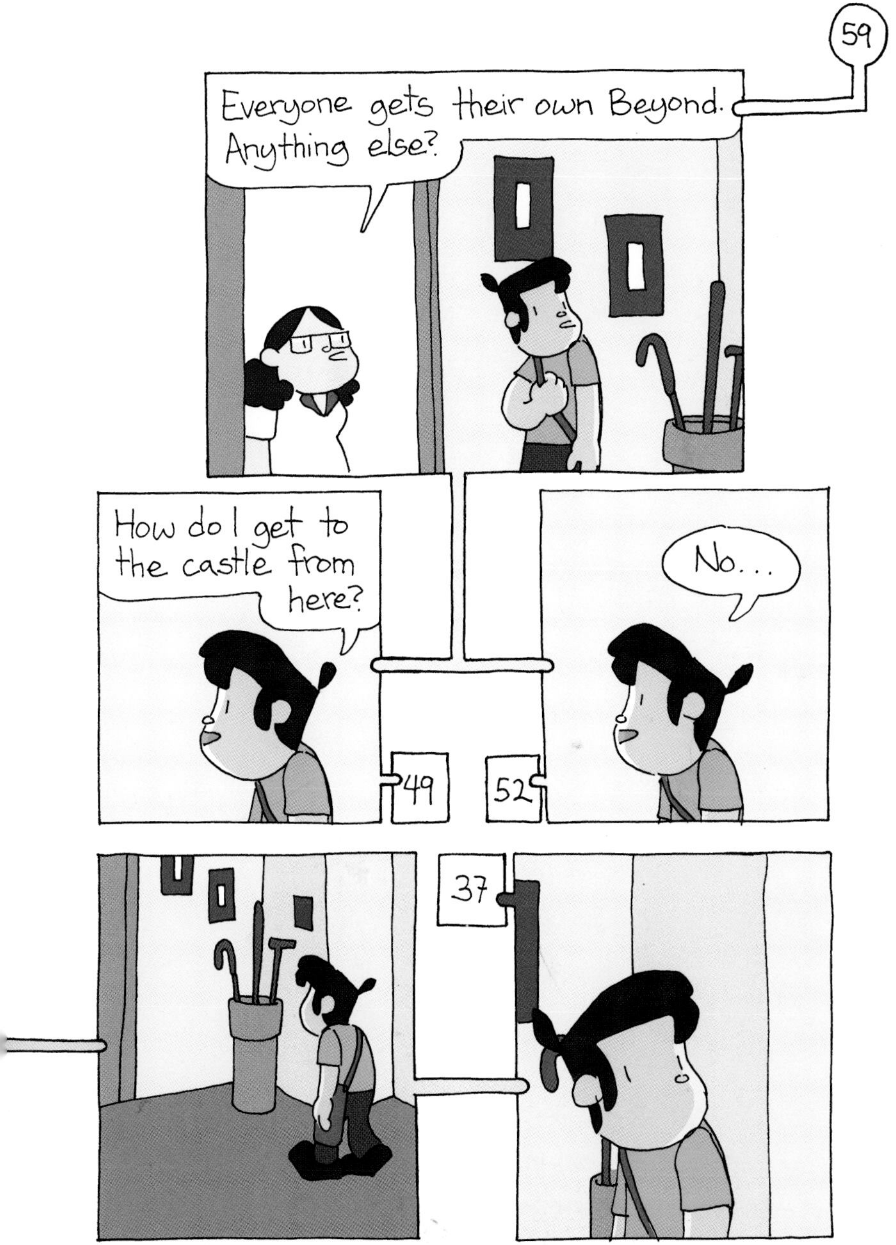
59
Everyone gets their own Beyond. Anything else?
How do I get to the castle from here?
No...
49
52
37

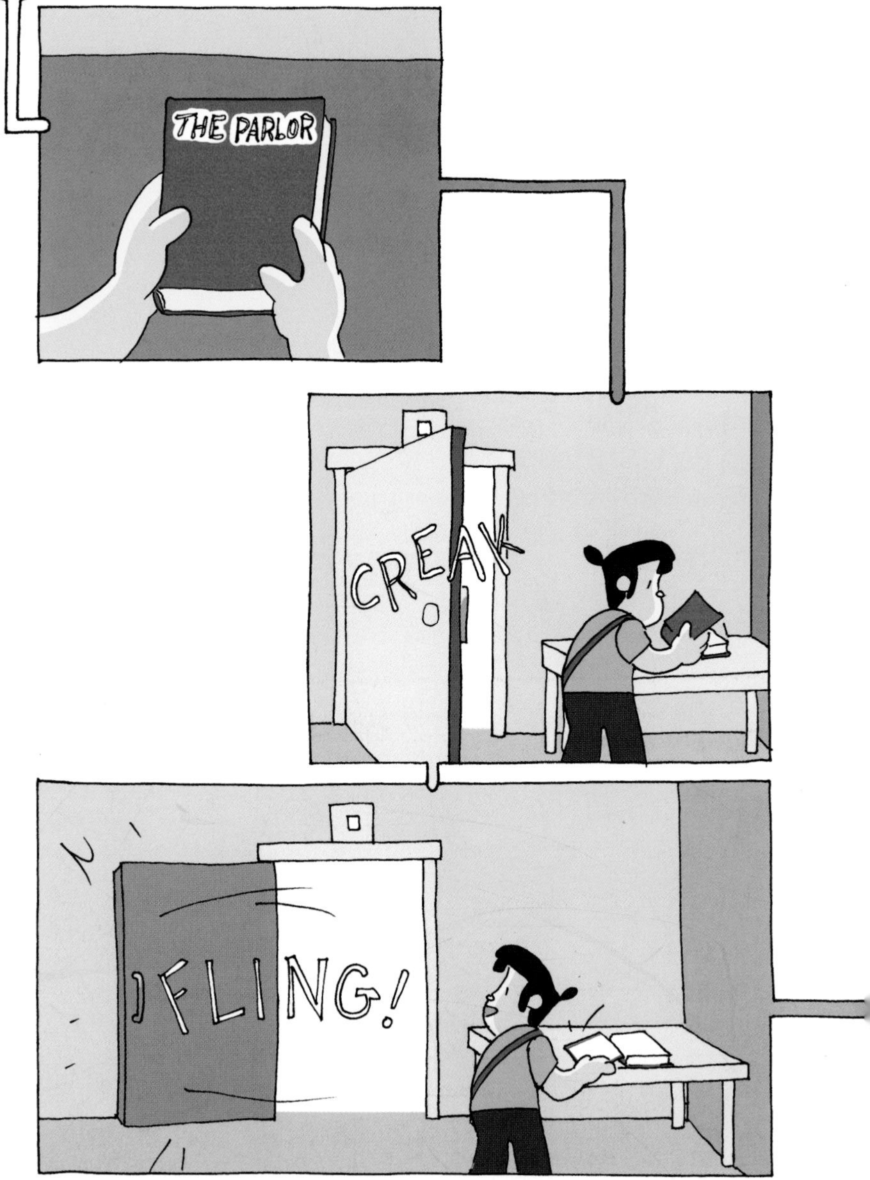
THE PARLOR
CREAK
FLING!

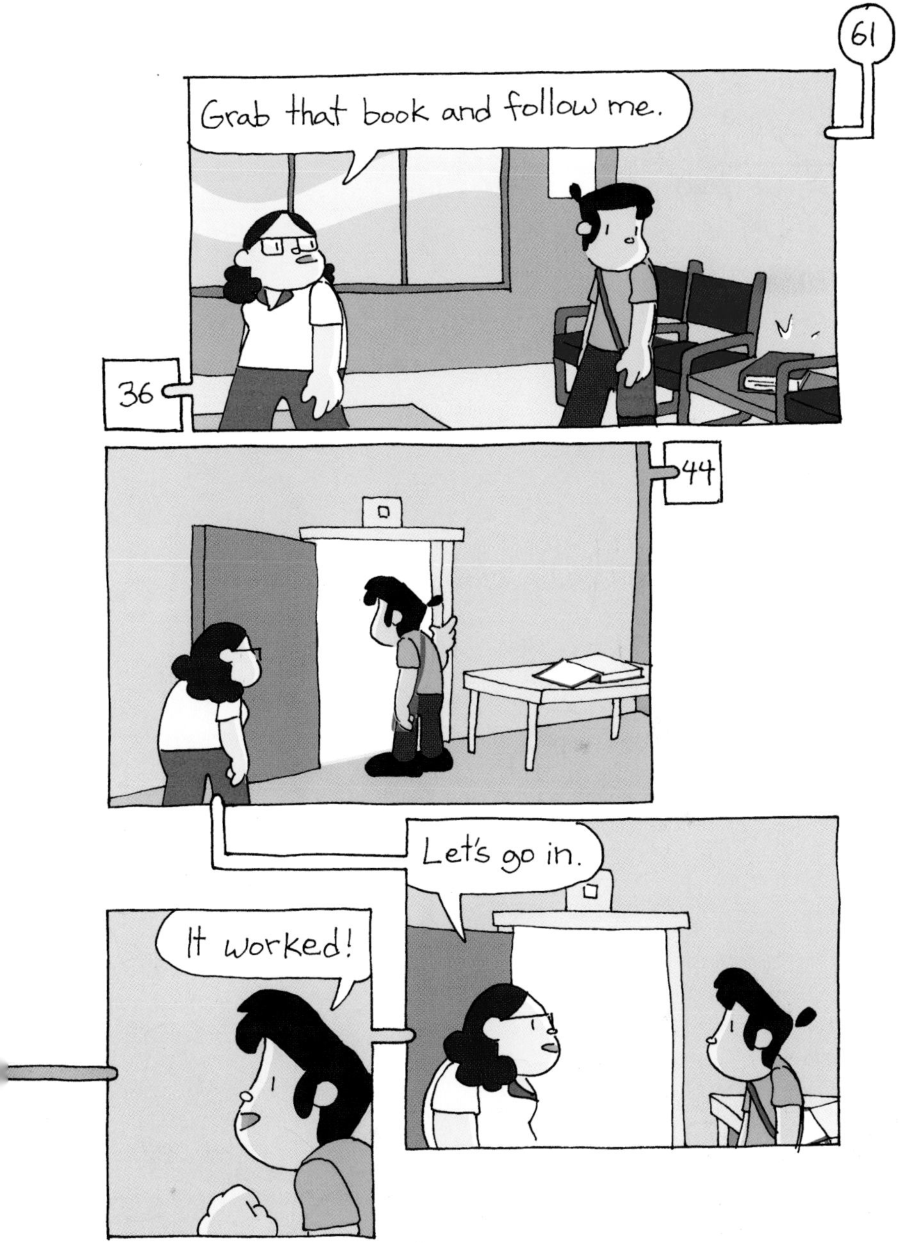
61
Grab that book and follow me.
36
44
Let's go in.
It worked!

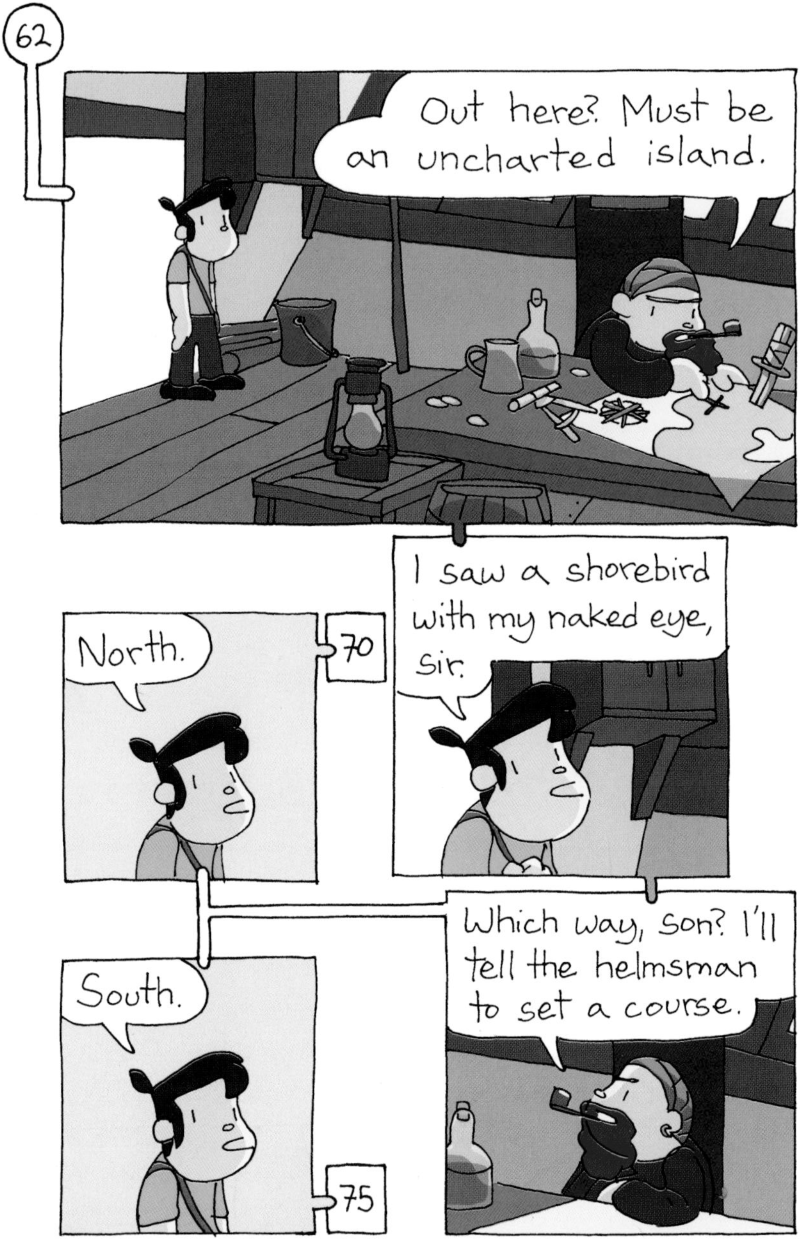
62
Out here? Must be an uncharted island.
I saw a shorebird with my naked eye, sir.
Which way, son? I'll tell the helmsman to set a course.
North.
70
South.
75

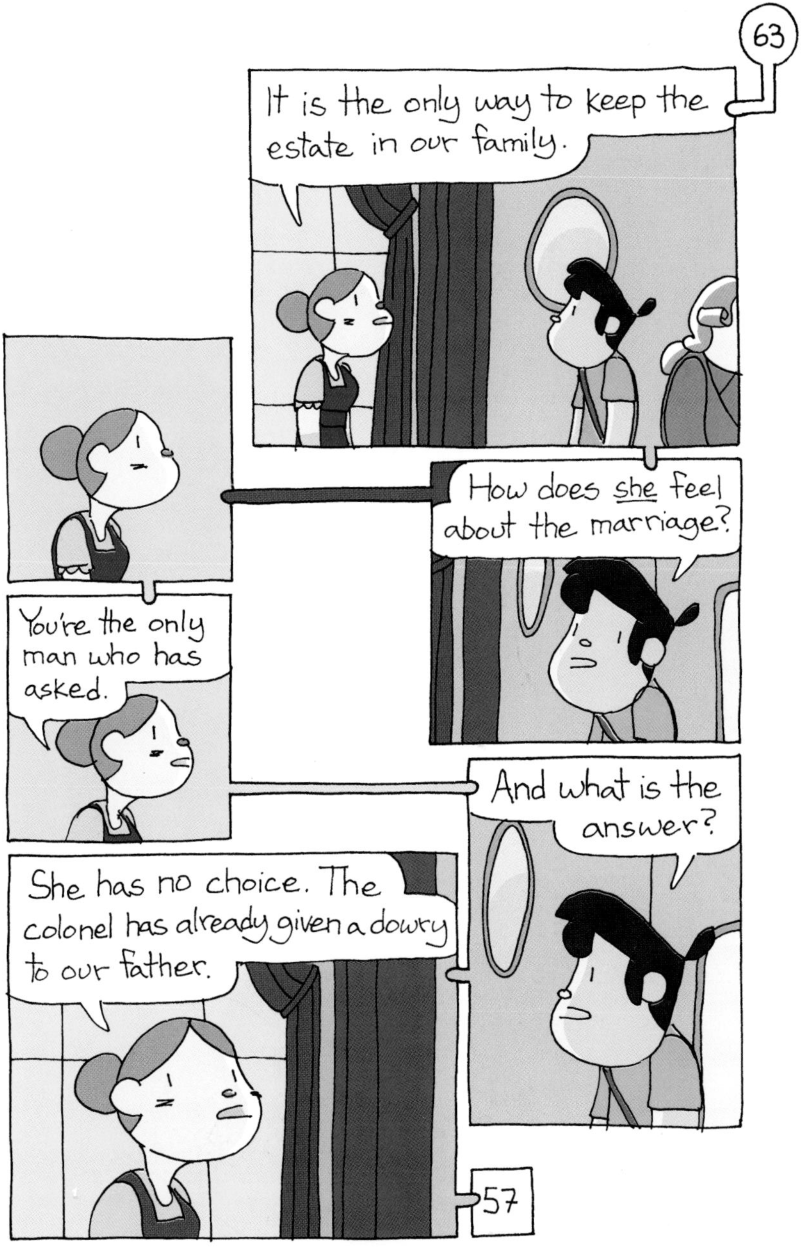
63
It is the only way to keep the estate in our family.
How does she feel about the marriage?
You're the only man who has asked.
And what is the answer?
She has no choice. The colonel has already given a dowry to our father.
57

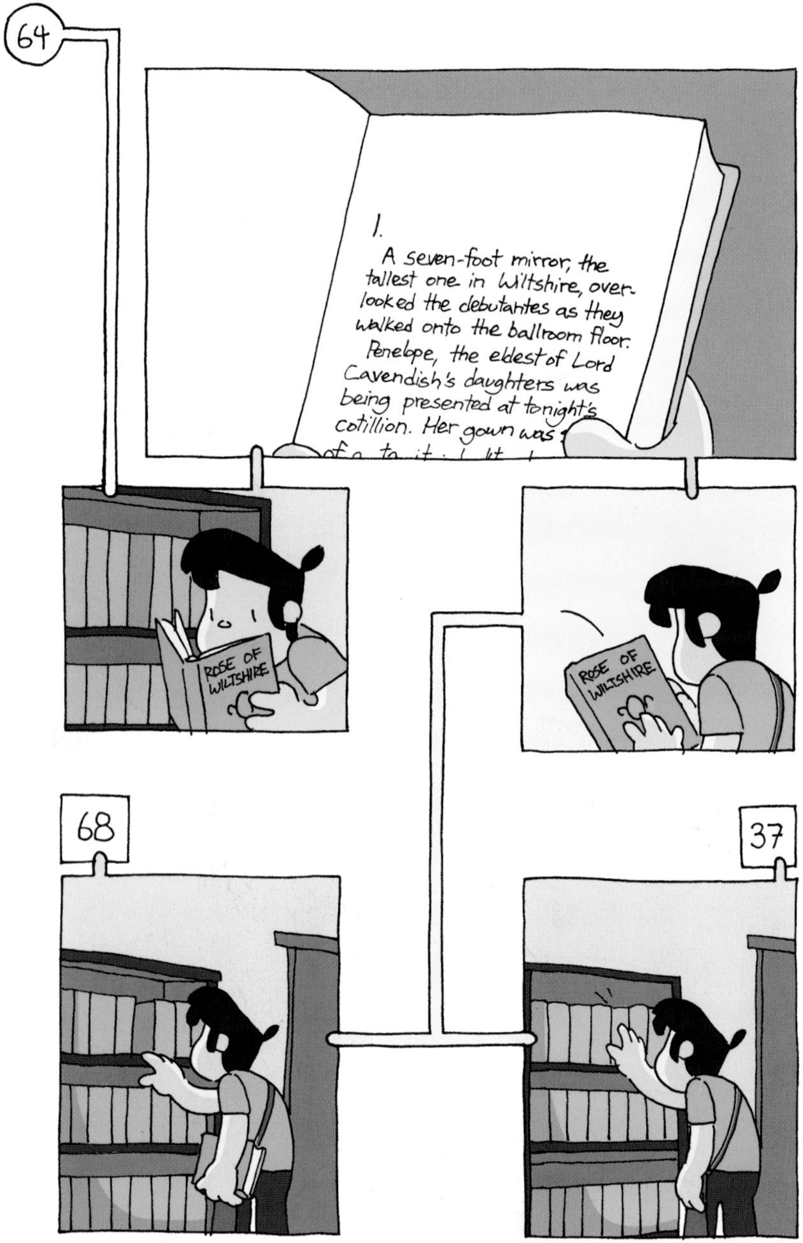
64
1.
A seven-foot mirror, the tallest one in Wiltshire, overlooked the debutantes as they walked onto the ballroom floor.
Penelope, the eldest of Lord Cavendish's daughters was being presented at tonight's cotillion. Her gown was
ROSE OF WILTSHIRE
ROSE OF WILTSHIRE
68
37

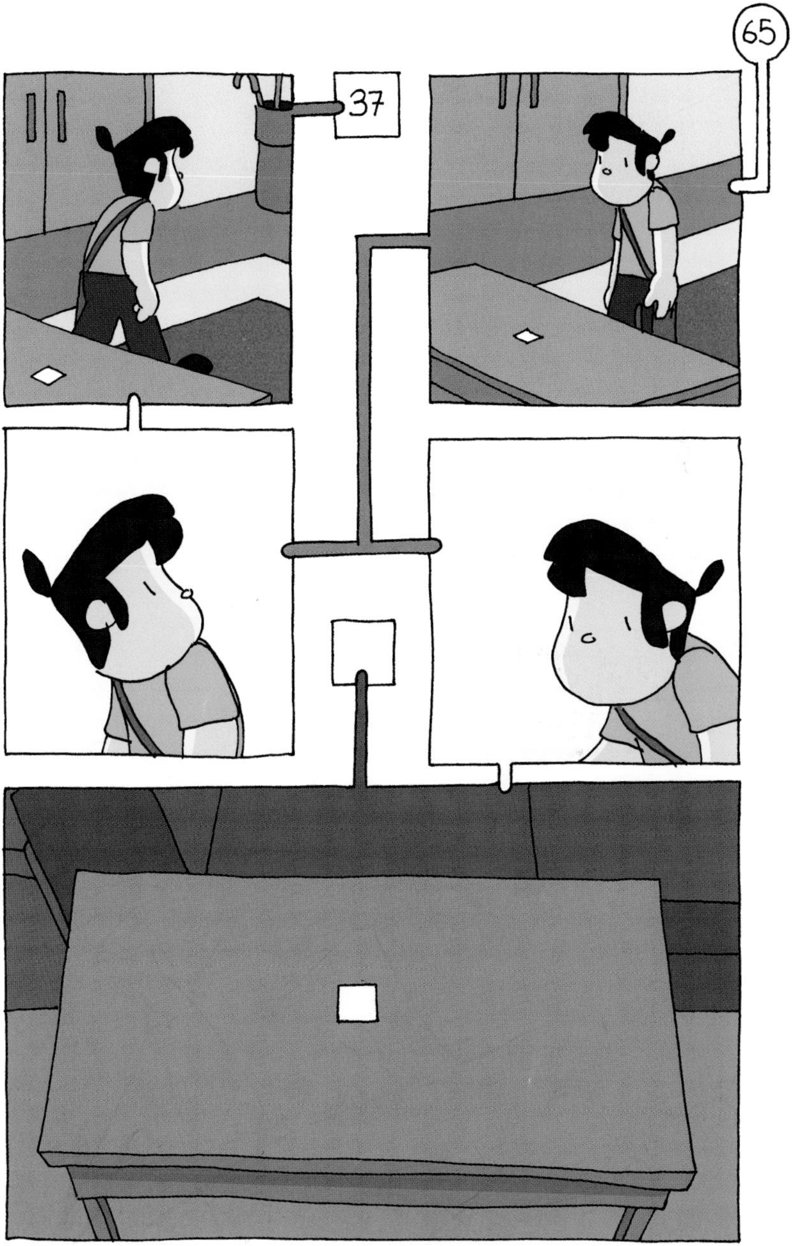
37
65

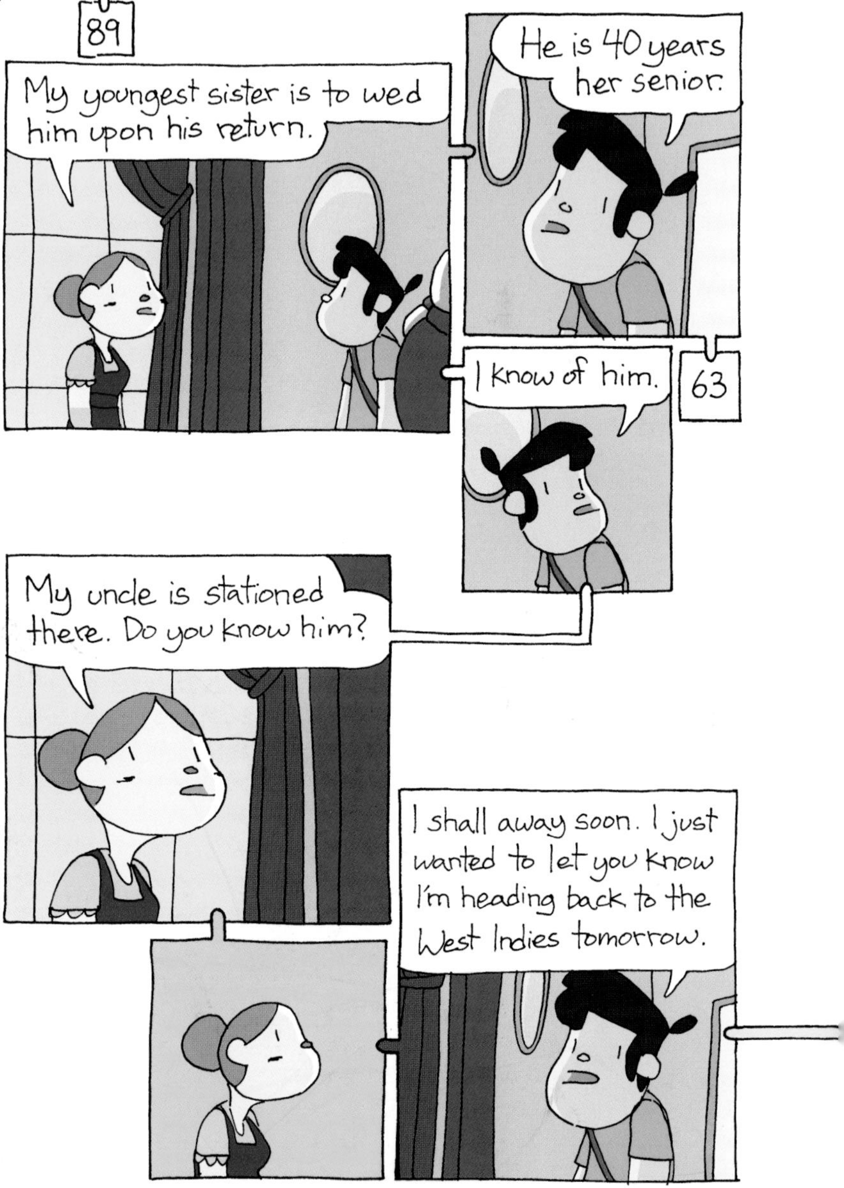
89
My youngest sister is to wed him upon his return.
He is 40 years her senior.
63
I know of him.
My uncle is stationed there. Do you know him?
I shall away soon. I just wanted to let you know I'm heading back to the West Indies tomorrow.

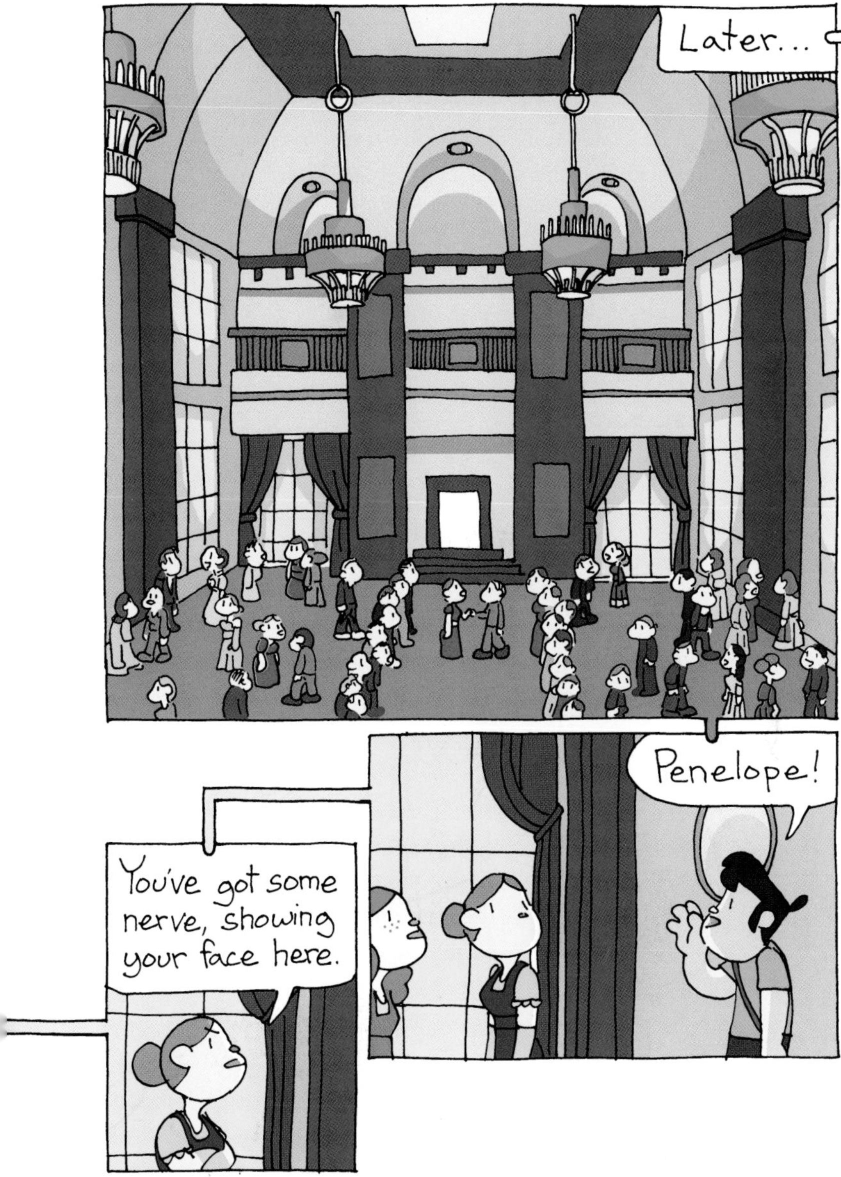
Later...
Penelope!
You've got some nerve, showing your face here.

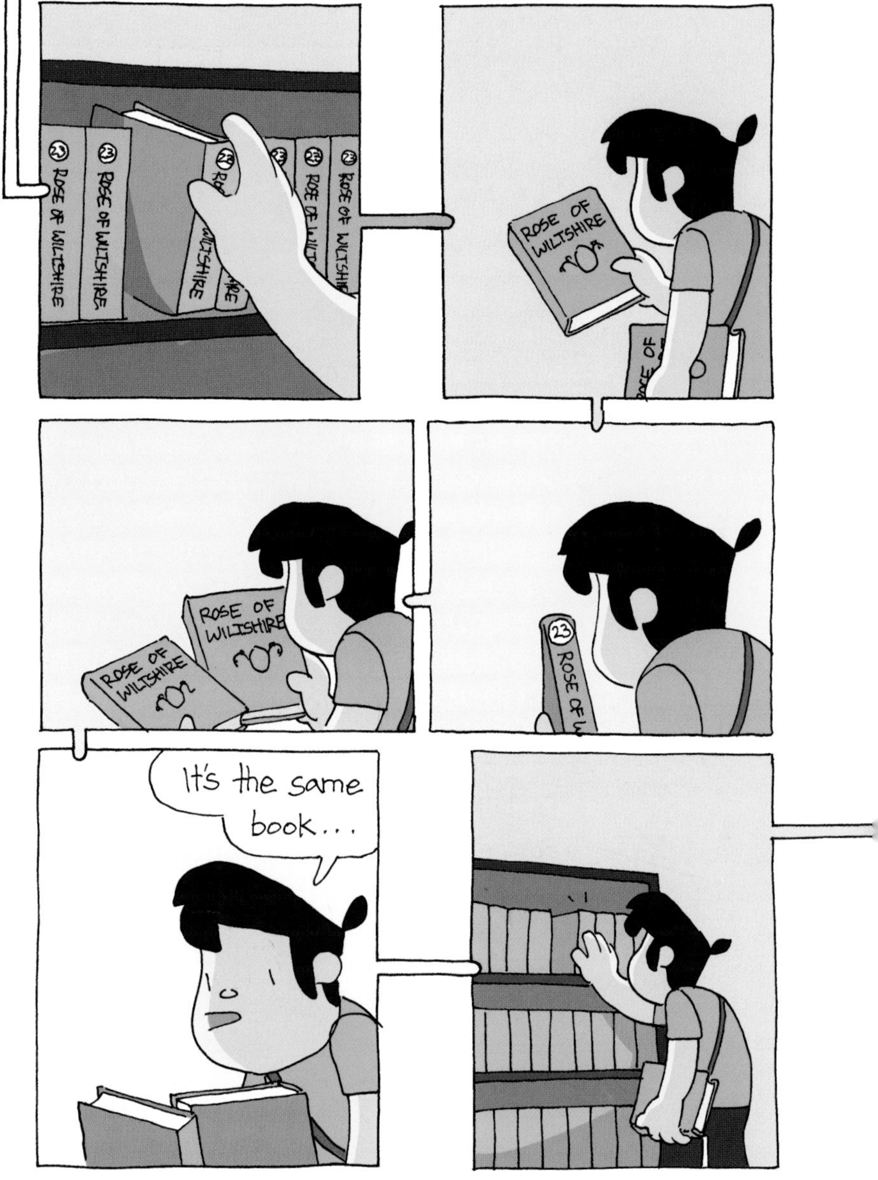
23 ROSE OF WILTSHIRE
ROSE OF WILTSHIRE
ROSE OF WILTSHIRE
ROSE OF WILTSHIRE
23 ROSE OF W
It's the same book...

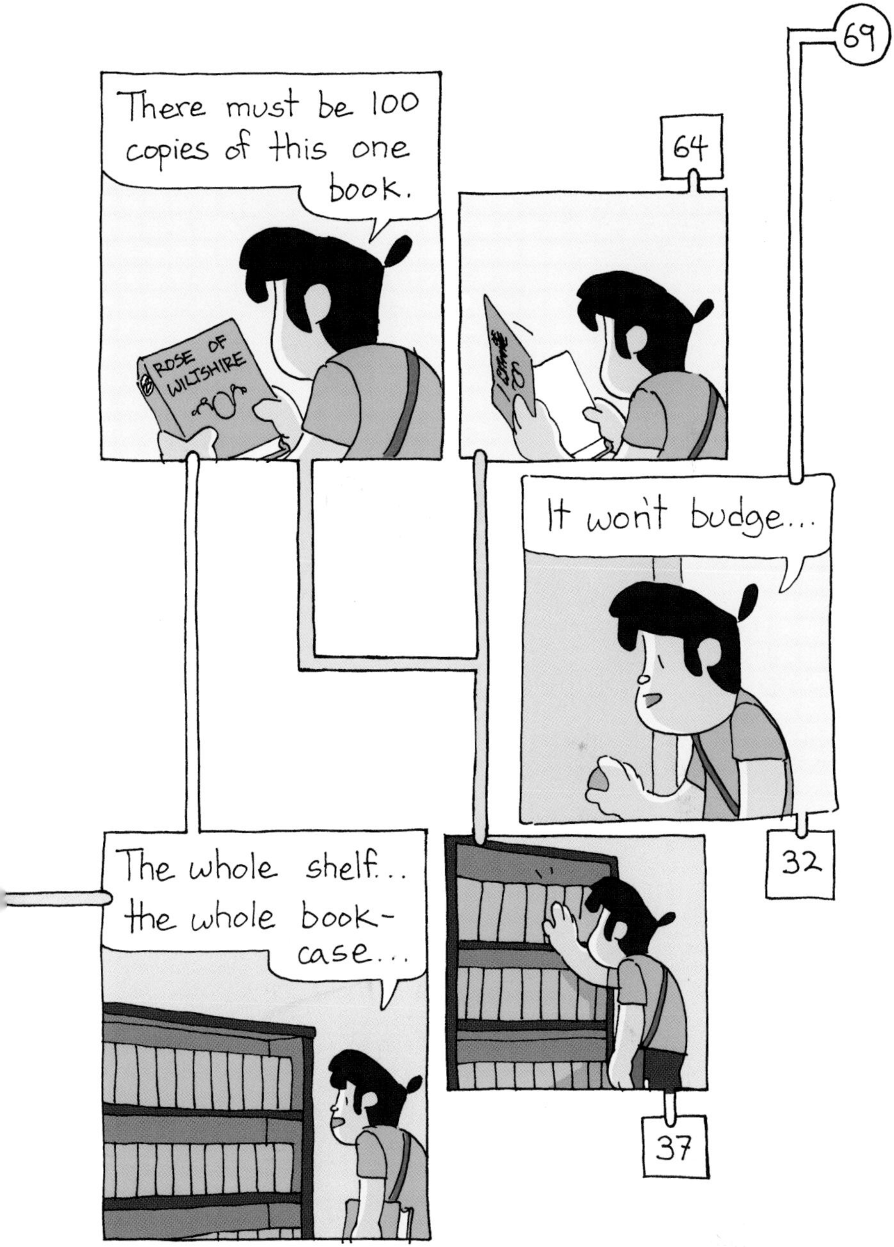
69
There must be 100 copies of this one book.
ROSE OF WILTSHIRE
64
It won't budge...
32
The whole shelf... the whole book-case...
37

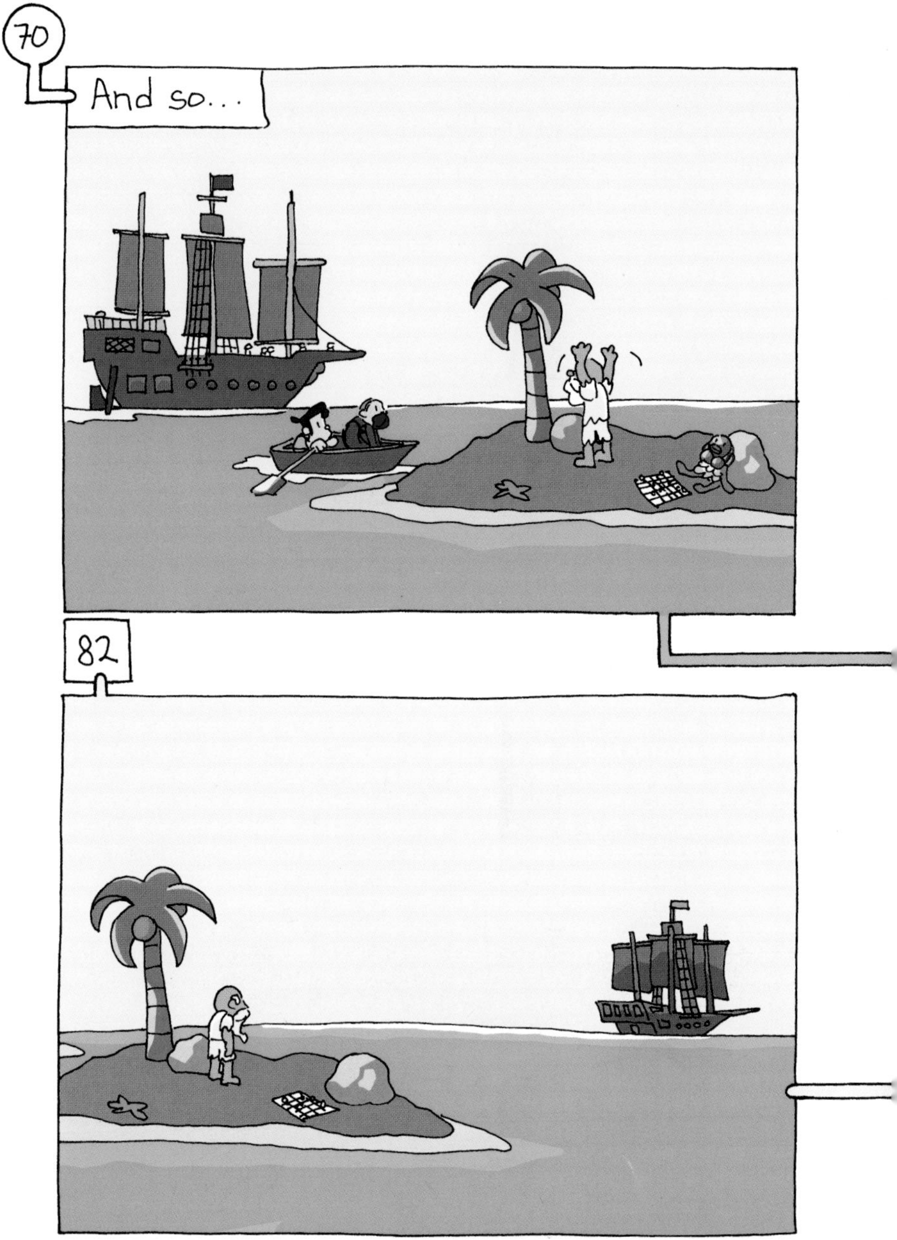
70
And so...
82

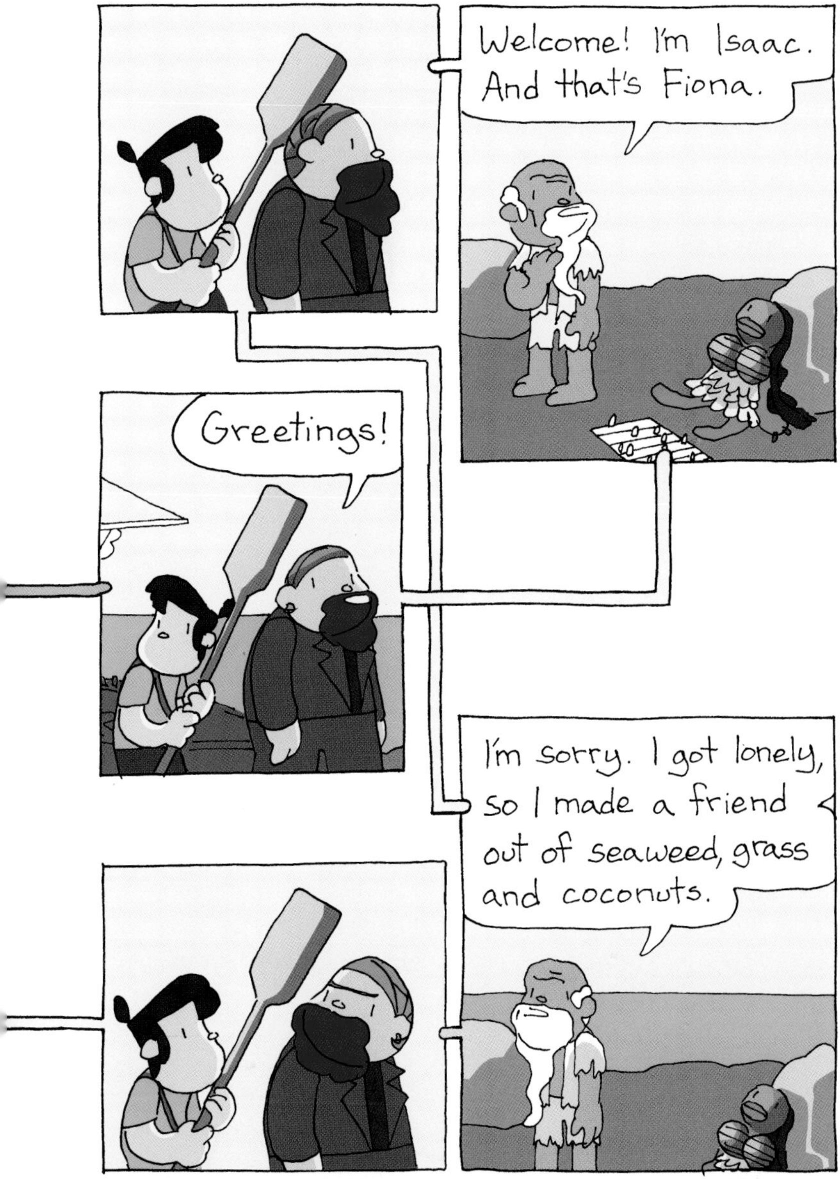
Welcome! I'm Isaac. And that's Fiona.
Greetings!
I'm sorry. I got lonely, so I made a friend out of seaweed, grass and coconuts.

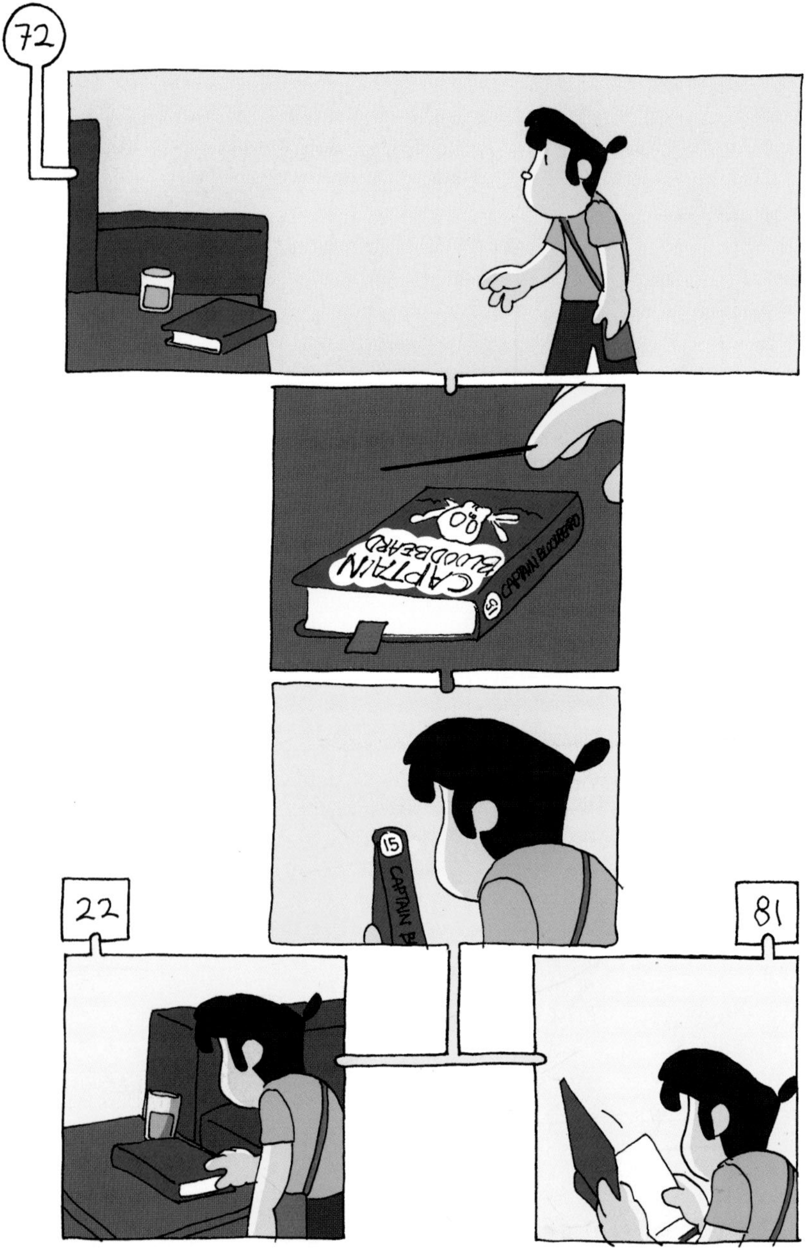

72
CAPTAIN BLOODBEARD
15
CAPTAIN BLOODBEARD
15
22
81

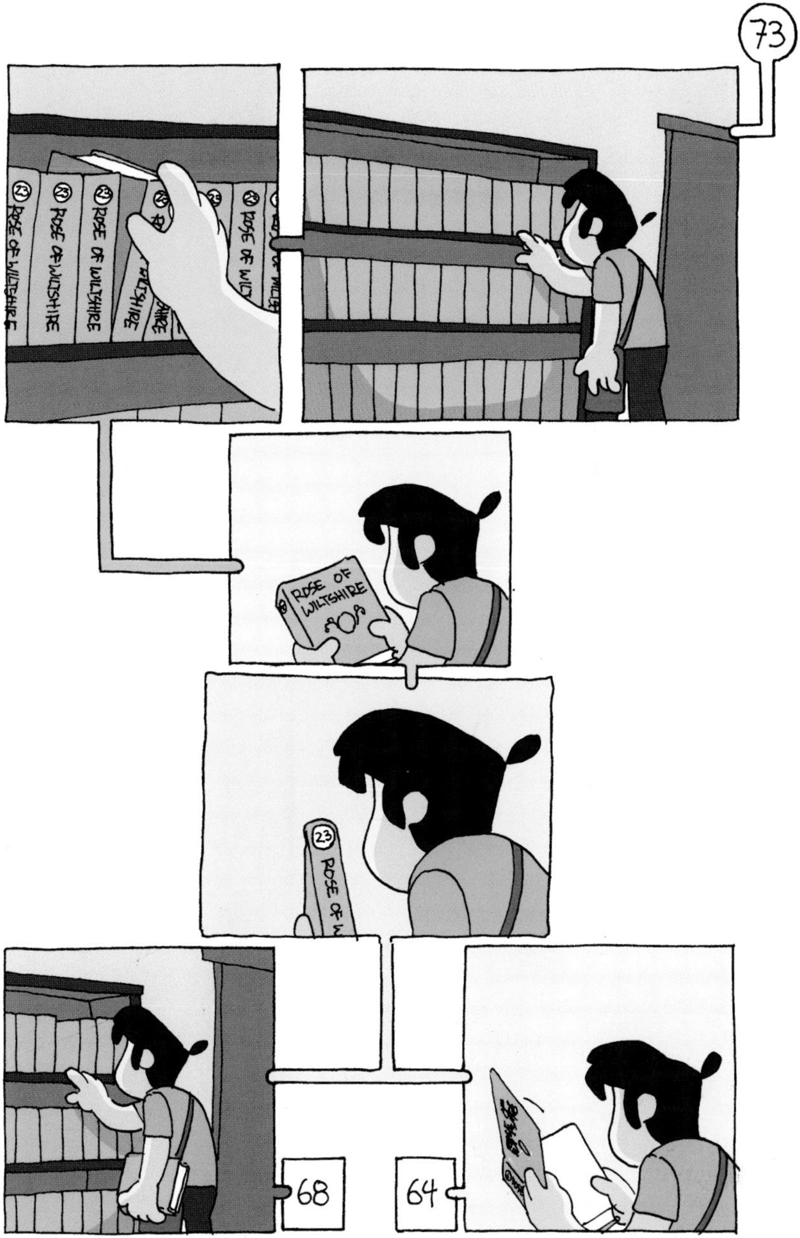
73
23 ROSE OF WILTSHIRE
23 ROSE OF WILTSHIRE
23 ROSE OF WILTSHIRE
ROSE OF WILTSHIRE
23 ROSE OF W
68
64

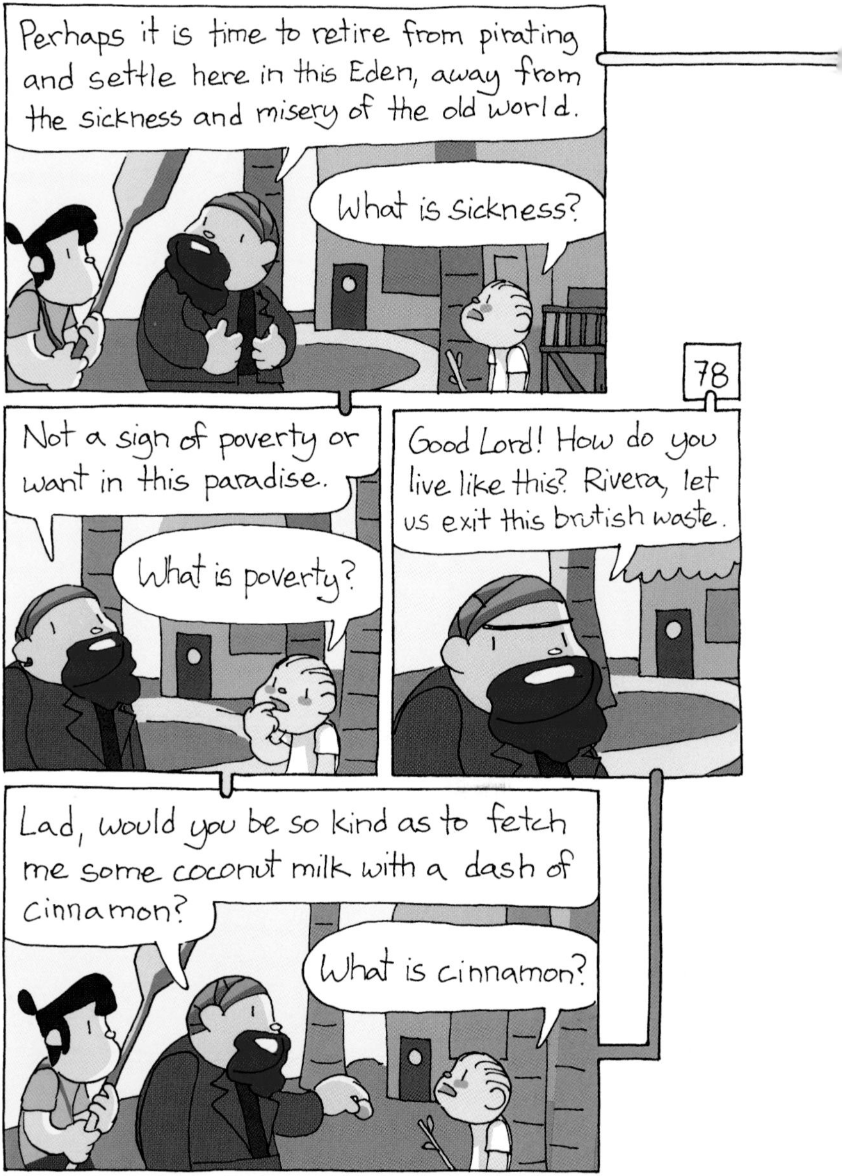
Perhaps it is time to retire from pirating and settle here in this Eden, away from the sickness and misery of the old world.
What is sickness?
78
Not a sign of poverty or want in this paradise.
What is poverty?
Good Lord! How do you live like this? Rivera, let us exit this brutish waste.
Lad, would you be so kind as to fetch me some coconut milk with a dash of cinnamon?
What is cinnamon?

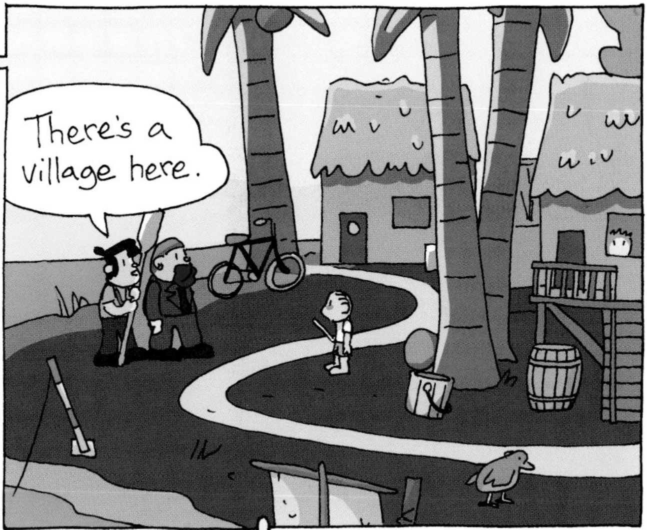
There's a village here.

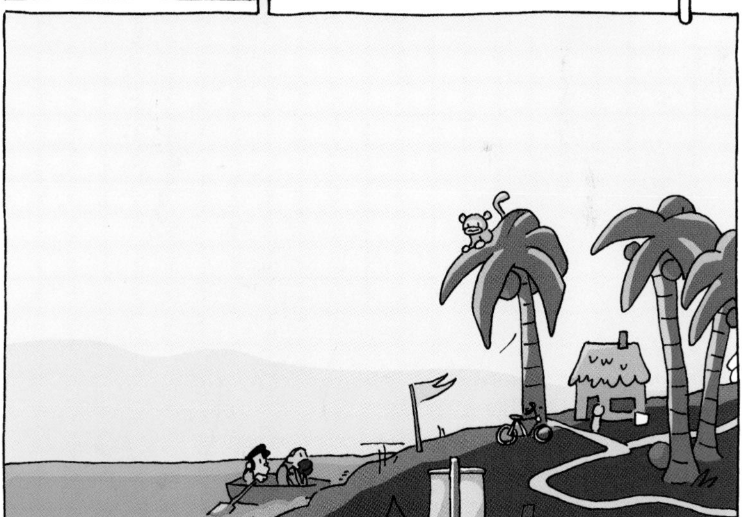

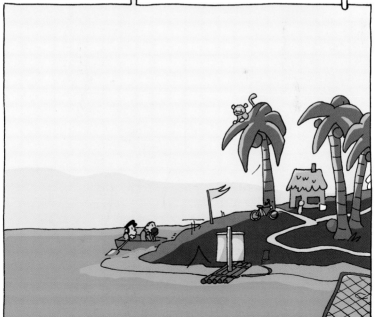

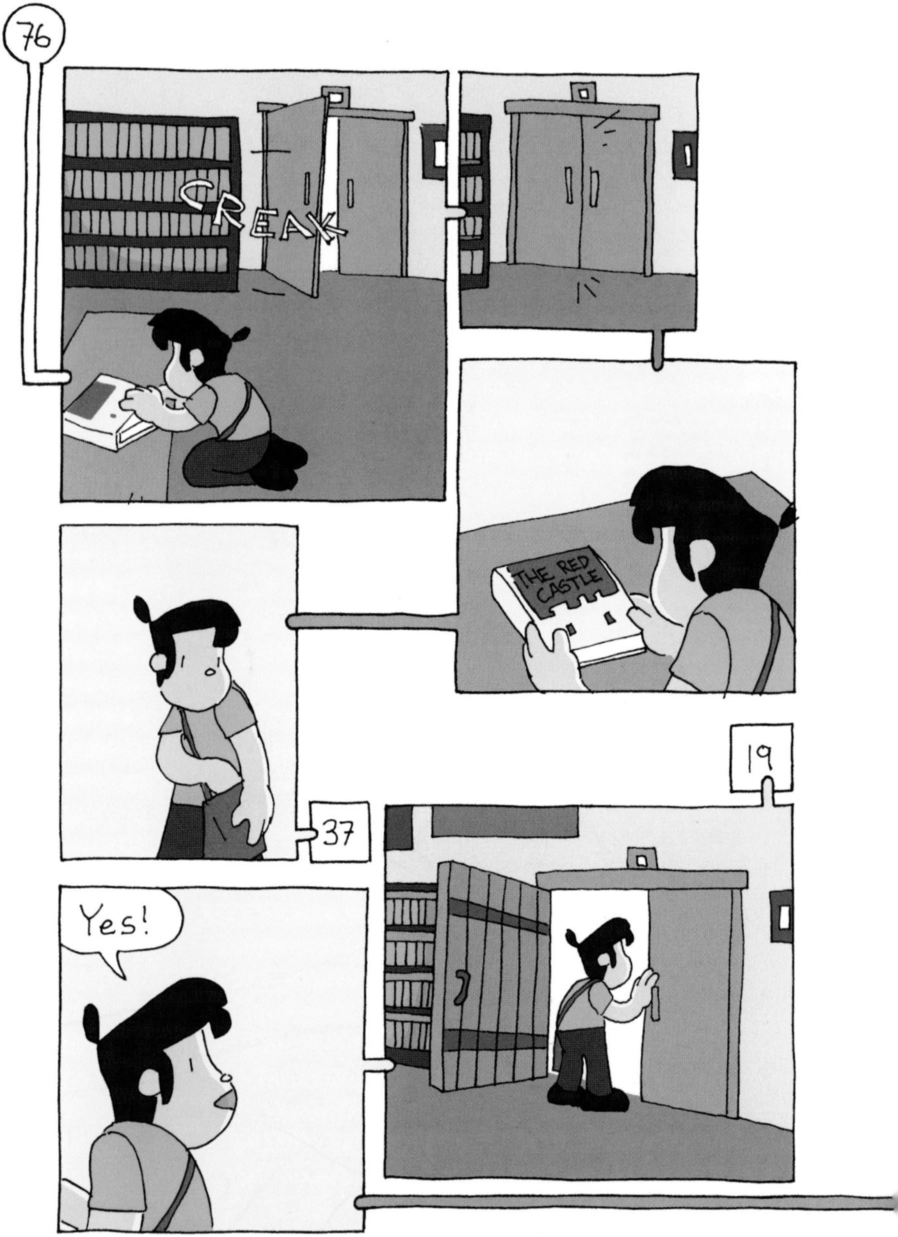
76
CREAK
THE RED CASTLE
37
19
Yes!

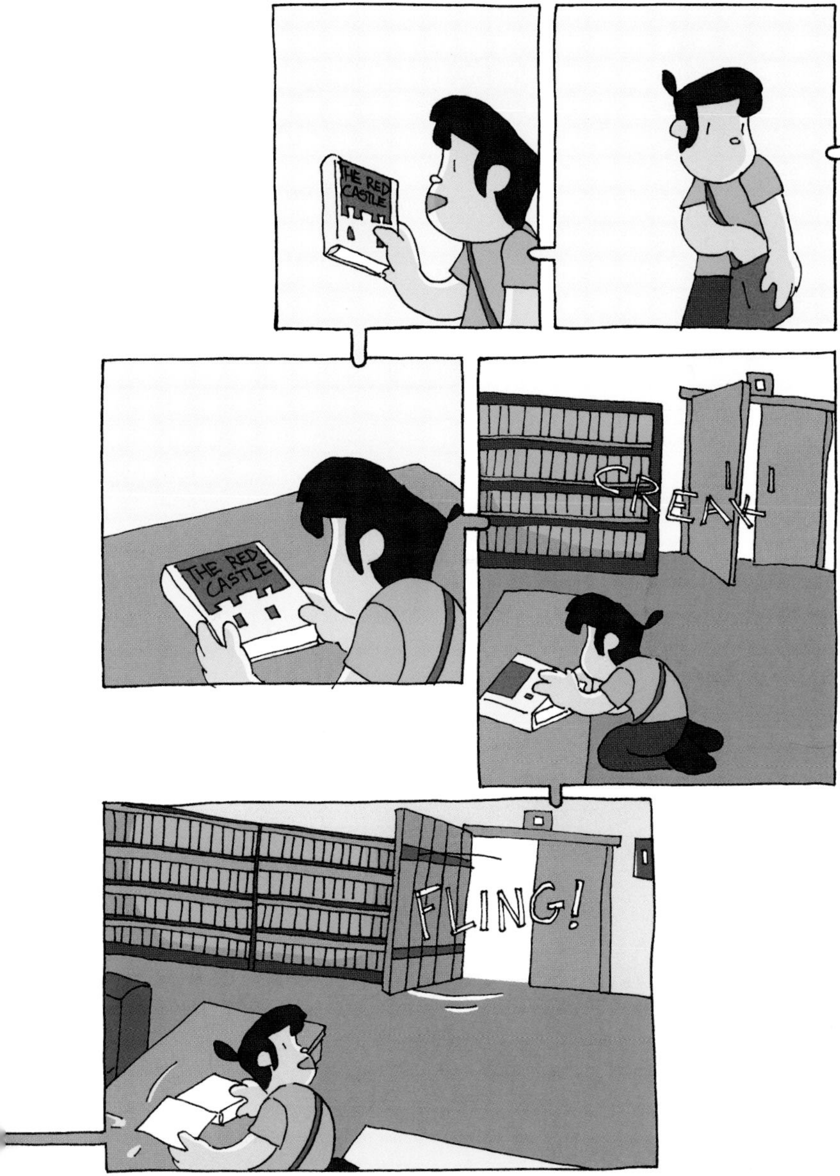
THE RED CASTLE
THE RED CASTLE
CREAK
FLING!

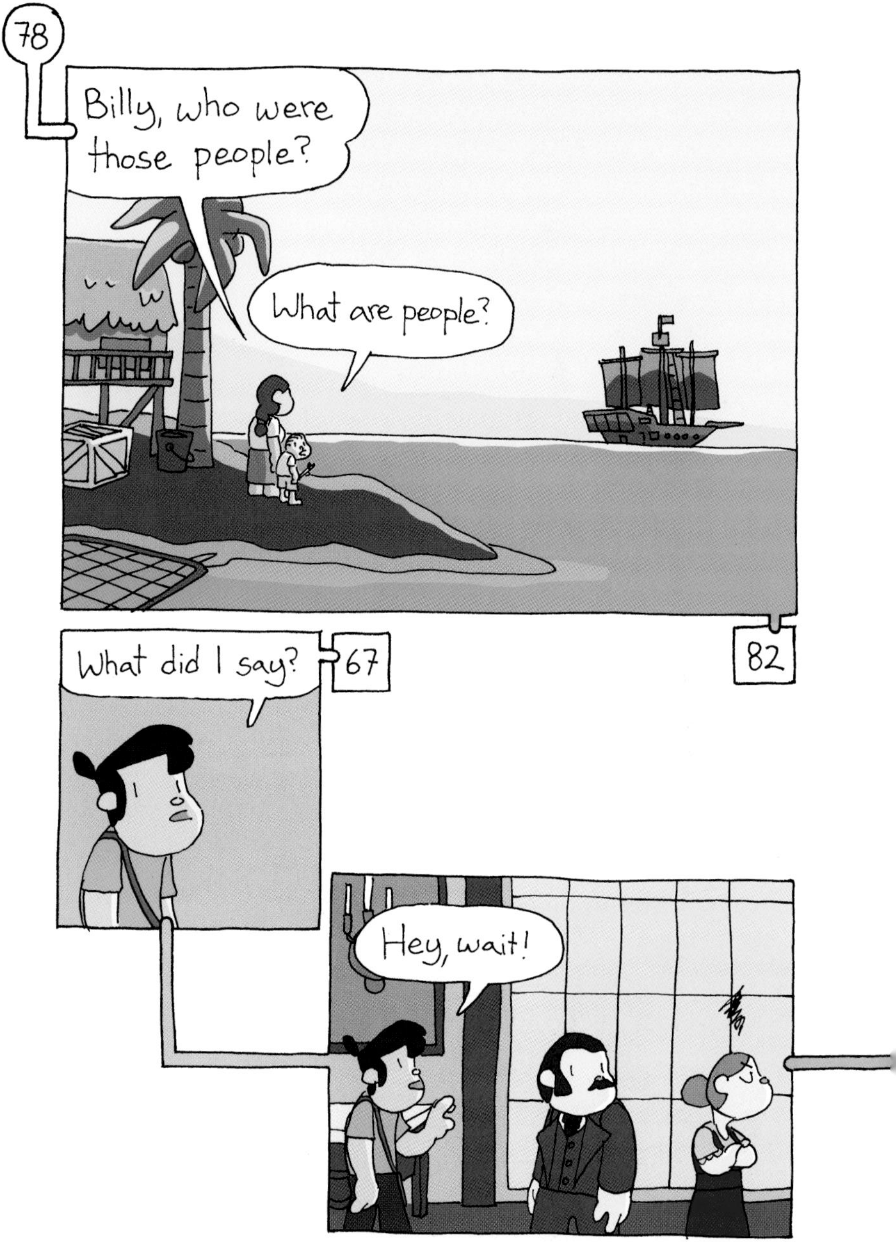
78
Billy, who were those people?
What are people?
82
What did I say?
67
Hey, wait!

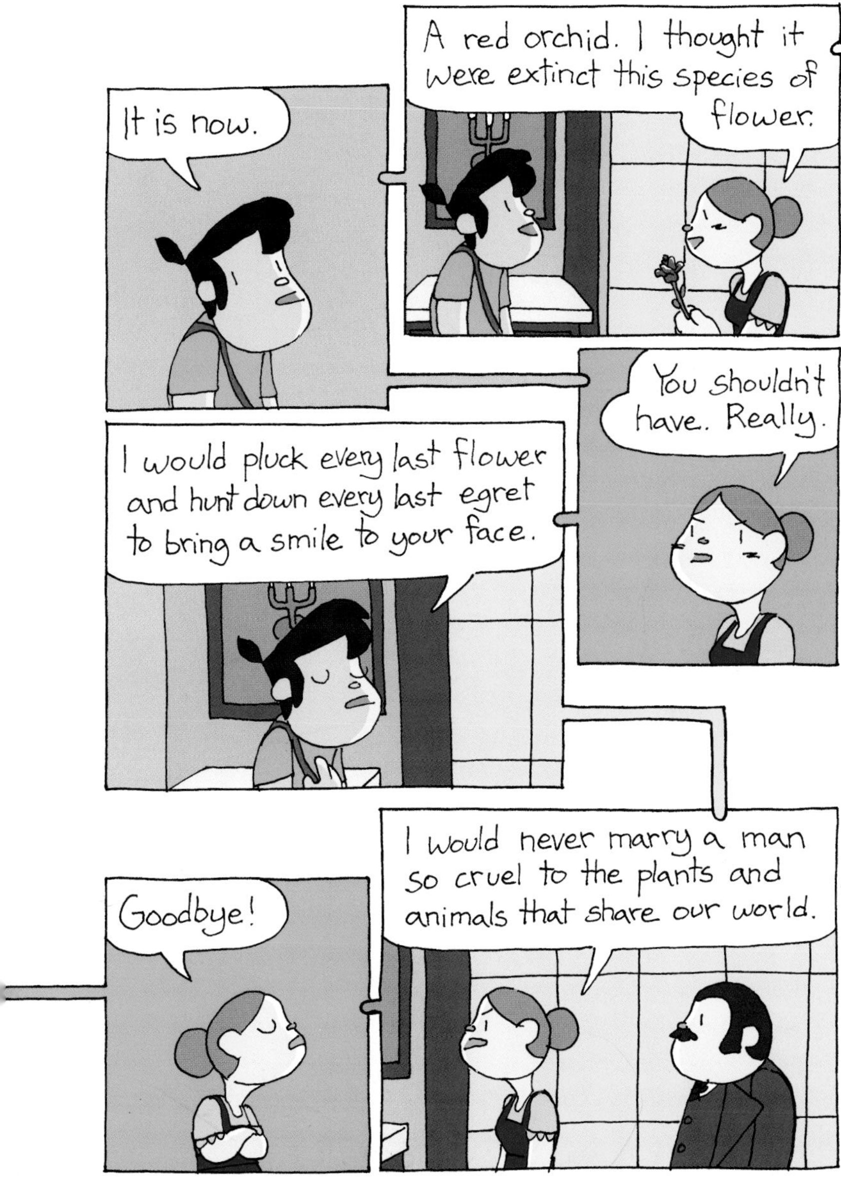
A red orchid. I thought it were extinct this species of flower.
It is now.
You shouldn't have. Really.
I would pluck every last flower and hunt down every last egret to bring a smile to your face.
I would never marry a man so cruel to the plants and animals that share our world.
Goodbye!

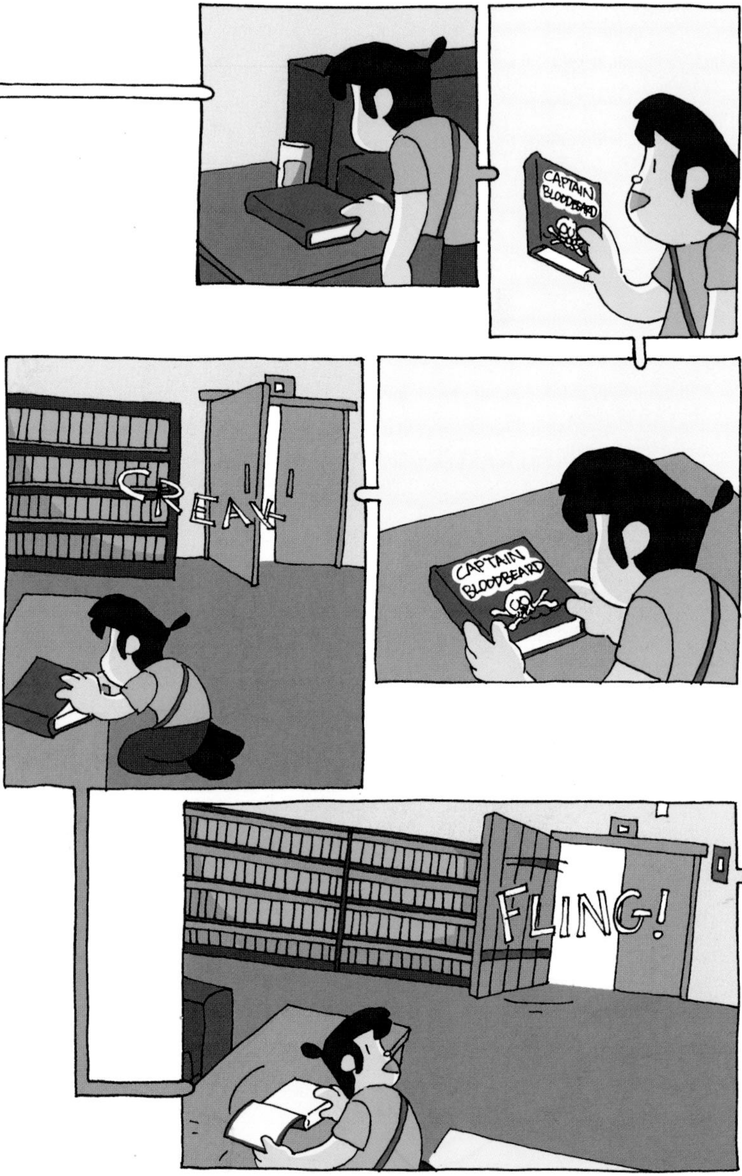
CAPTAIN BLOODBEARD
CAPTAIN BLOODBEARD
CREAK
FLING!

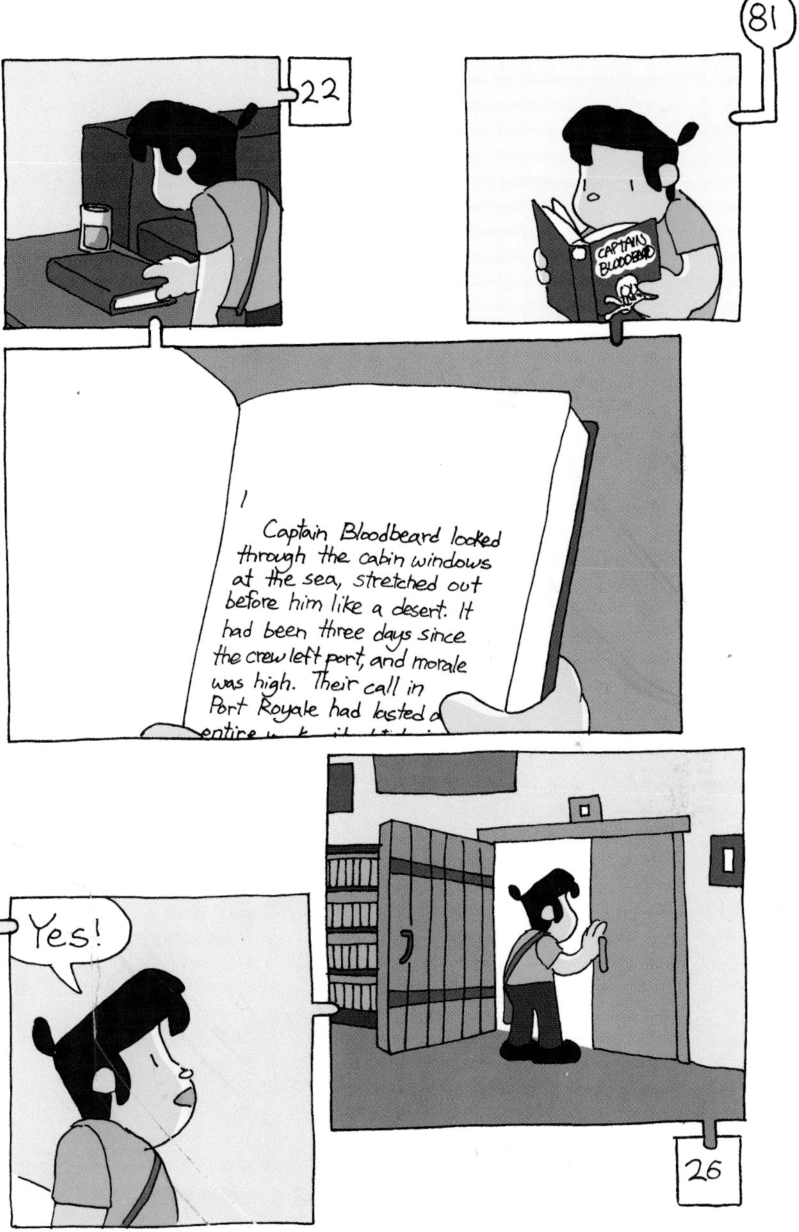
81
22
CAPTAIN BLOODBEARD
1
Captain Bloodbeard looked through the cabin windows at the sea, stretched out before him like a desert. It had been three days since the crew left port, and morale was high. Their call in Port Royale had lasted a
Yes!
26

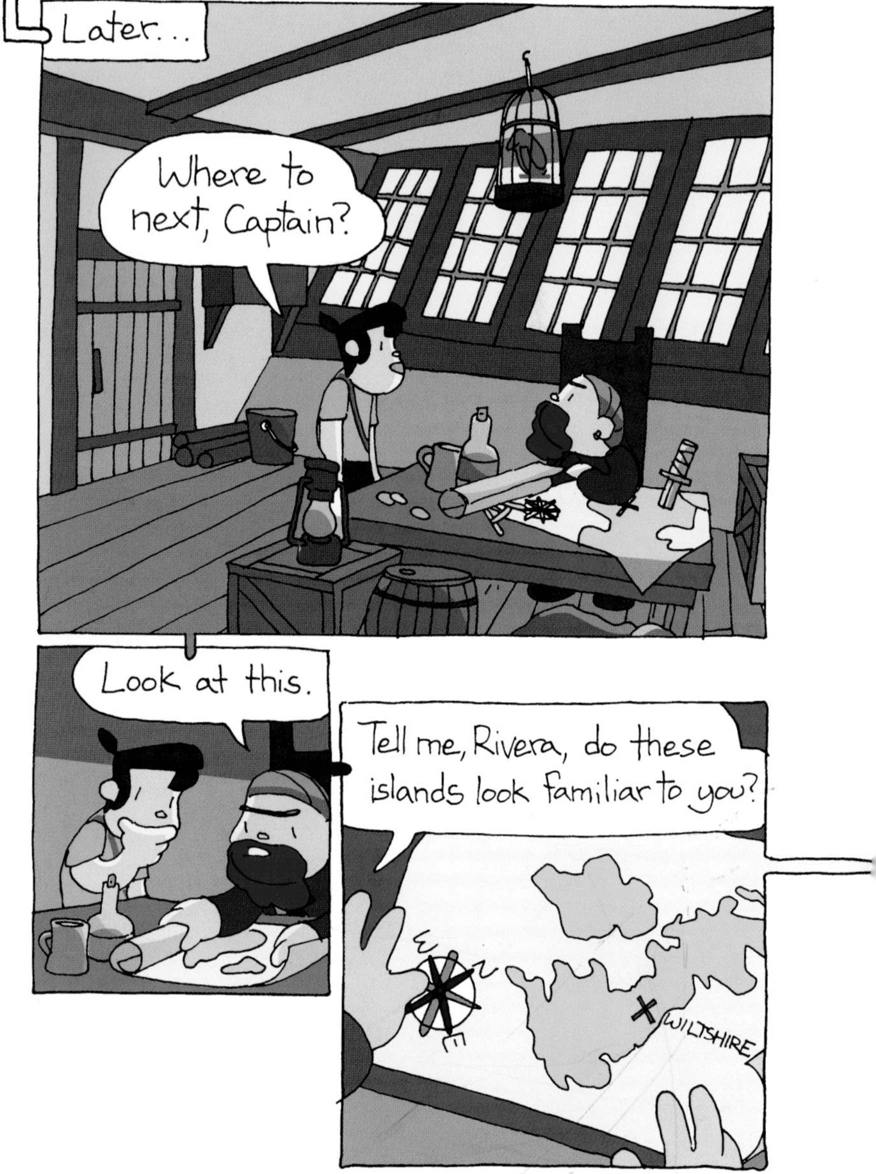
Later...
Where to next, Captain?
Look at this.
Tell me, Rivera, do these islands look familiar to you?
WILTSHIRE

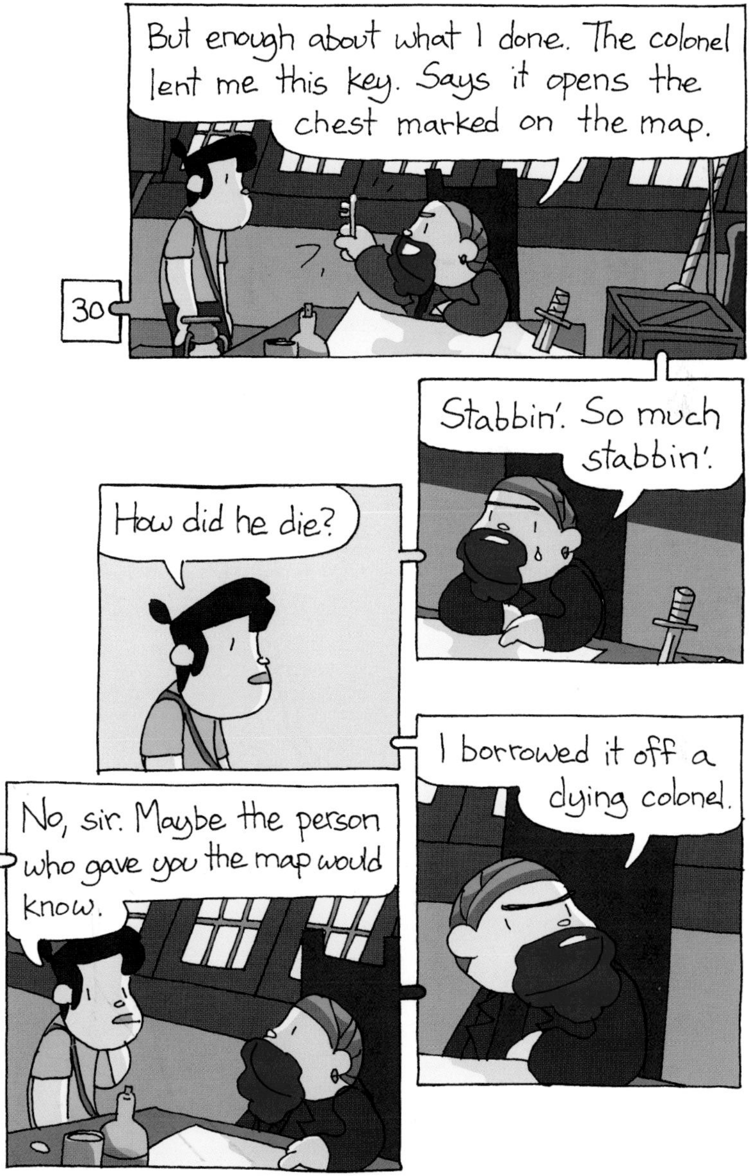
But enough about what I done. The colonel lent me this key. Says it opens the chest marked on the map.
30
Stabbin'. So much stabbin'.
How did he die?
I borrowed it off a dying colonel.
No, sir. Maybe the person who gave you the map would know.

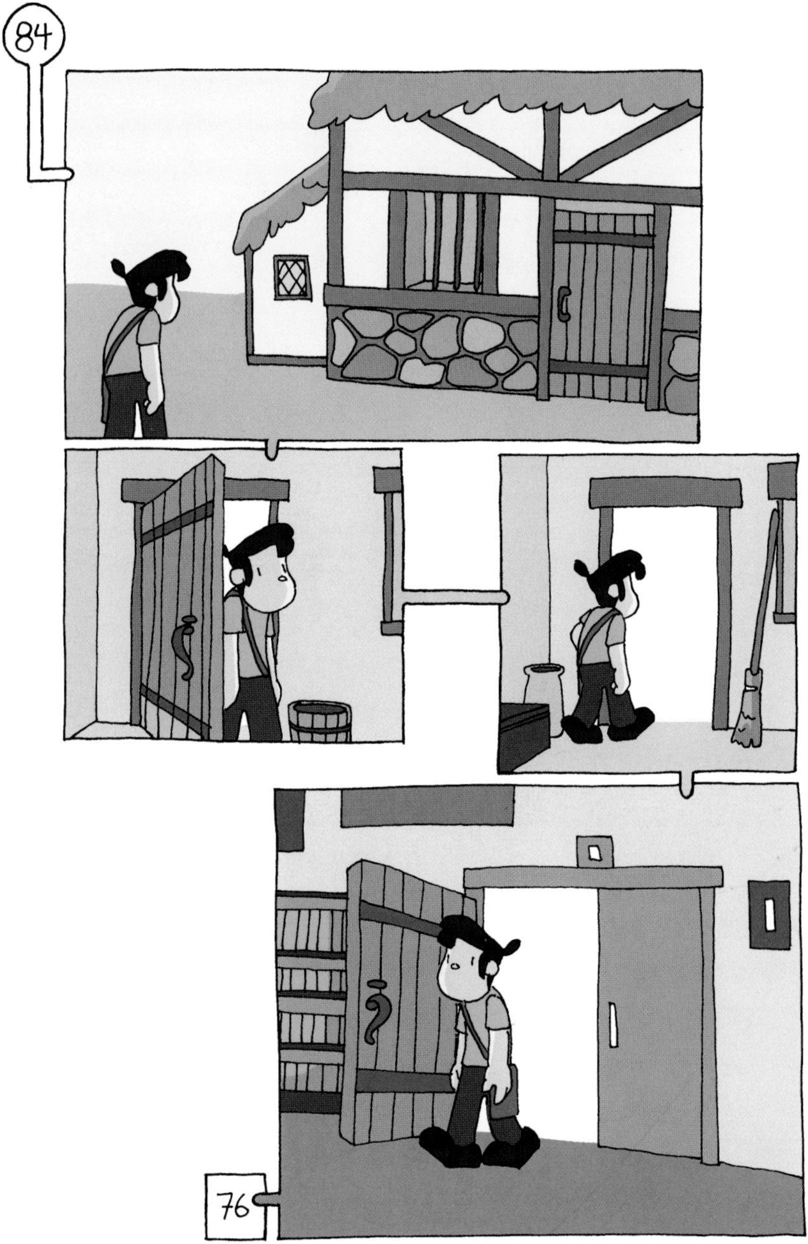
84
76

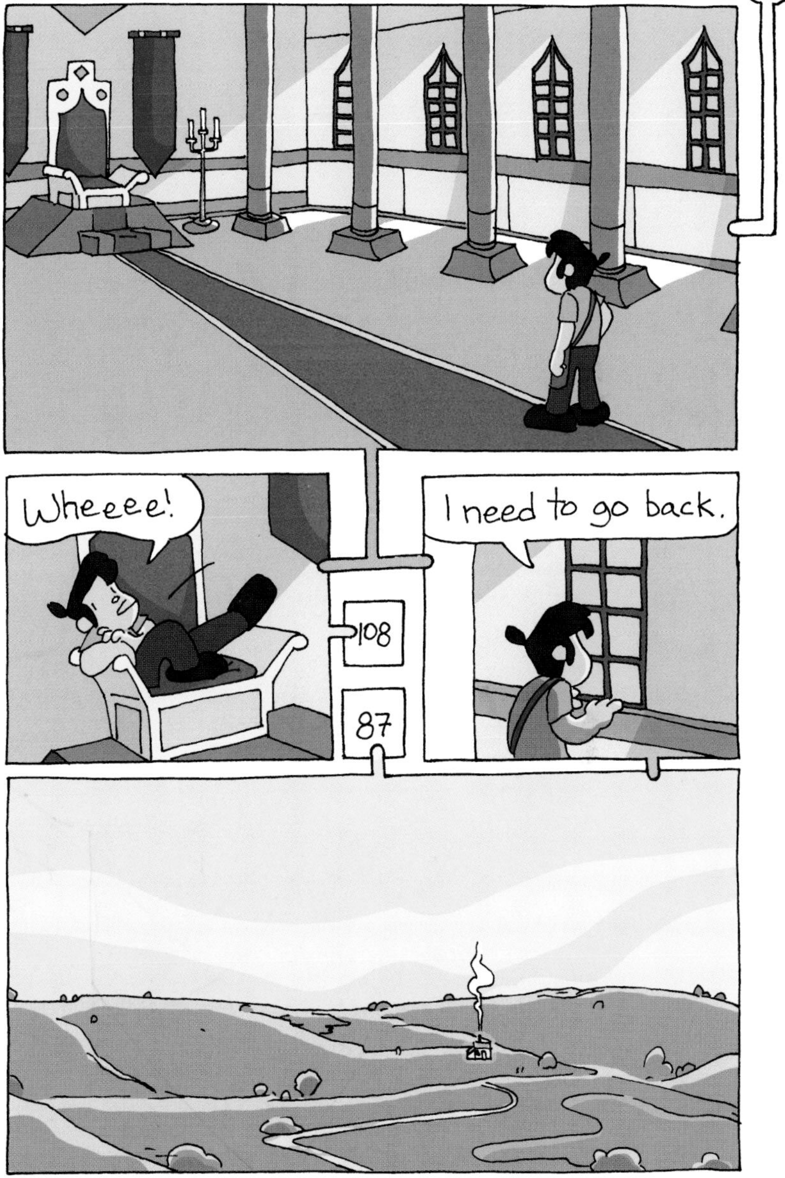
Wheeee!
108
87
I need to go back.

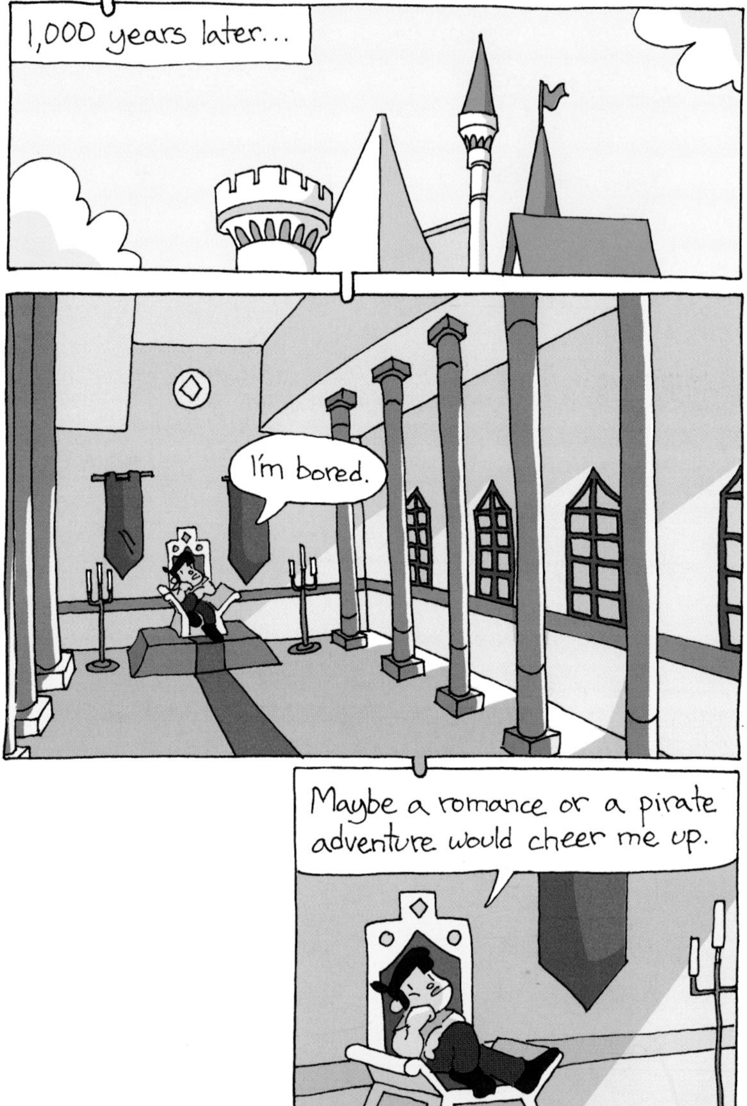
1,000 years later...
I'm bored.
Maybe a romance or a pirate adventure would cheer me up.

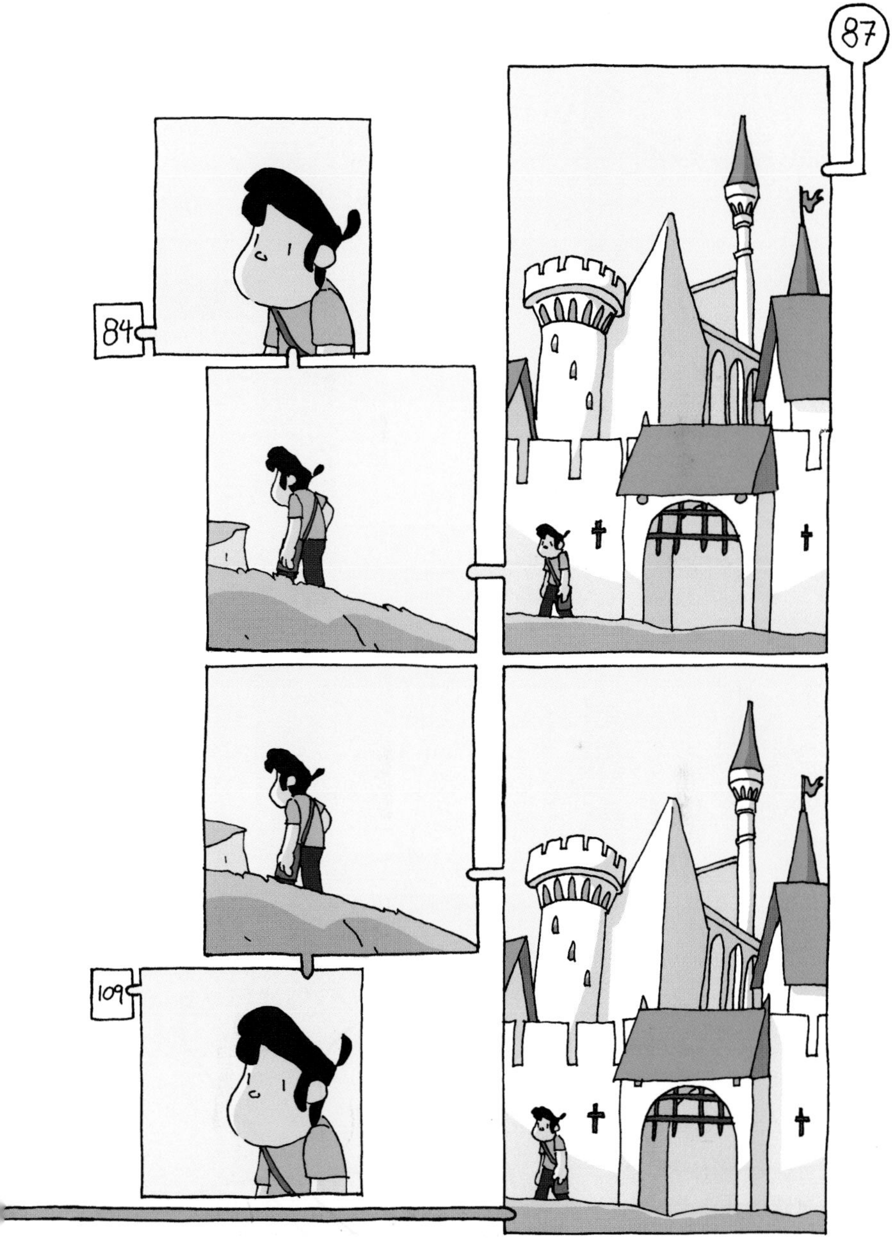
87
84
109

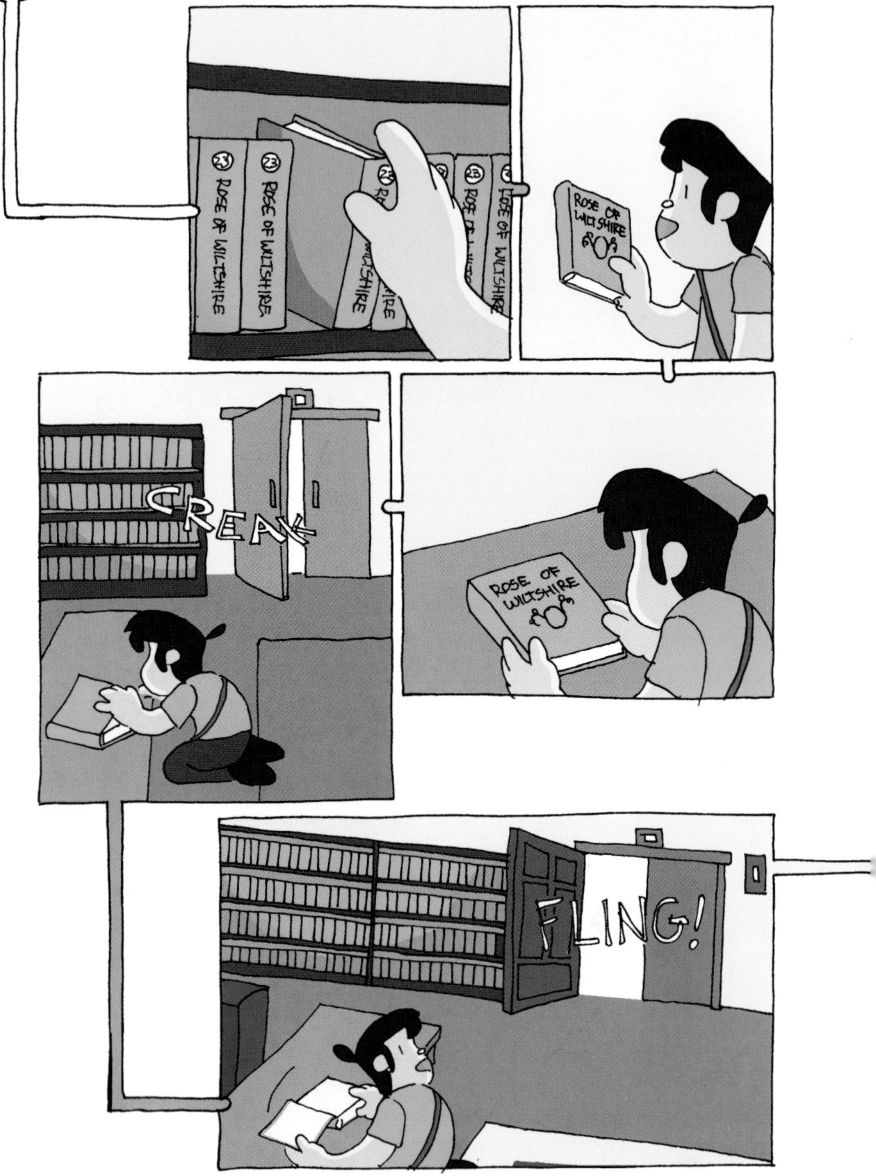
ROSE OF WILTSHIRE
ROSE OF WILTSHIRE
ROSE OF WILTSHIRE
ROSE OF WILTSHIRE
ROSE OF WILTSHIRE
CREAK
FLING!

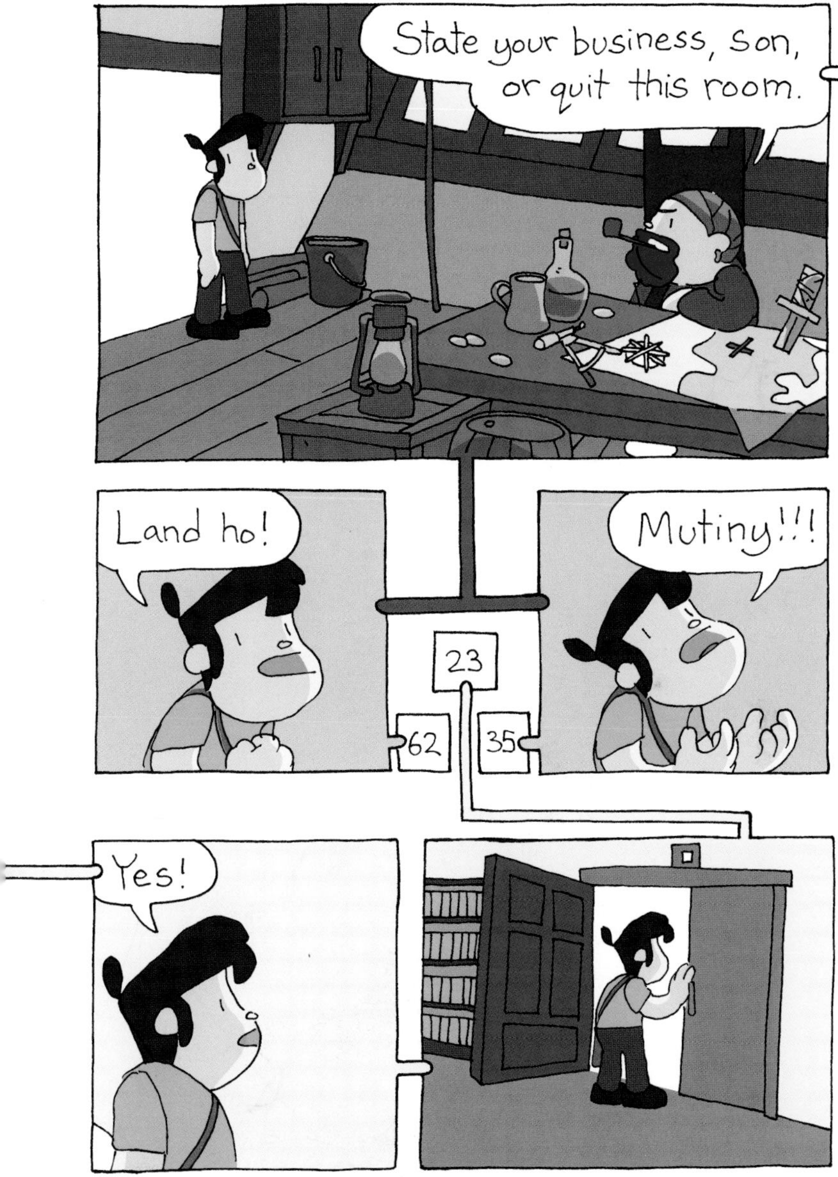
State your business, son, or quit this room.
Land ho!
Mutiny!!!
23
62
35
Yes!

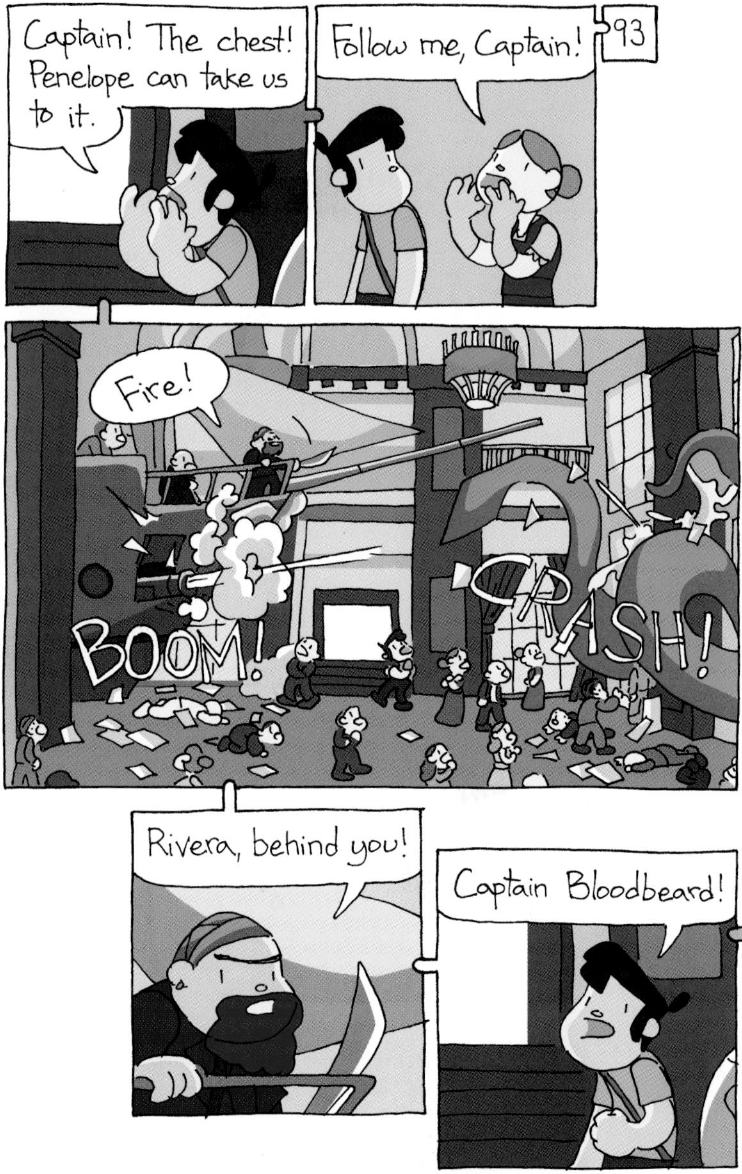
Captain! The chest! Penelope can take us to it.
Follow me, Captain!
93
Fire!
BOOM!
CRASH!
Rivera, behind you!
Captain Bloodbeard!

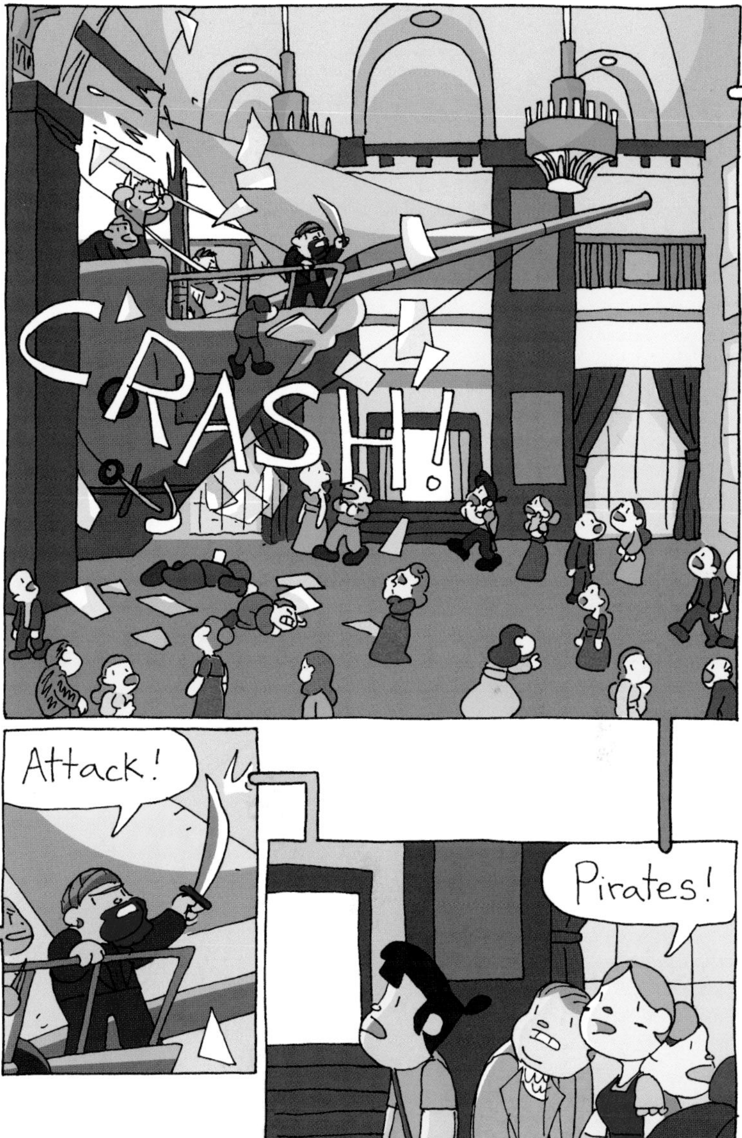
CRASH!
Attack!
Pirates!

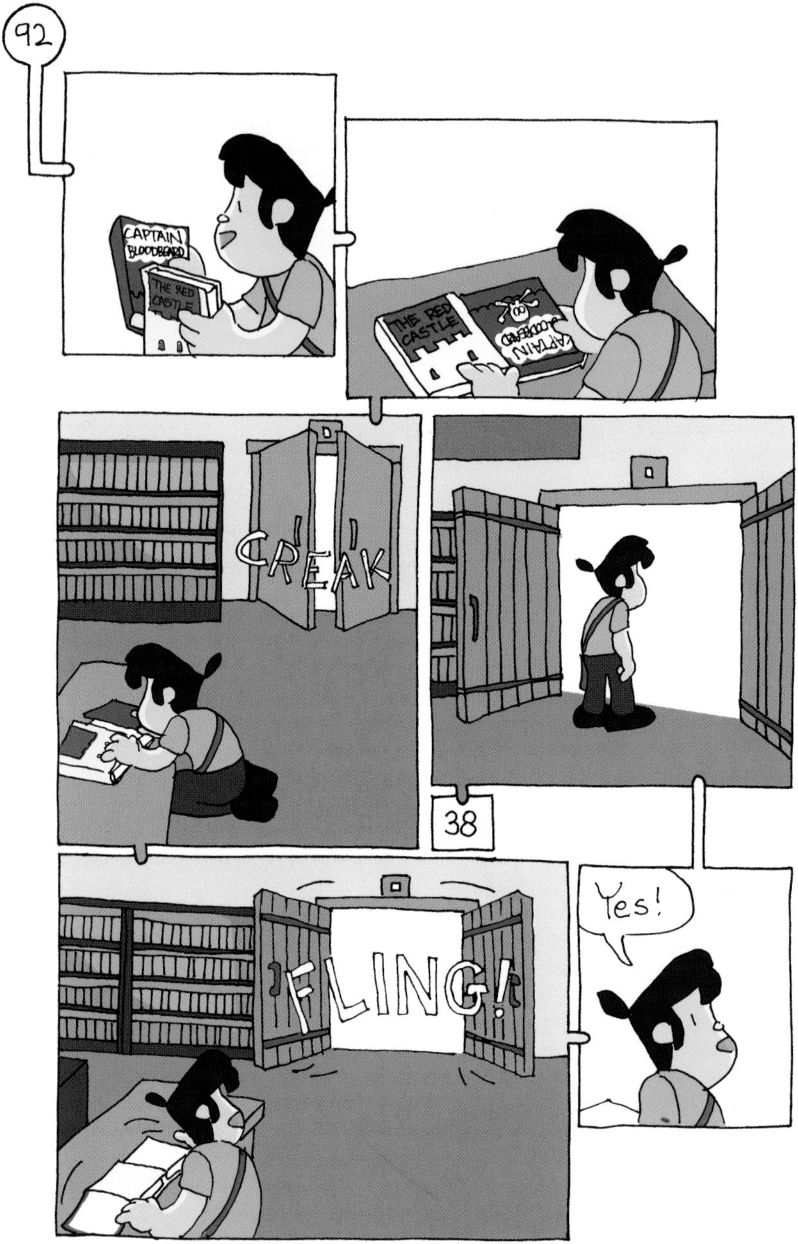
92
CAPTAIN BLOODBEARD
THE RED CASTLE
THE RED CASTLE
CAPTAIN BLOODBEARD
CREAK
38
FLING!
Yes!

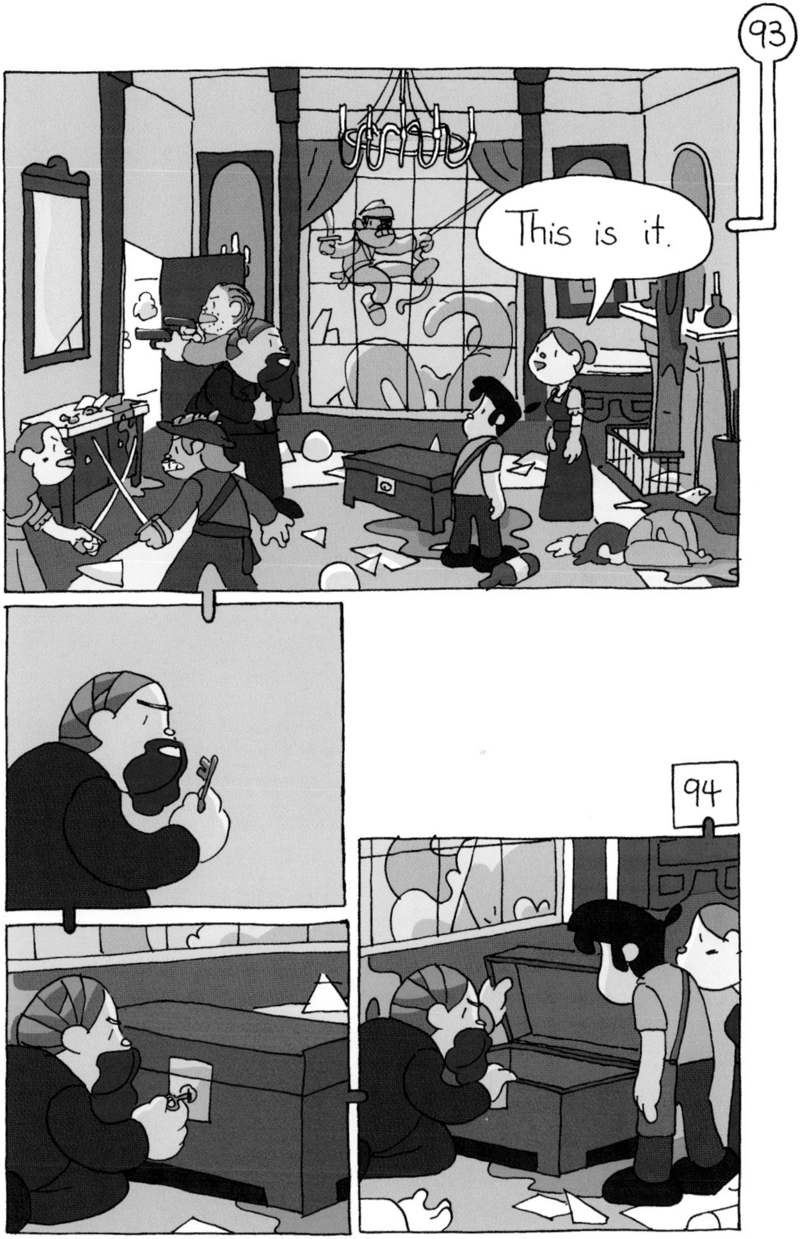
93
This is it.
94

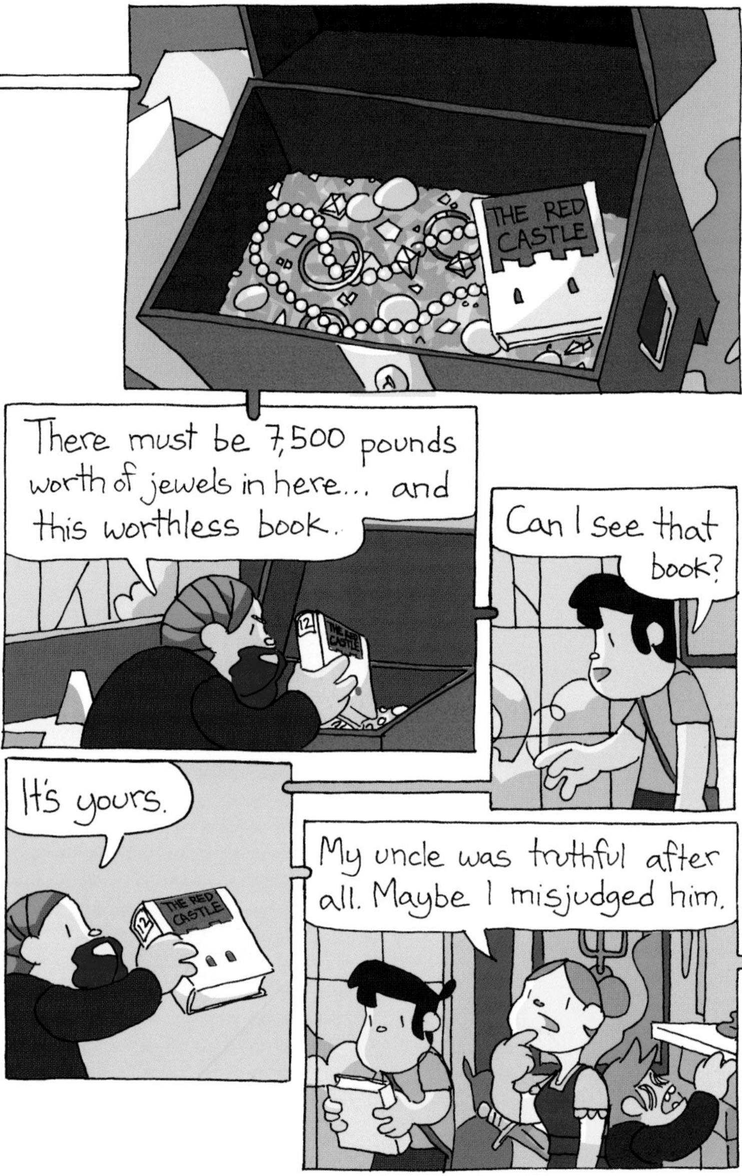
THE RED CASTLE
There must be 7,500 pounds worth of jewels in here... and this worthless book..
12 THE RED CASTLE
Can I see that book?
It's yours.
12 THE RED CASTLE
My uncle was truthful after all. Maybe I misjudged him.

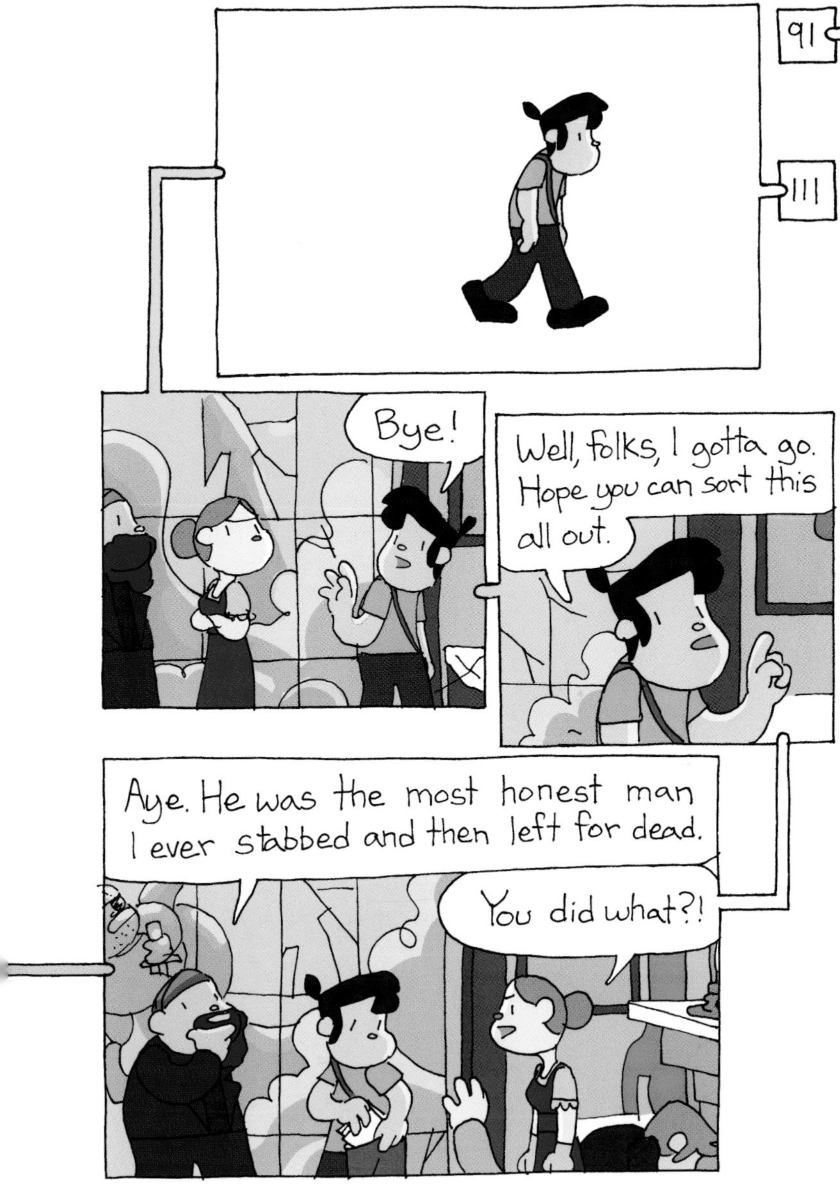
91
111
Bye!
Well, folks, I gotta go. Hope you can sort this all out.
Aye. He was the most honest man I ever stabbed and then left for dead.
You did what?!

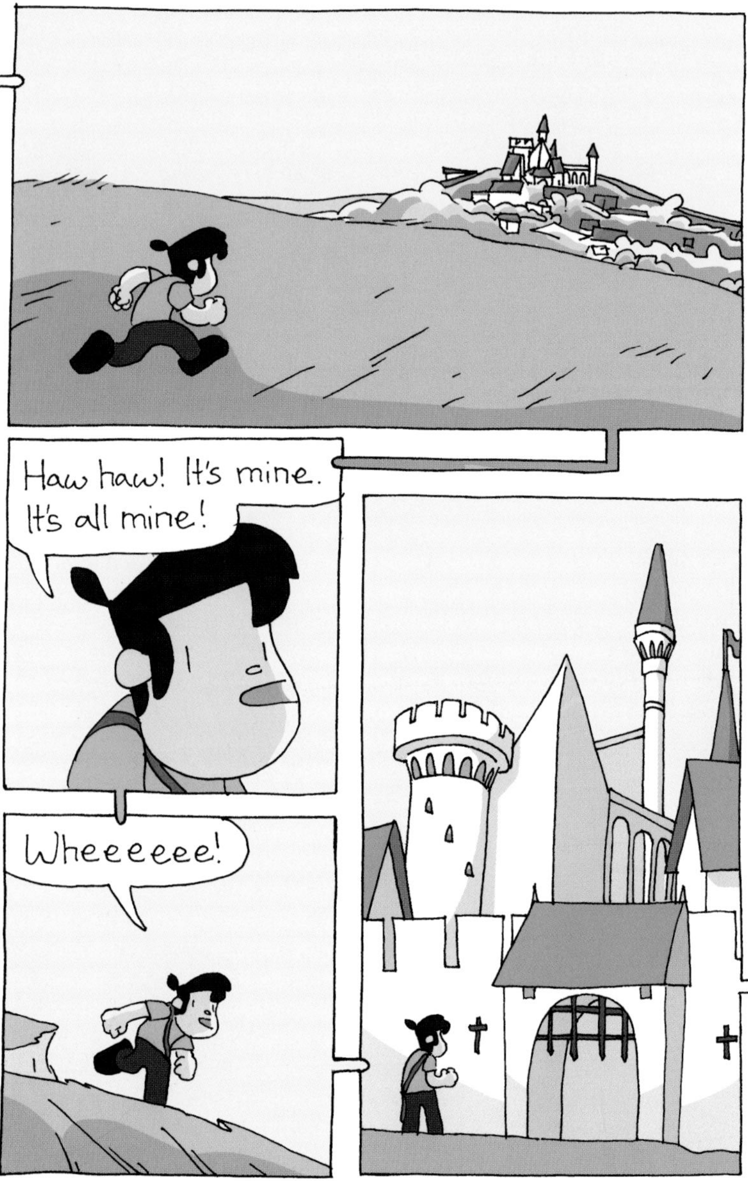
Haw haw! It's mine. It's all mine!
Wheeeeee!

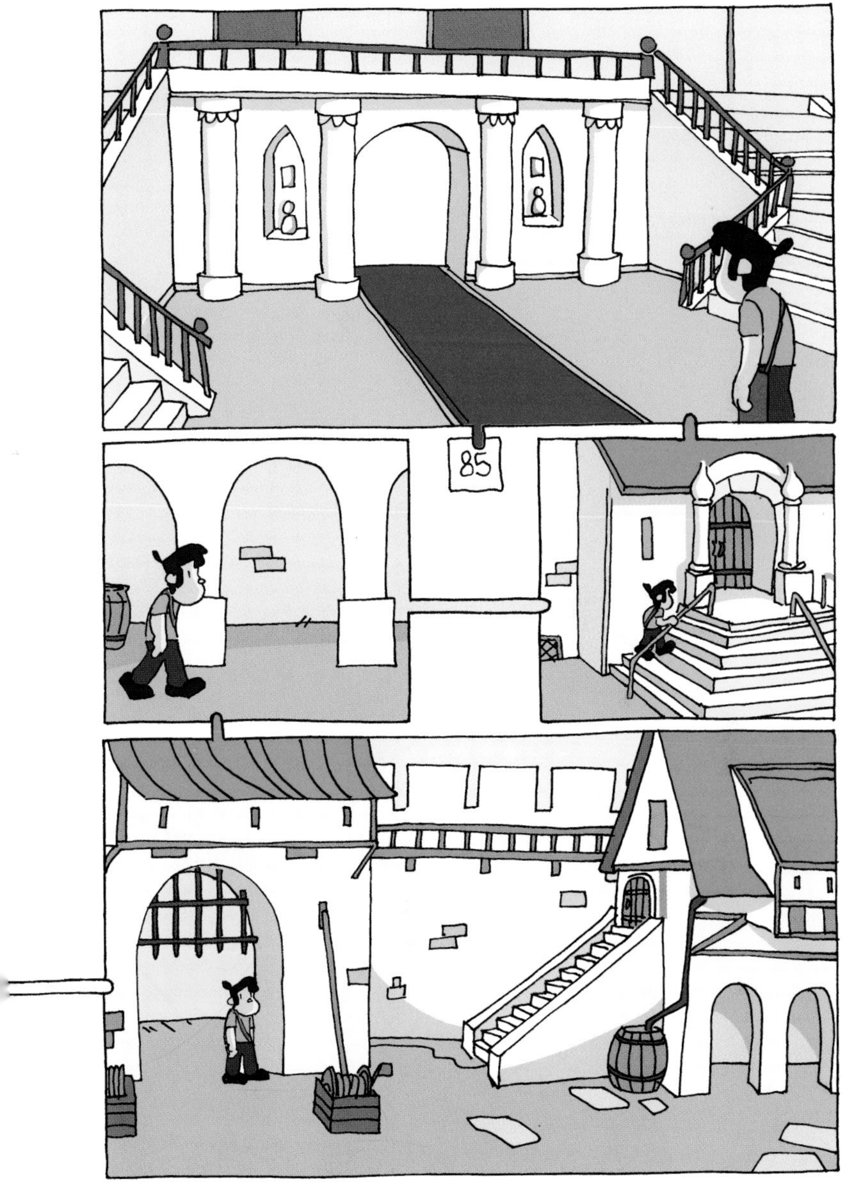
85

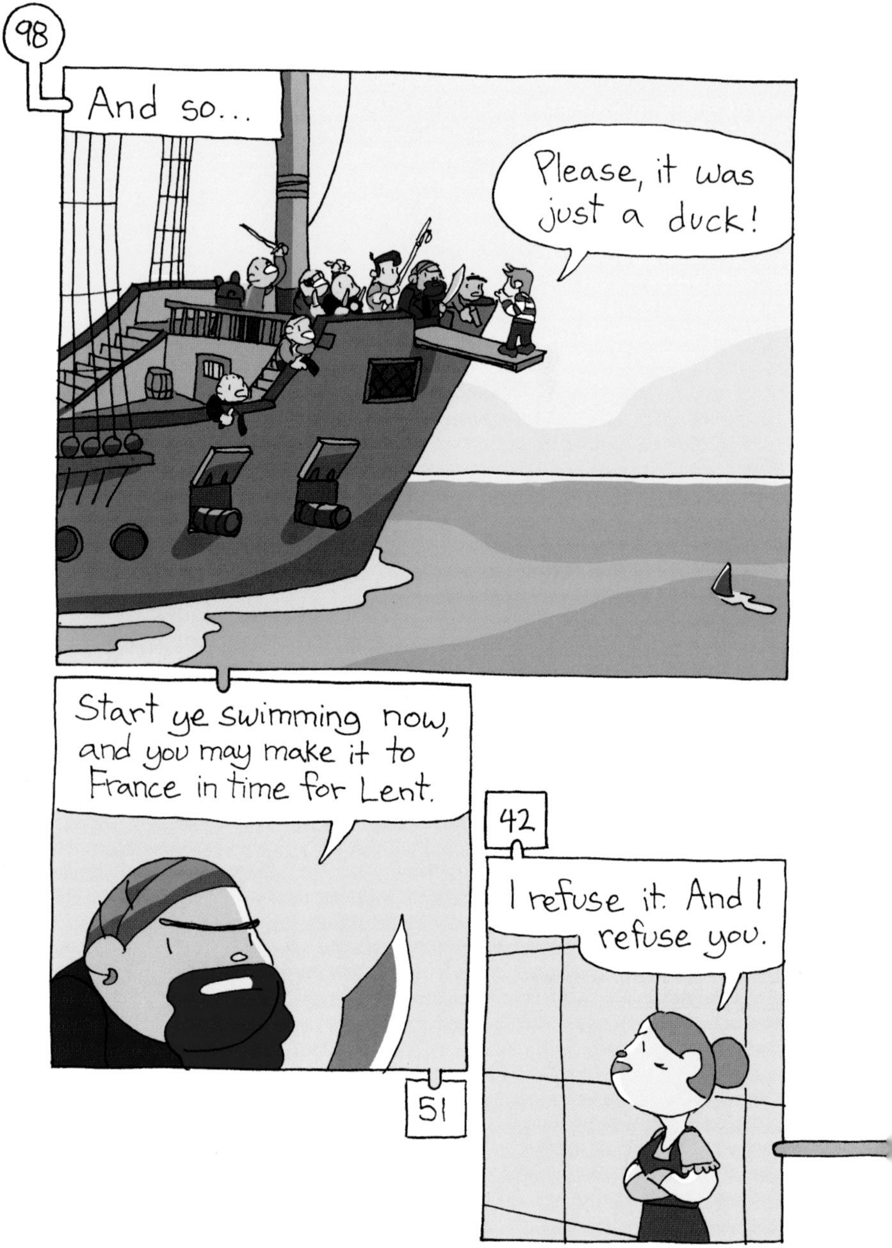
98
And so...
Please, it was just a duck!
Start ye swimming now, and you may make it to France in time for Lent.
51
42
I refuse it. And I refuse you.

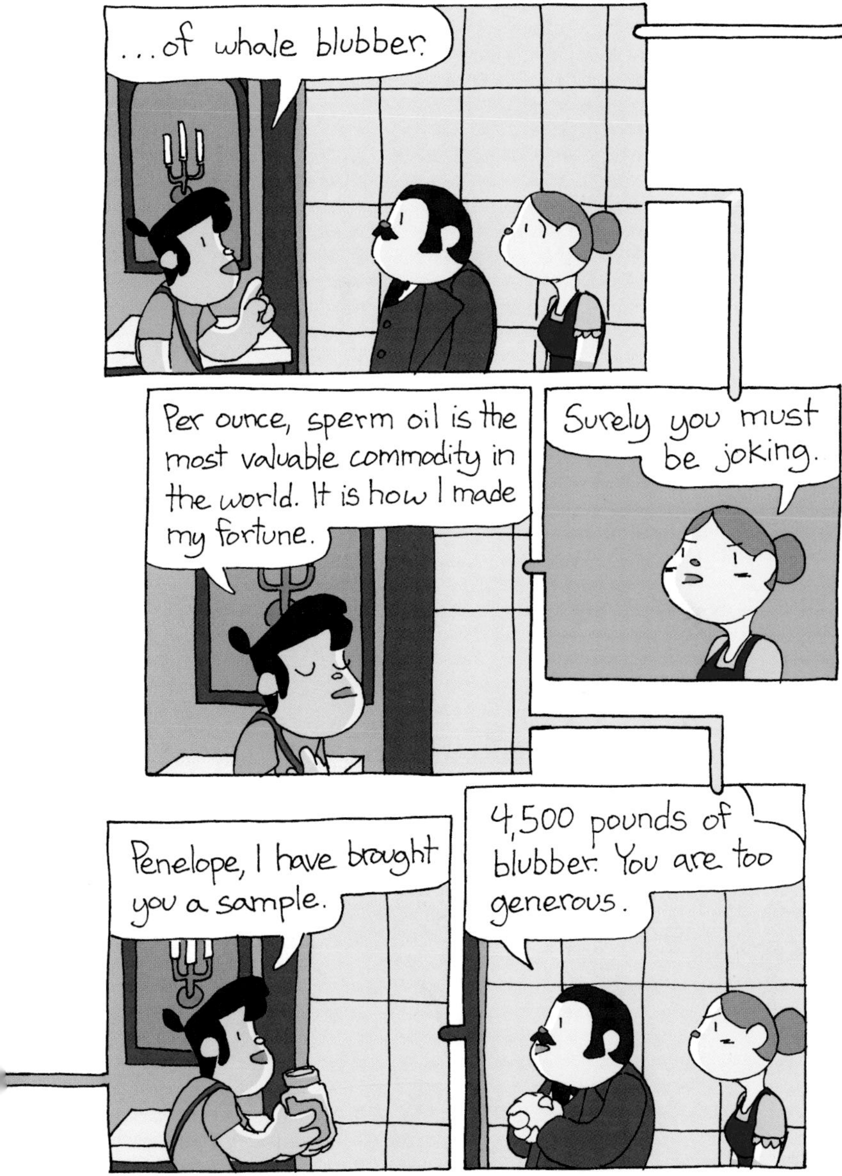
...of whale blubber.
Per ounce, sperm oil is the most valuable commodity in the world. It is how I made my fortune.
Surely you must be joking.
Penelope, I have brought you a sample.
4,500 pounds of blubber. You are too generous.

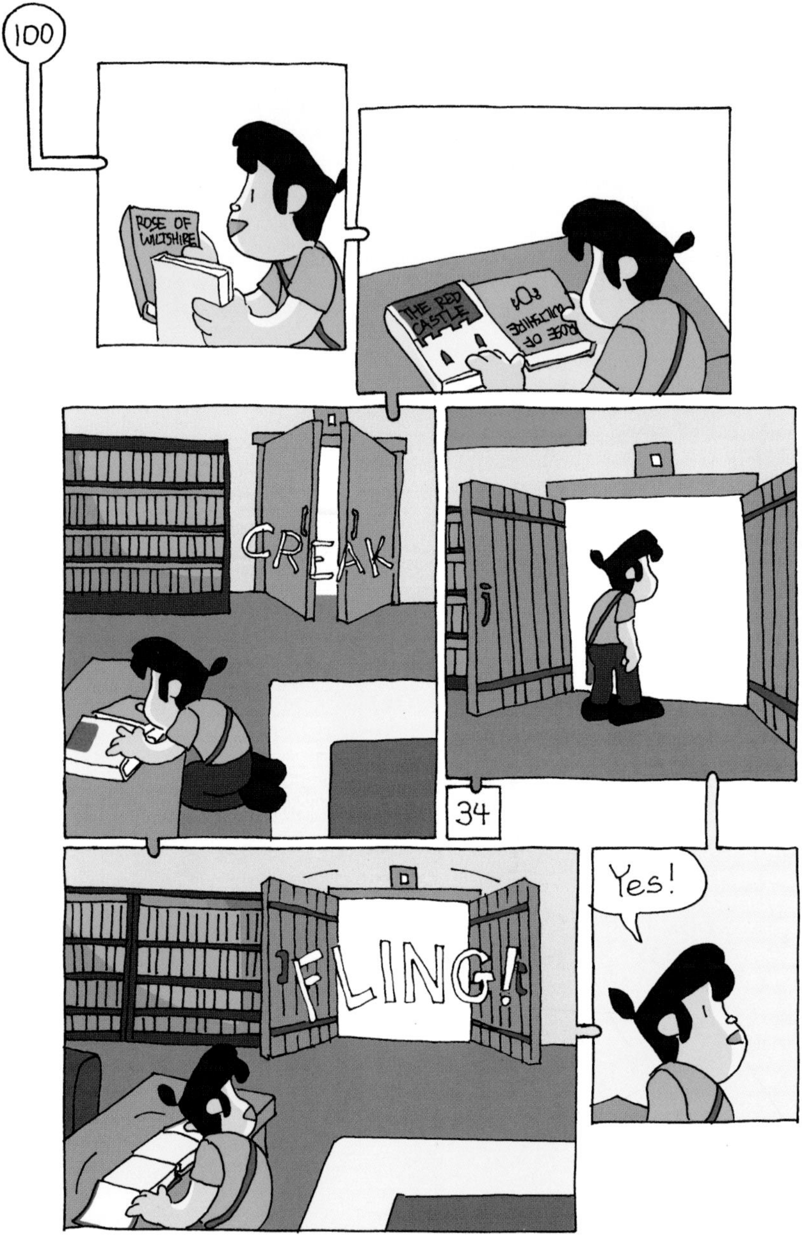
100
ROSE OF WILTSHIRE
THE RED CASTLE
ROSE OF WILTSHIRE
CREAK
34
FLING!
Yes!

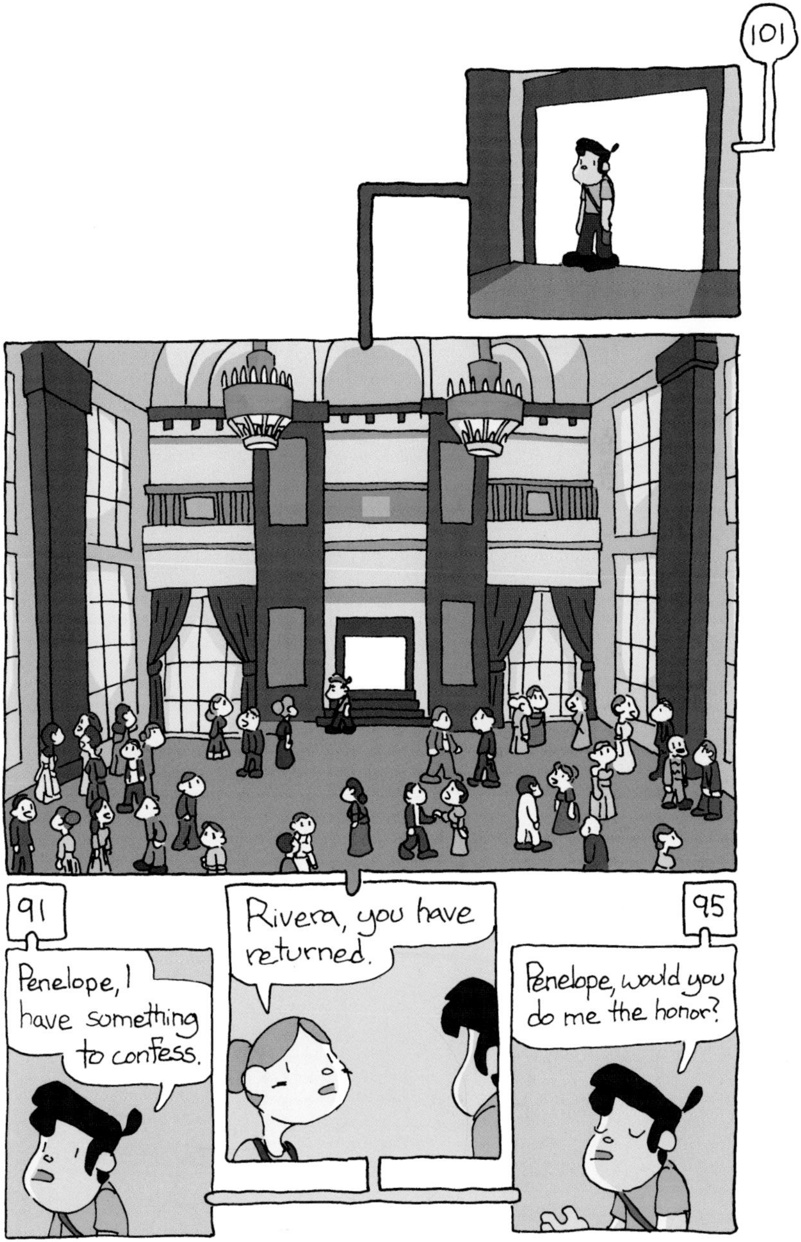
101
91
Penelope, I have something to confess.
Rivera, you have returned.
95
Penelope, would you do me the honor?

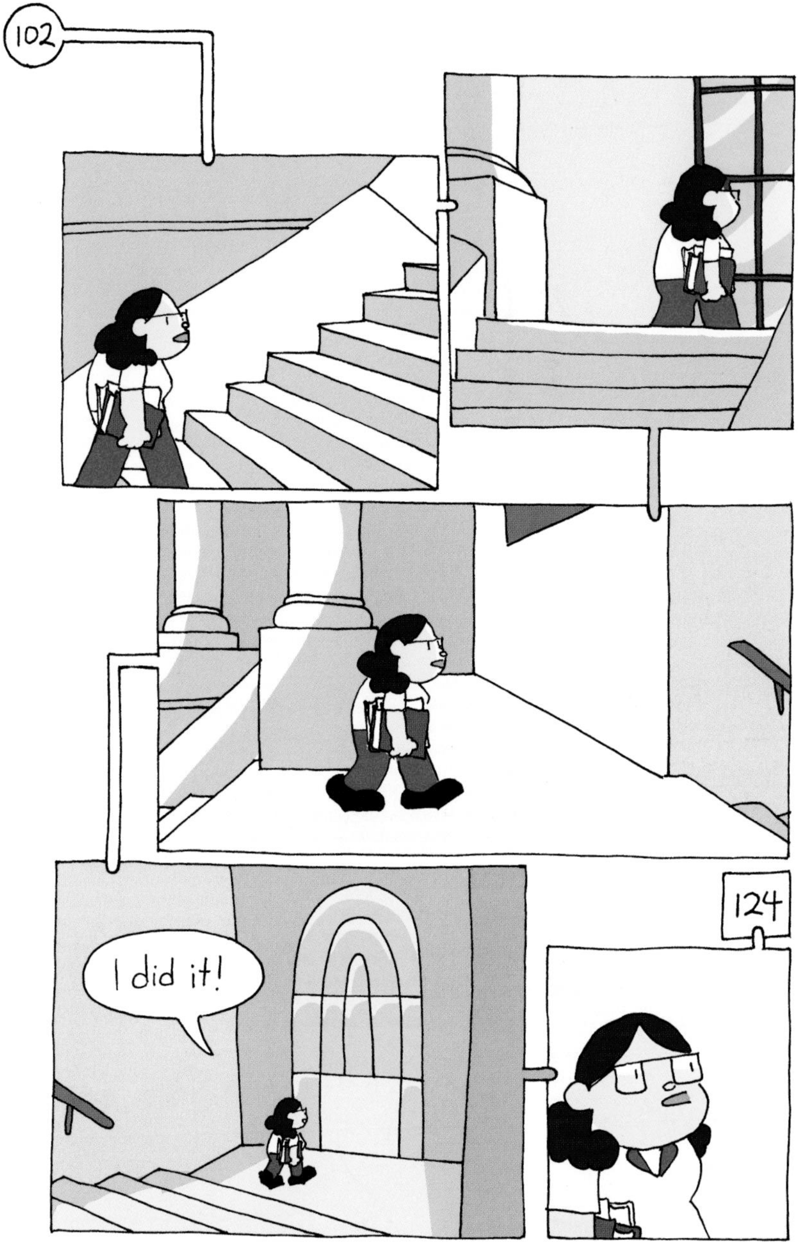
102
I did it!
124

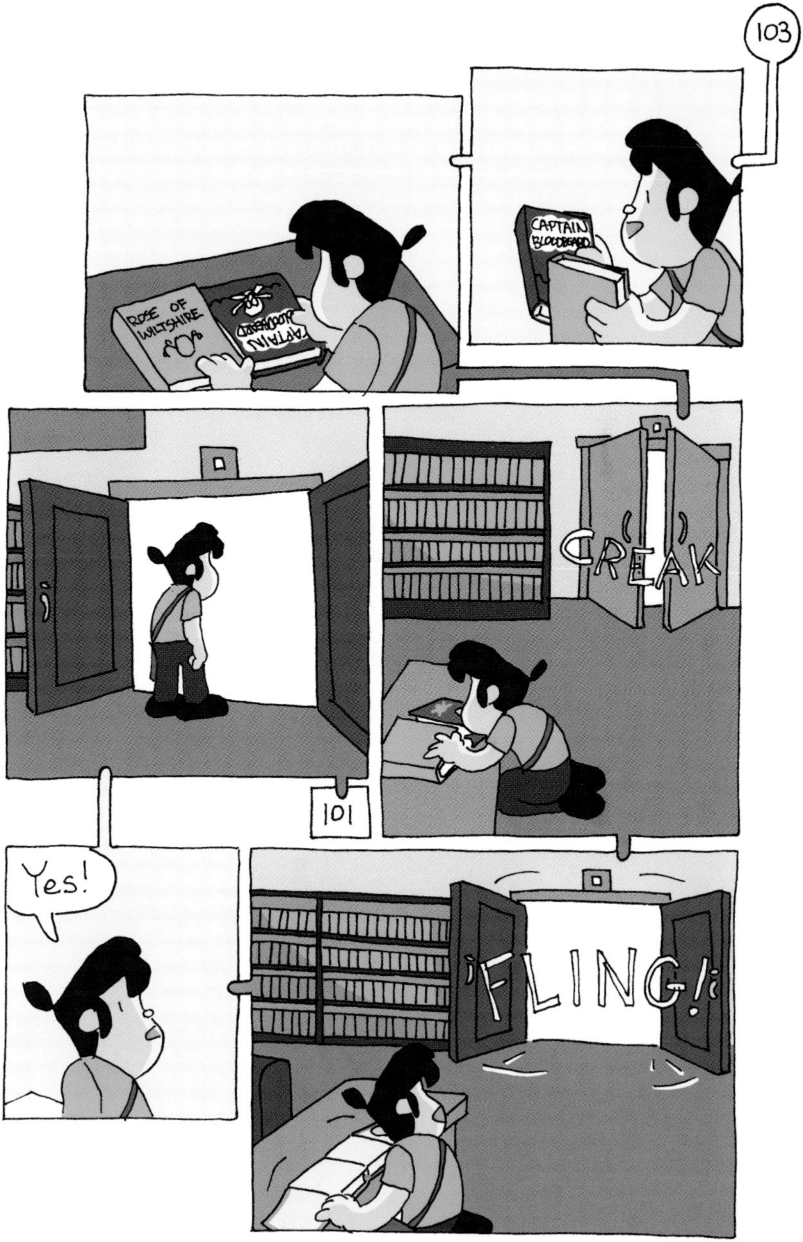
103
ROSE OF WILTSHIRE
CAPTAIN BLOODBEARD
CAPTAIN BLOODBEARD
CREAK
101
Yes!
FLING!

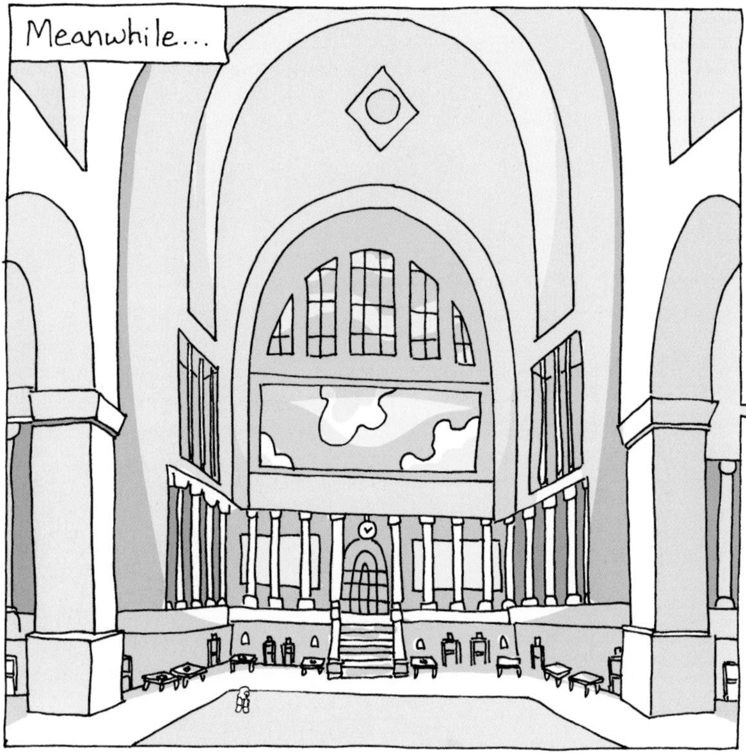
Meanwhile...

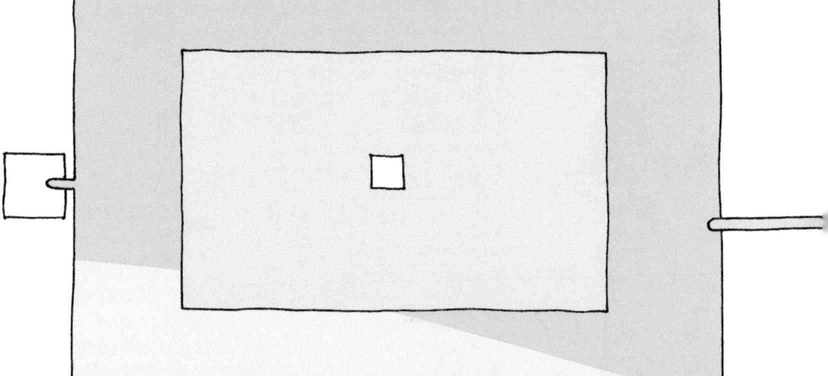

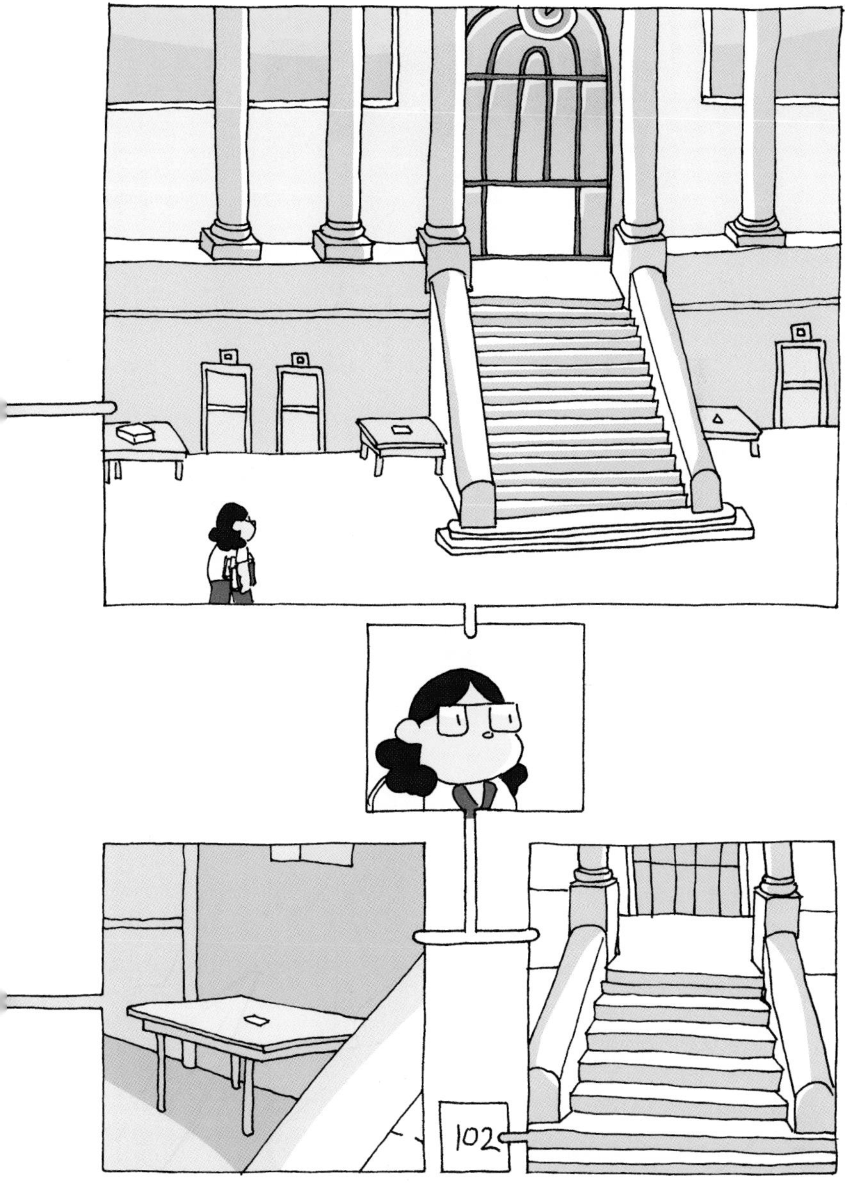
102

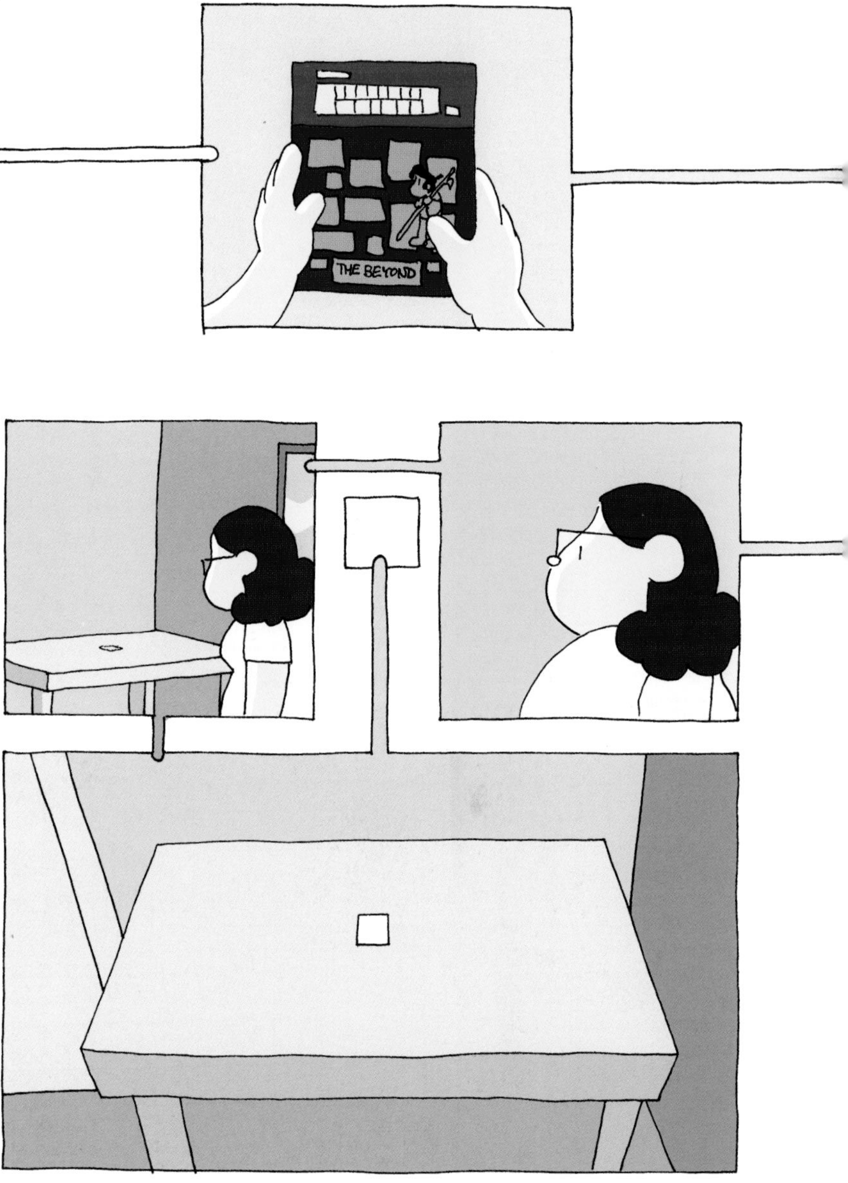
THE BEYOND

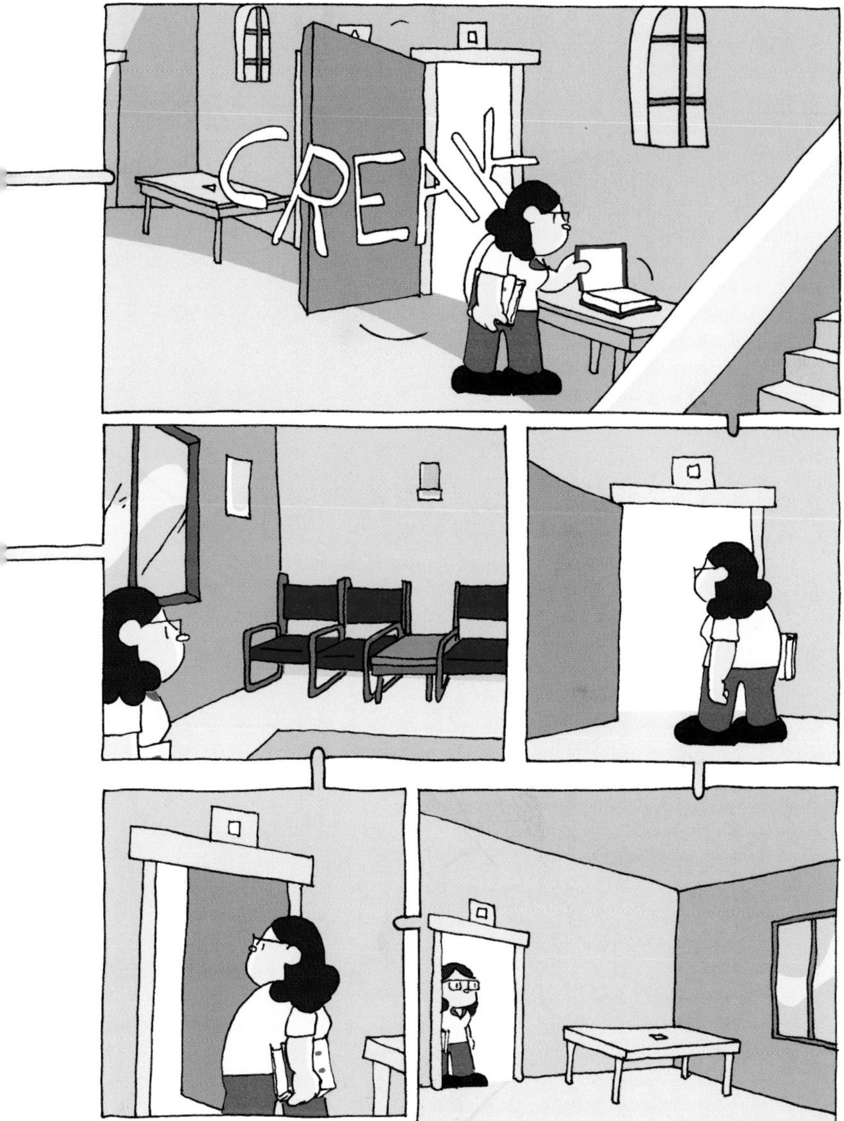
CREAK

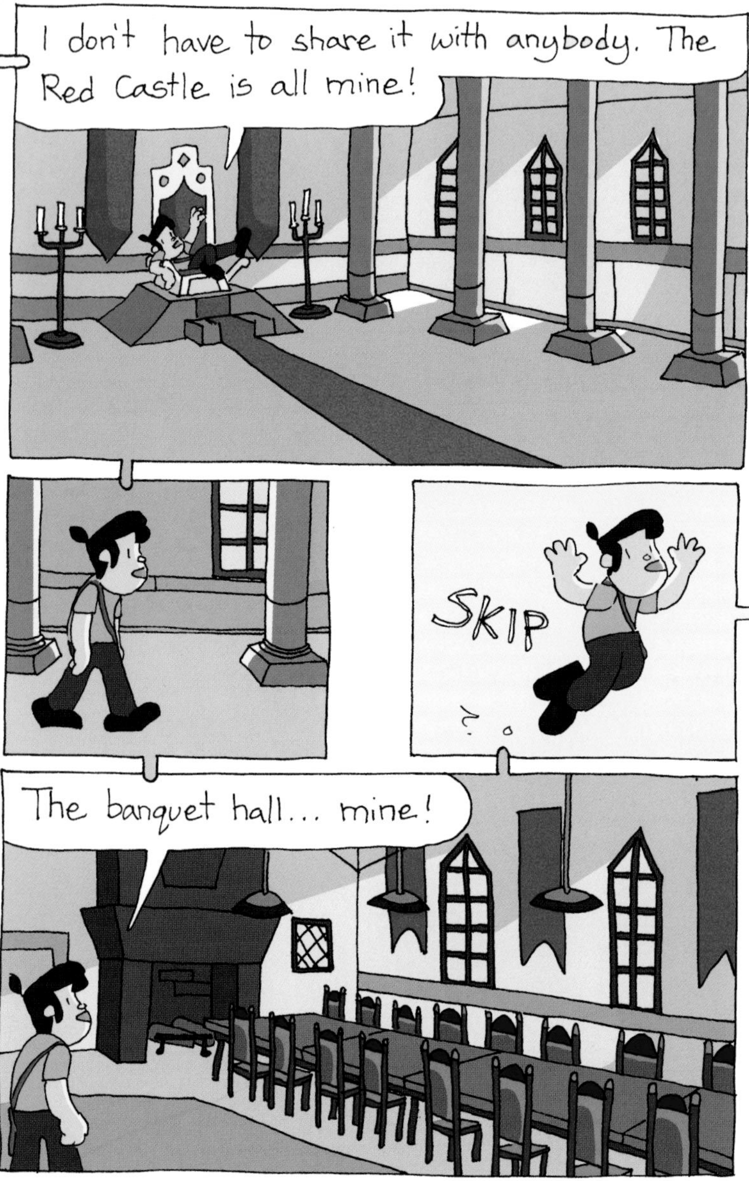
I don't have to share it with anybody. The Red Castle is all mine!
SKIP
The banquet hall... mine!

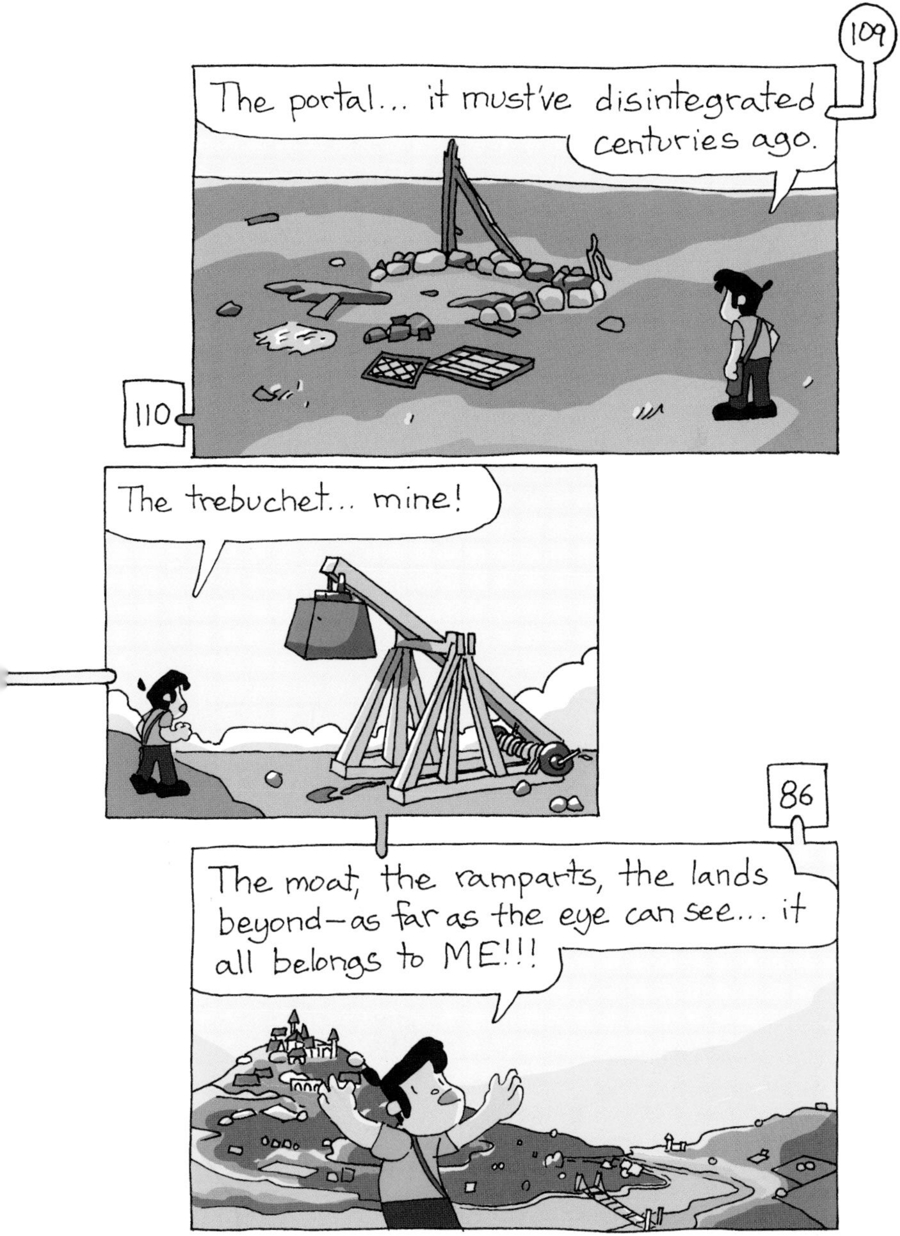

109
The portal... it must've disintegrated centuries ago.
110
The trebuchet... mine!
86
The moat, the ramparts, the lands beyond—as far as the eye can see... it all belongs to ME!!!

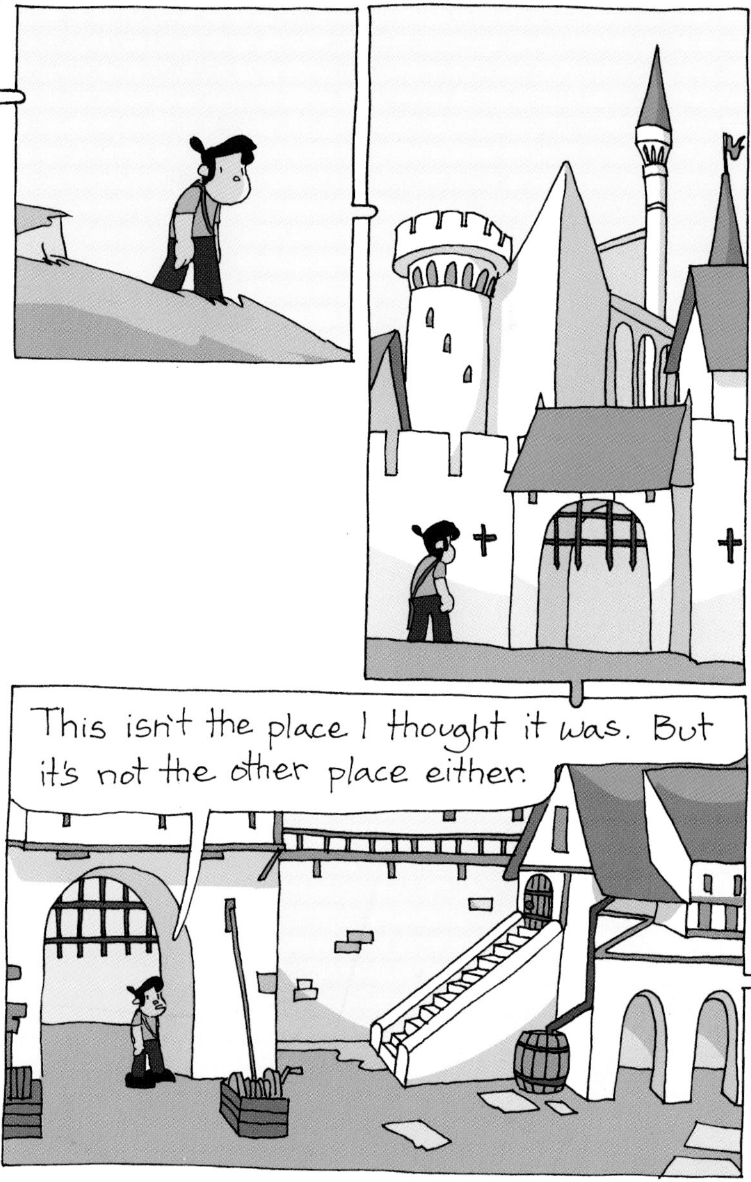
This isn't the place I thought it was. But it's not the other place either.

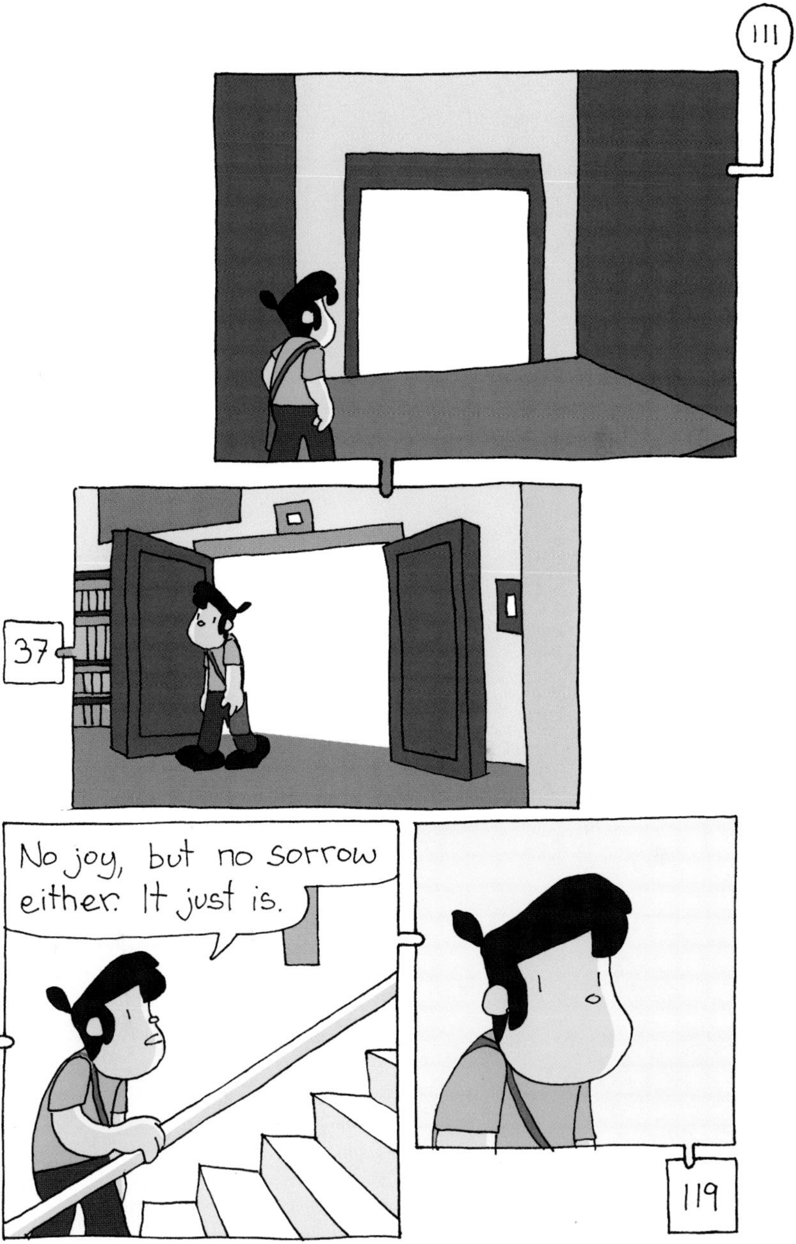
111
37
No joy, but no sorrow either. It just is.
119

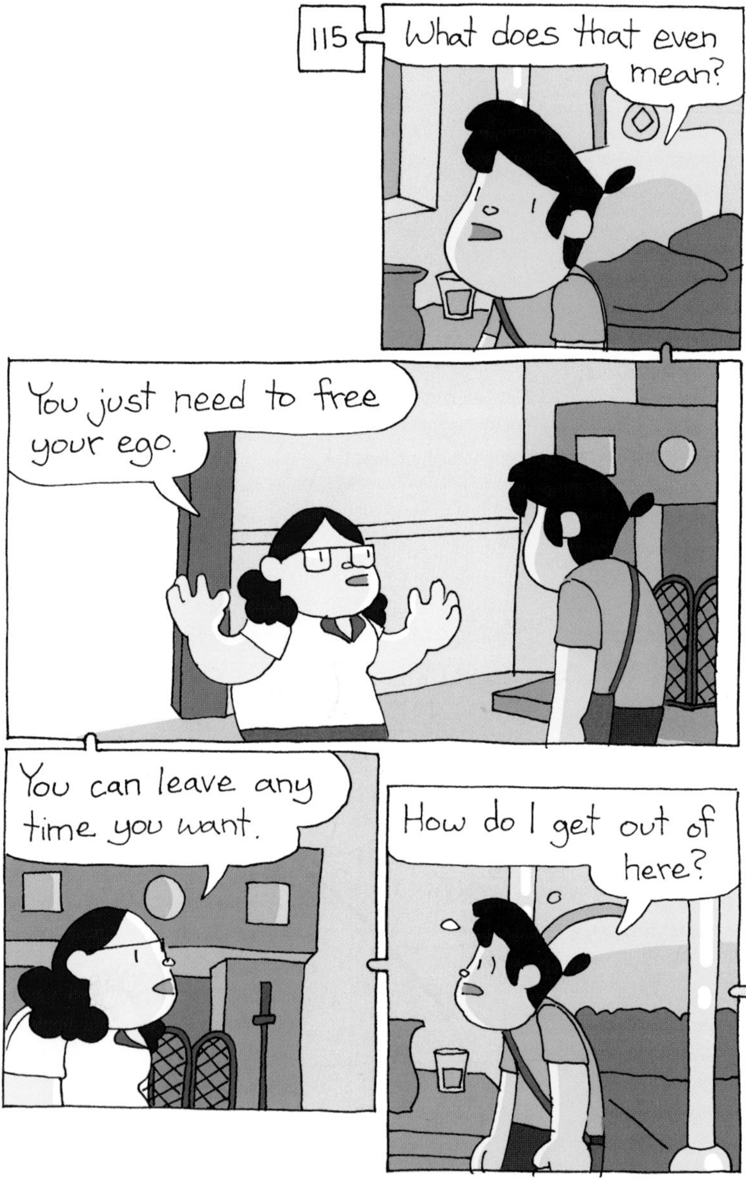
115
What does that even mean?
You just need to free your ego.
You can leave any time you want.
How do I get out of here?

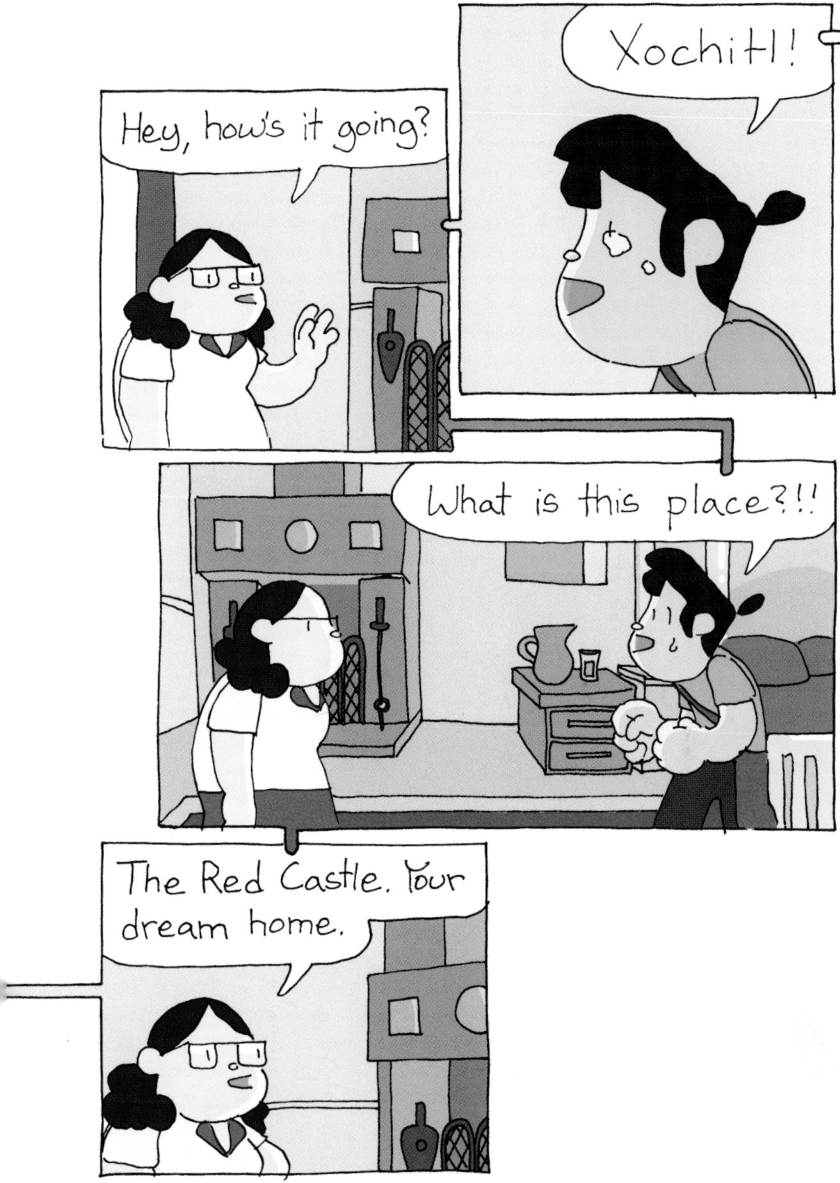
Hey, how's it going?
Xochitl!
What is this place?!!
The Red Castle. Your dream home.

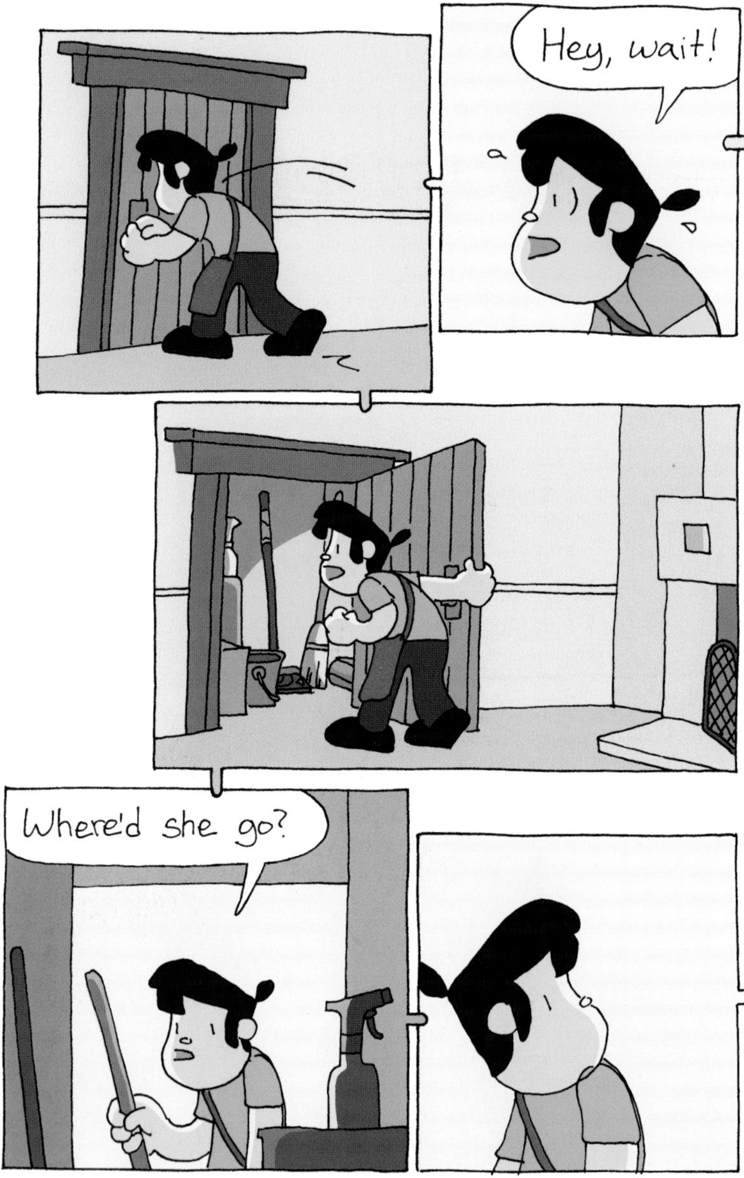
Hey, wait!
Where'd she go?

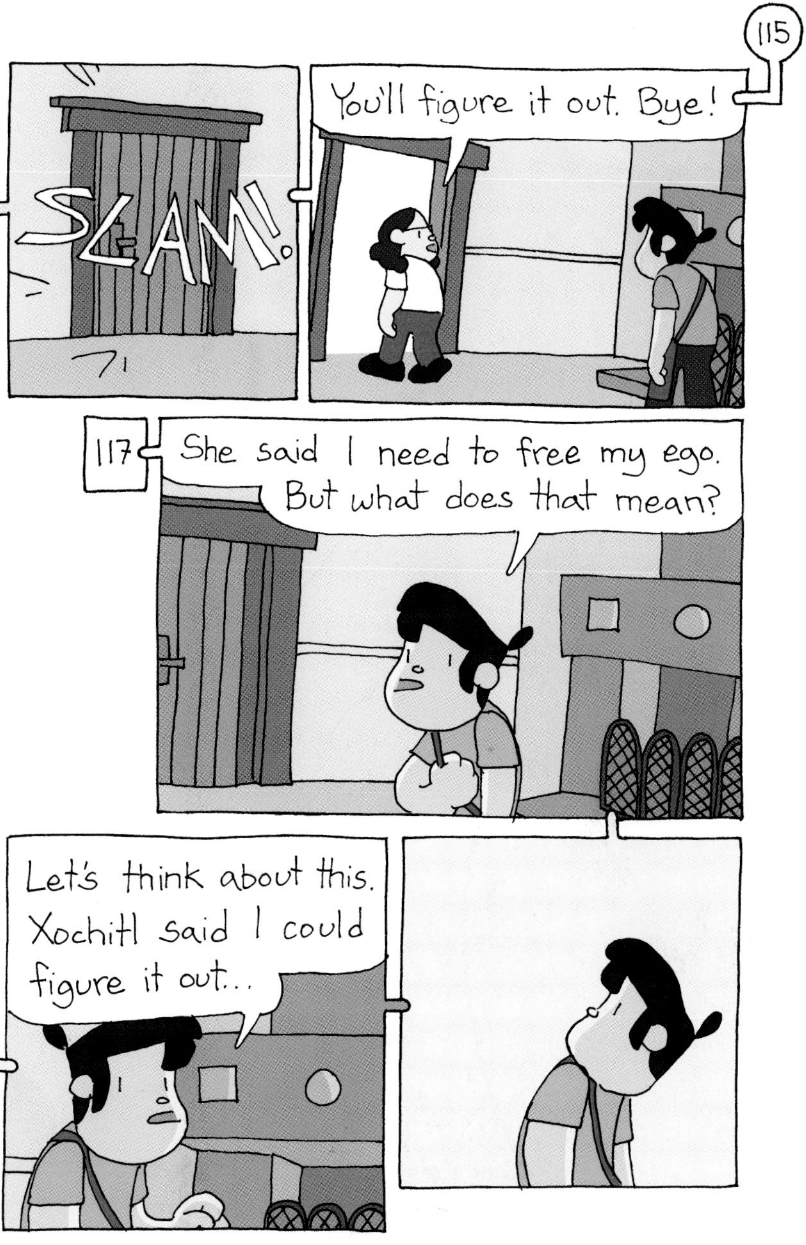
115
SLAM!
You'll figure it out. Bye!
117
She said I need to free my ego. But what does that mean?
Let's think about this. Xochitl said I could figure it out...

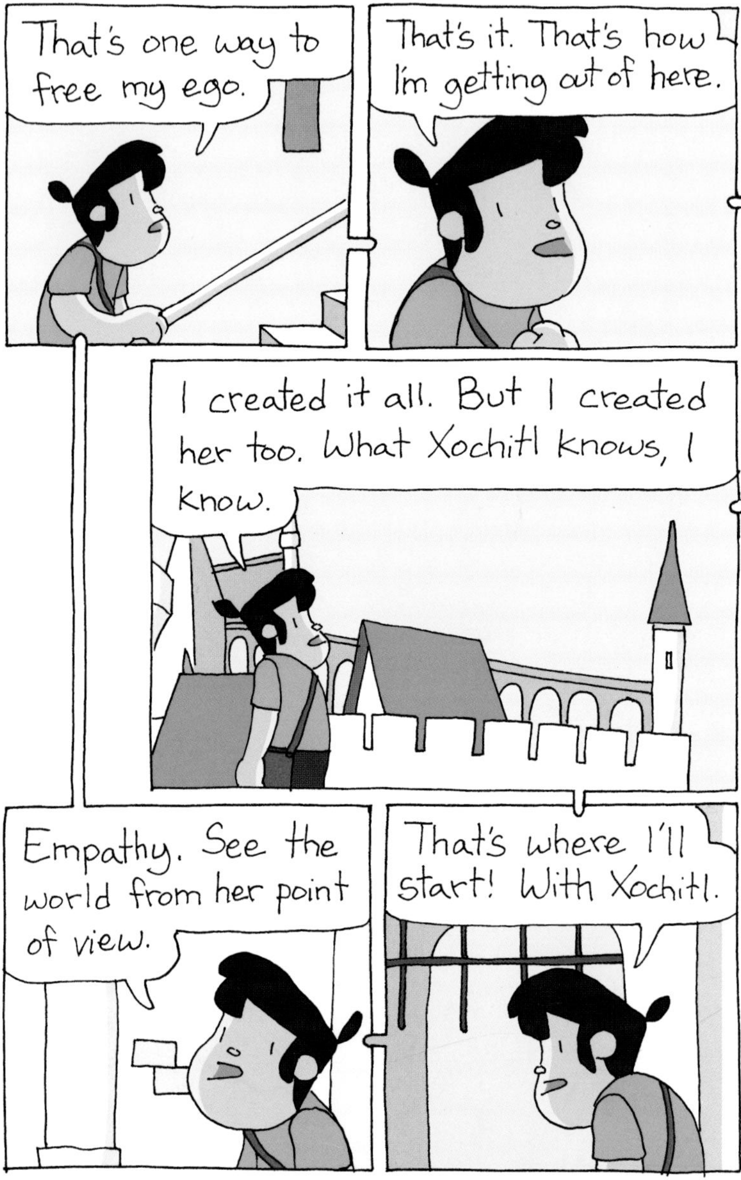
That's one way to free my ego.
That's it. That's how I'm getting out of here.
I created it all. But I created her too. What Xochitl knows, I know.
Empathy. See the world from her point of view.
That's where I'll start! With Xochitl.

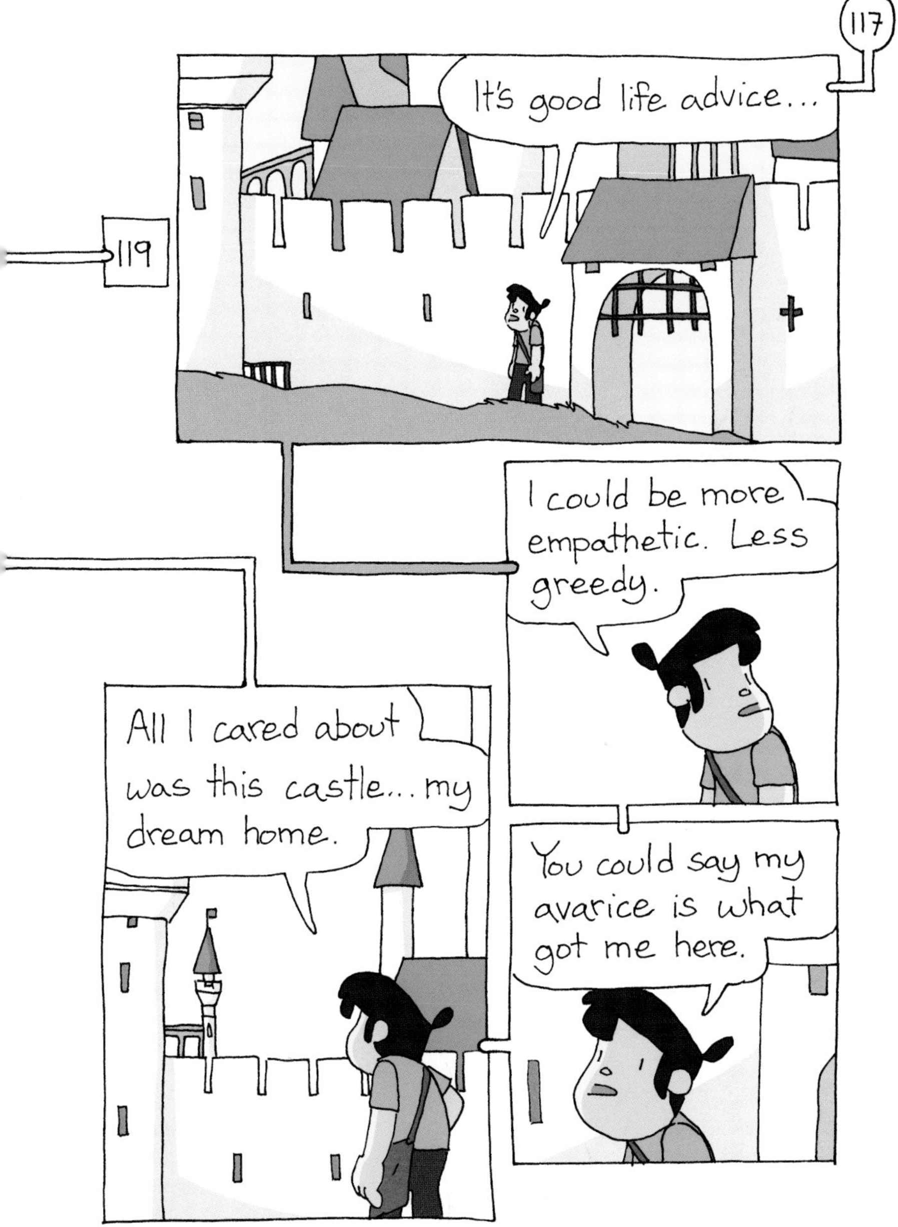
117
119
It's good life advice...
I could be more empathetic. Less greedy.
You could say my avarice is what got me here.
All I cared about was this castle... my dream home.

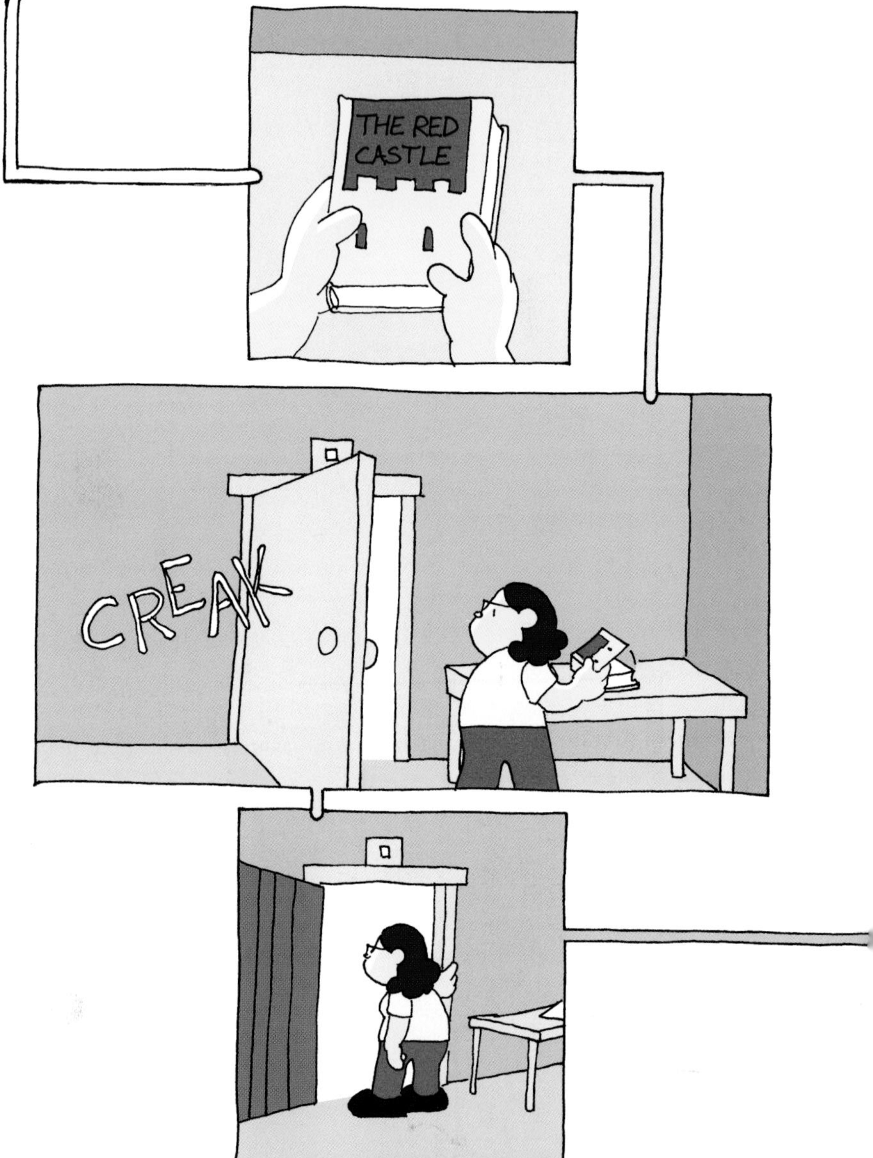
THE RED CASTLE
CREAK

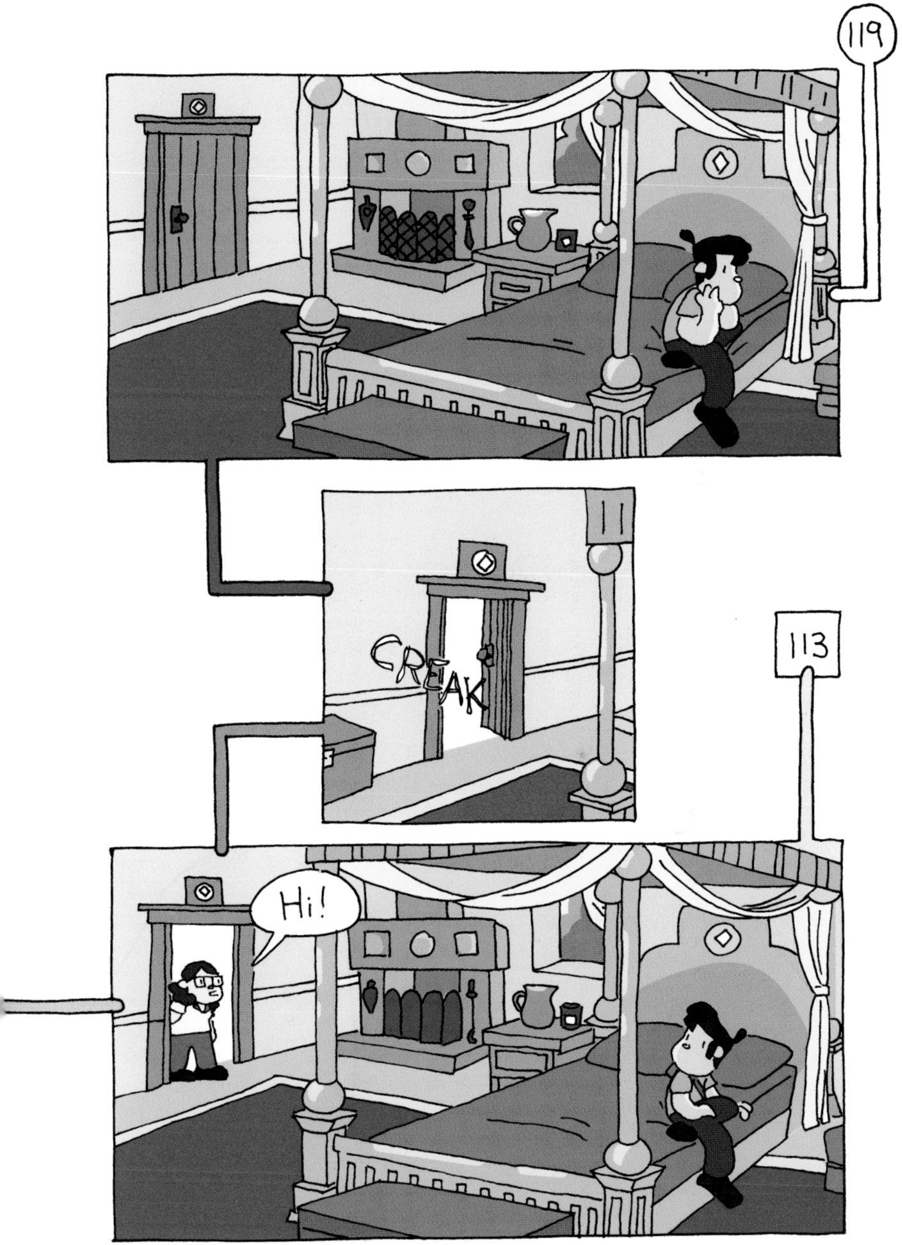
119
CREAK
113
Hi!

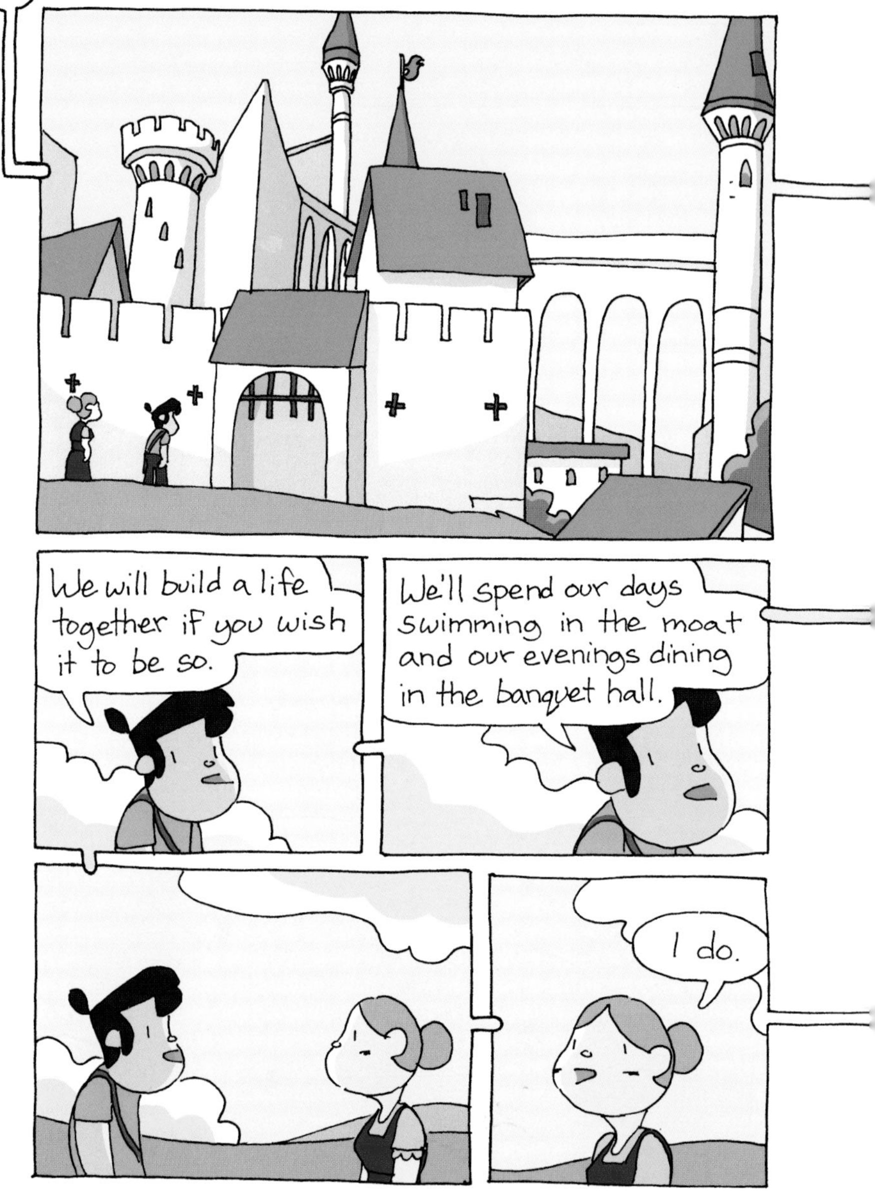
We will build a life together if you wish it to be so.
We'll spend our days swimming in the moat and our evenings dining in the banquet hall.
I do.

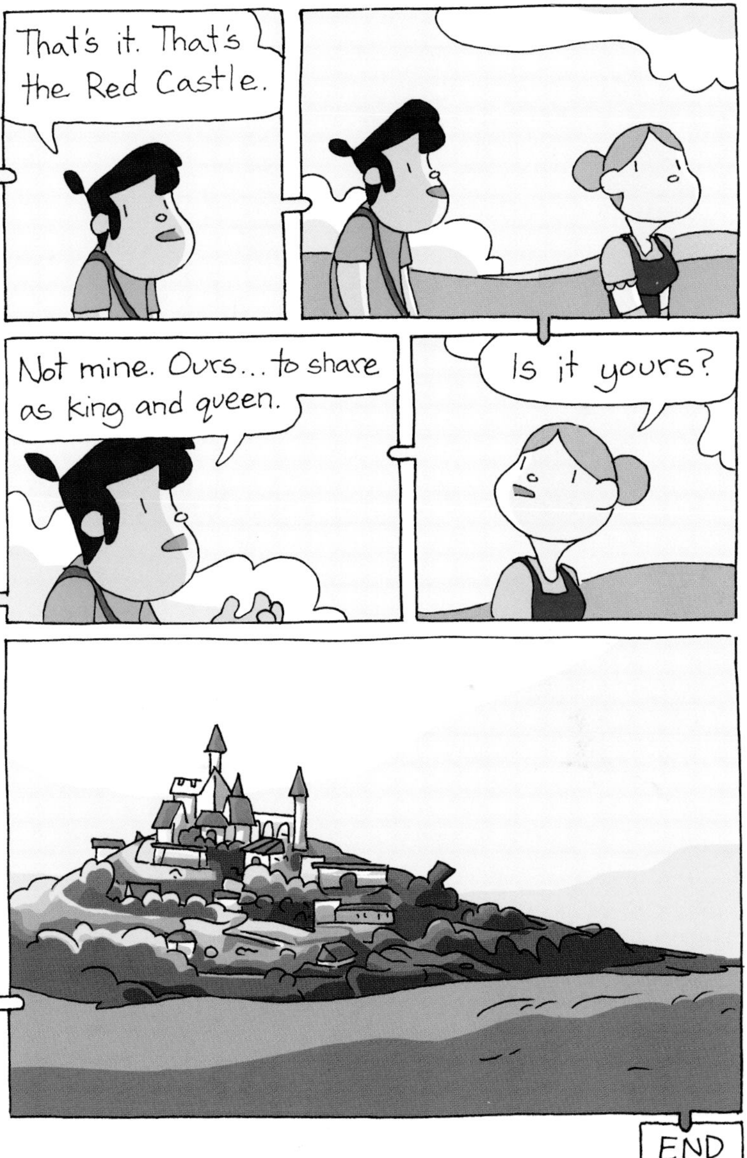
That's it. That's the Red Castle.
Is it yours?
Not mine. Ours... to share as king and queen.
END

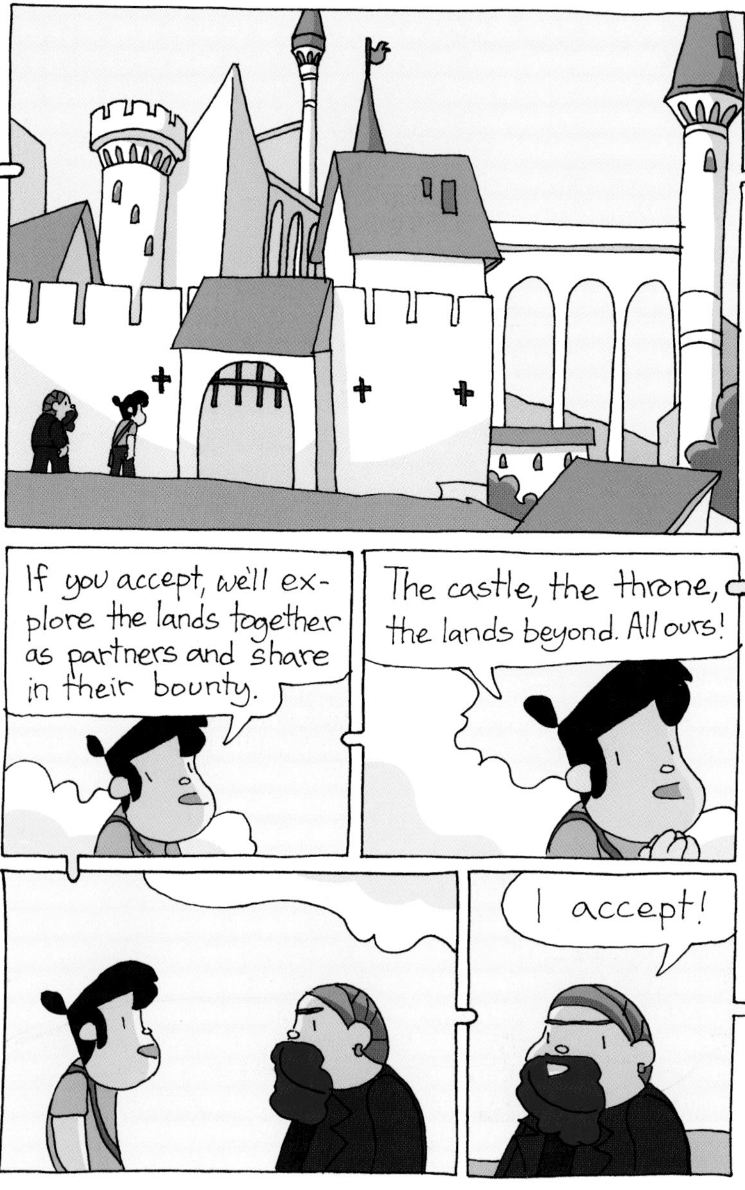
If you accept, we'll explore the lands together as partners and share in their bounty.
The castle, the throne, the lands beyond. All ours!
I accept!

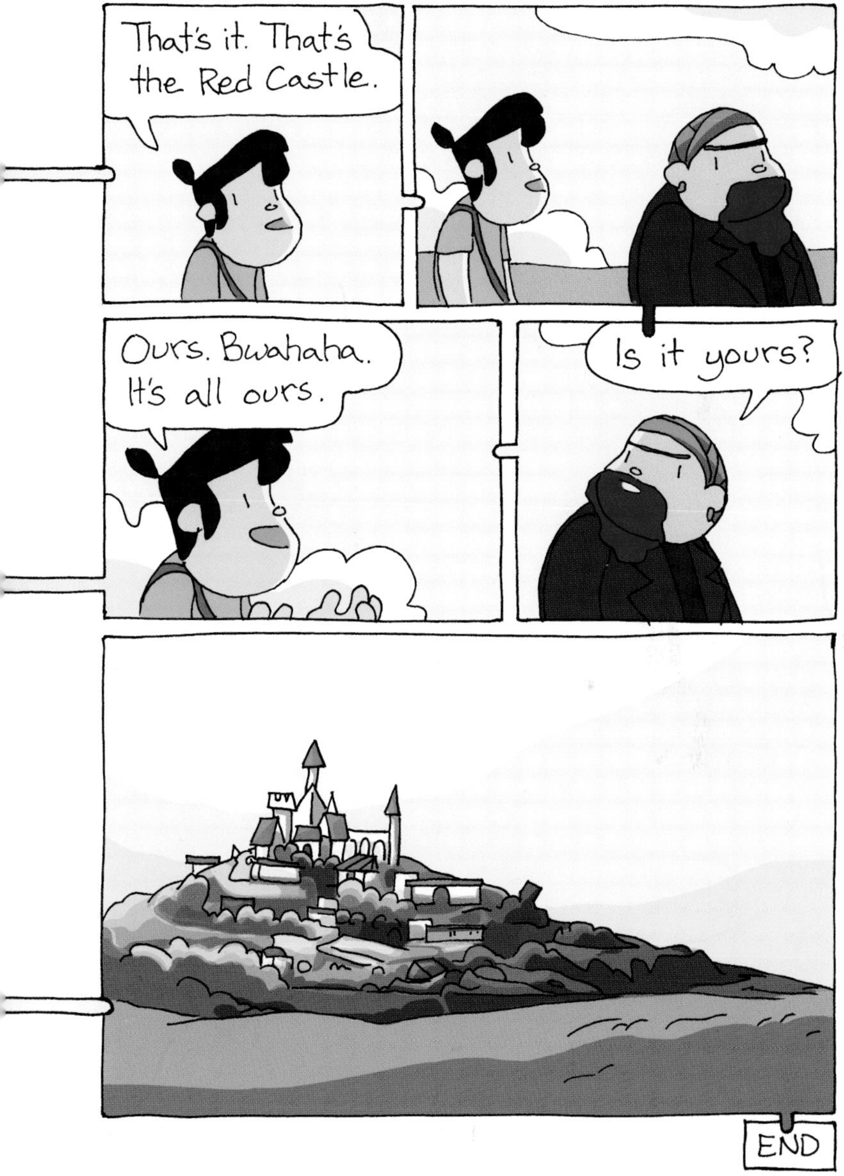
That's it. That's the Red Castle.
Is it yours?
Ours. Bwahaha. It's all ours.
END

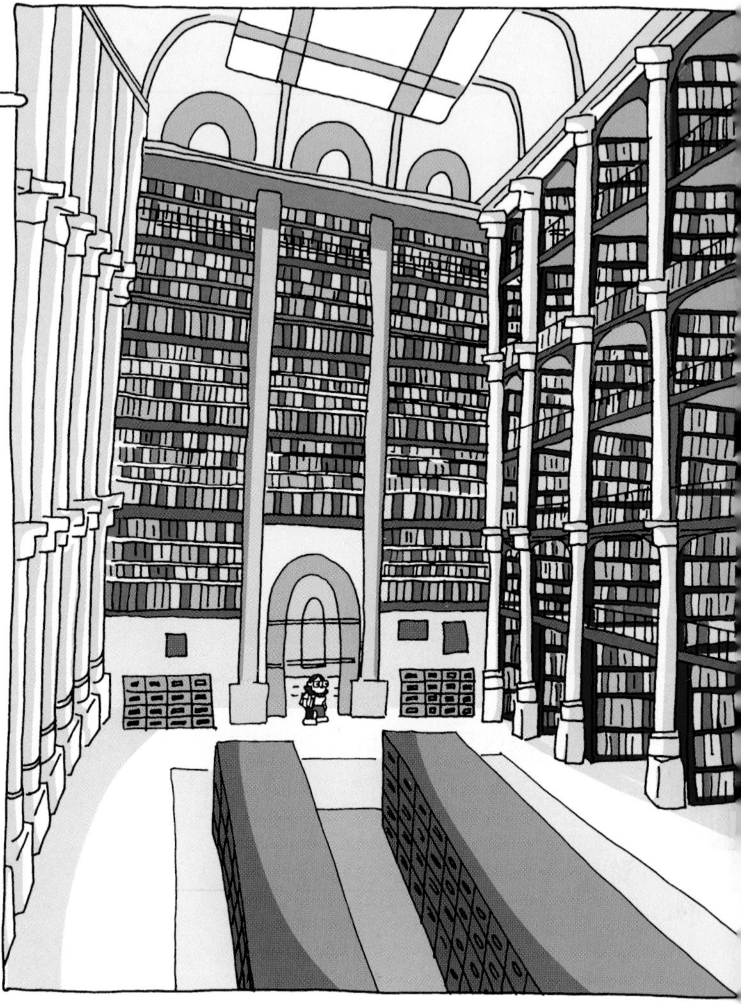

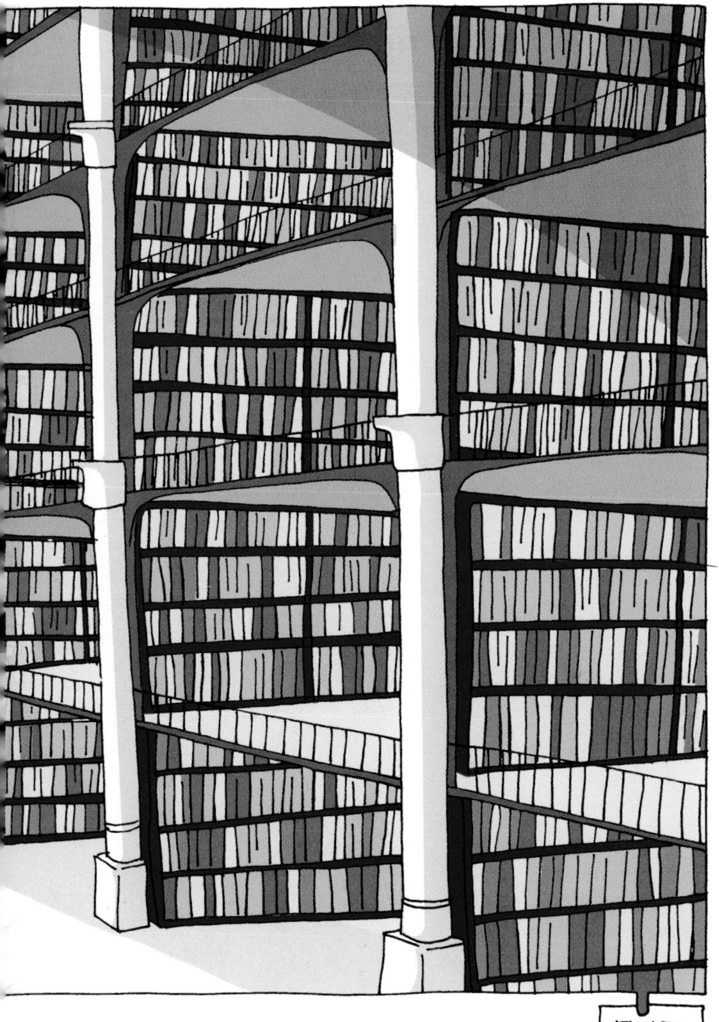
END

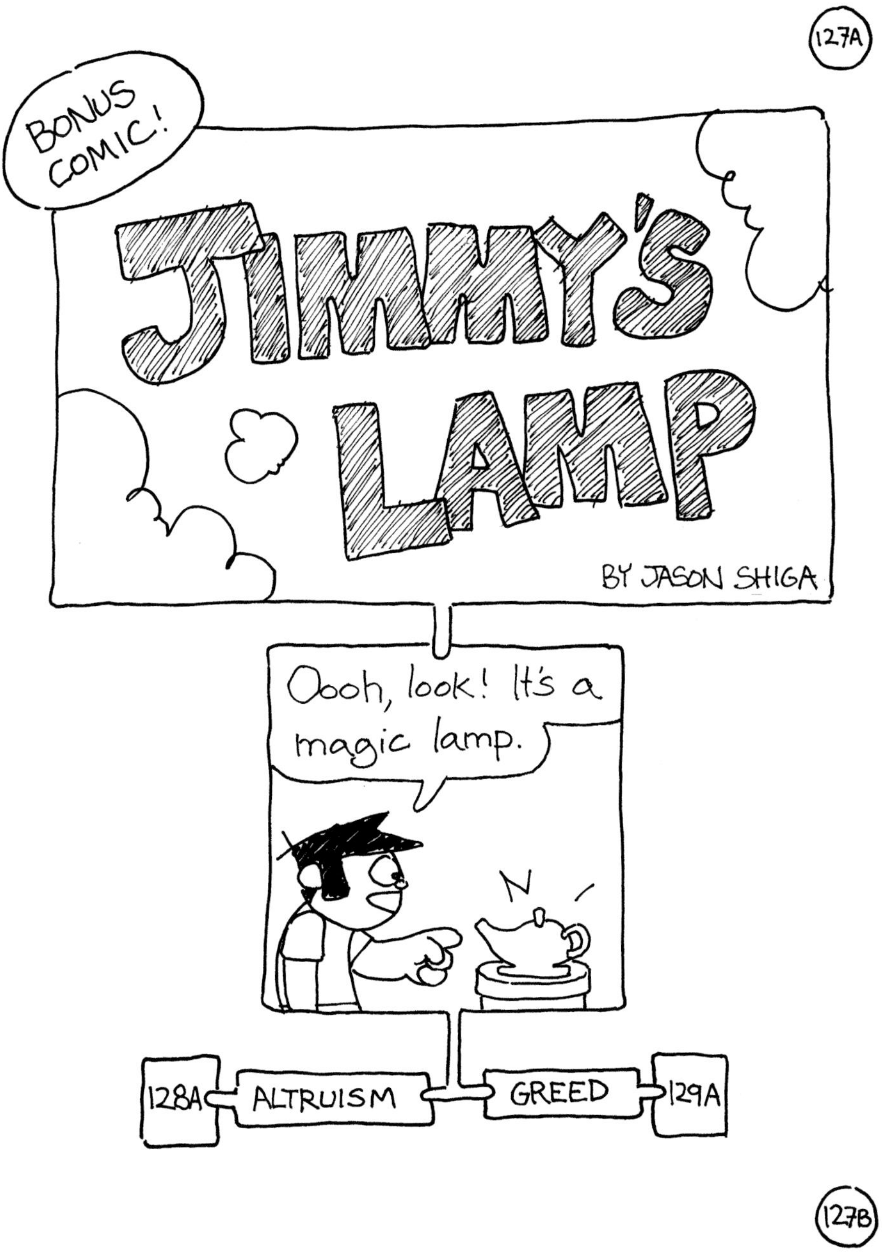
BONUS COMIC!
JIMMY'S LAMP
BY JASON SHIGA
Oooh, look! It's a magic lamp.
128A
ALTRUISM
GREED
129A

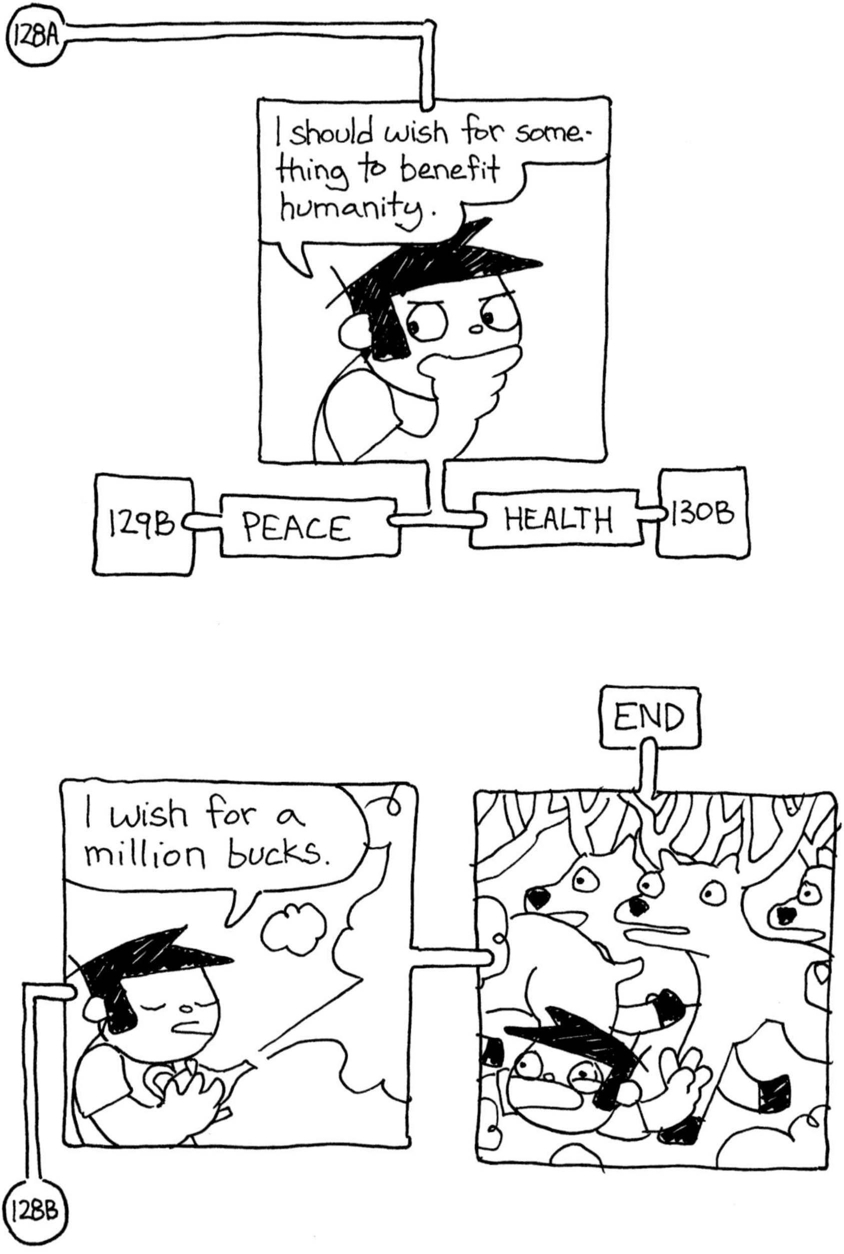
128A
I should wish for some-thing to benefit humanity.
129B
PEACE
HEALTH
130B
128B
I wish for a million bucks.
END

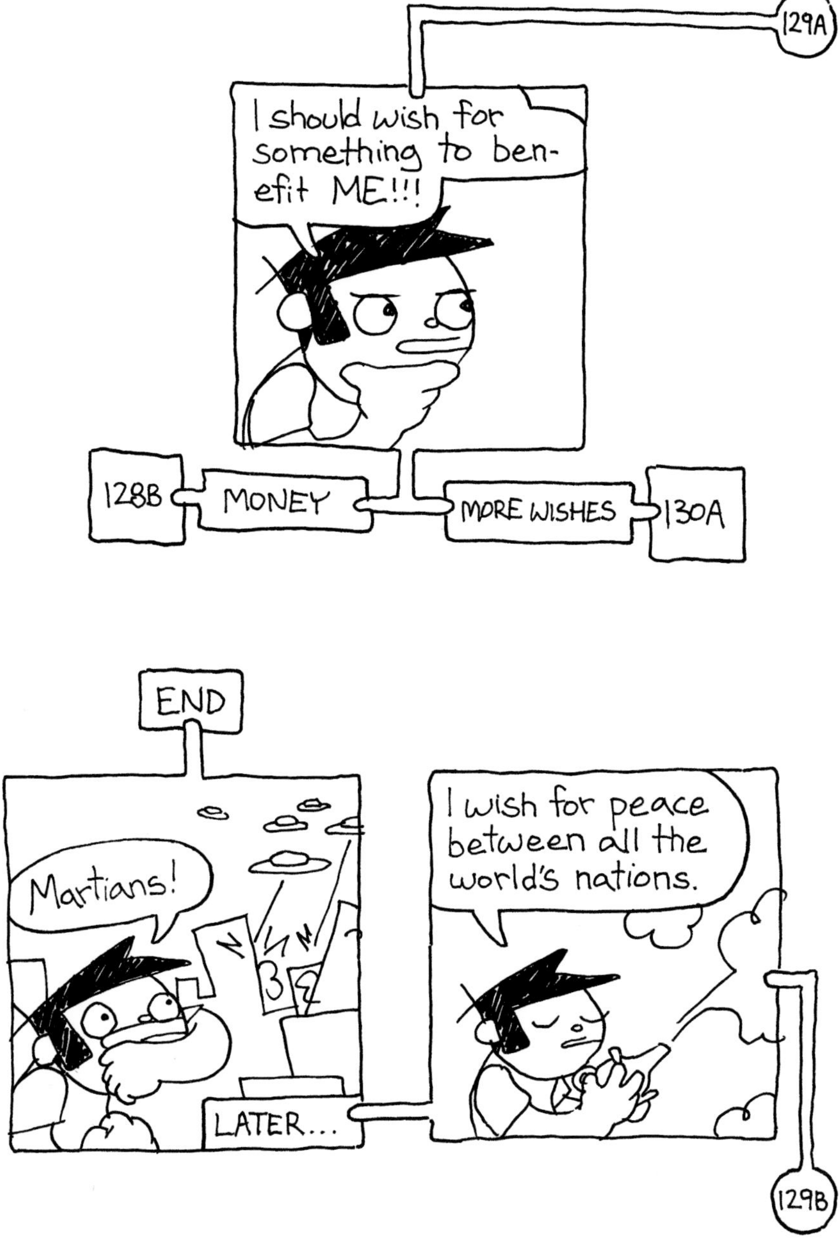
129A
I should wish for something to ben-efit ME!!!
MONEY
128B
MORE WISHES
130A
129B
I wish for peace between all the world's nations.
LATER...
Martians!
END

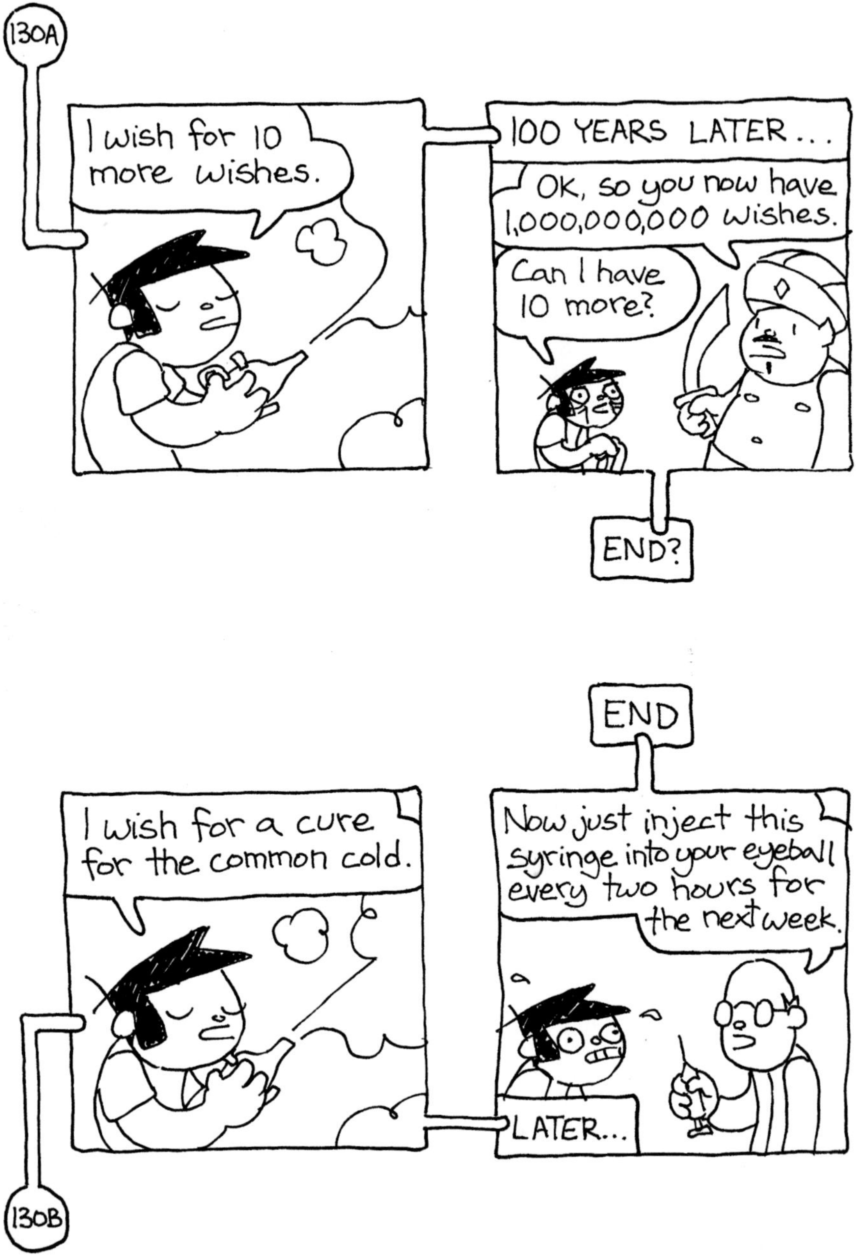
130A
I wish for 10 more wishes.
100 YEARS LATER...
OK, so you now have 1,000,000,000 wishes.
Can I have 10 more?
END?
I wish for a cure for the common cold.
LATER...
Now just inject this syringe into your eyeball every two hours for the next week.
END
130B